Also By Francesca Lia Block

HOUSE *of* HEARTS

Francesca Lia Block

RARE BIRD
LOS ANGELES, CALIF.

RARE BIRD

THIS IS A GENUINE RARE BIRD BOOK

Rare Bird Books
6044 North Figueroa Street
Los Angeles, CA 90042
rarebirdbooks.com

FIRST HARDCOVER EDITION

Also available in e-book and unabridged audiobook,
as well as a limited edition vinyl audiobook
narrated by Scout laRue Willis

Set in Warnock
Printed in the United States

Cover Photograph by Algirdas Grigaitis
Cover Design by Robert Schlofferman
Interior Design by Hailie Johnson

10 9 8 7 6 5 4 3 2 1

Library of Congress Cataloging-in-Publication Data

Names: Block, Francesca Lia, author.
Title: House of hearts / by Francesca Lia Block.
Description: First Hardcover Edition. | Los Angeles, Calif. : Rare Bird, [2022]
Identifiers: LCCN 2021059619 | ISBN 9781644282625 (hardcover)
Classification: LCC PS3552.L617 H67 2022 | DDC 813/.54—dc23

LC record available at https://lccn.loc.gov/2021059619

I've traveled over
Dry earth and floods
Hell and high water
To bring you my love.

—PJ Harvey

Part I

I See a Darkness

Bad things can happen in the desert. Beneath the horned head graffitied on a burned and gutted building in Bombay Beach, the scrawled words read: "It didn't always used to be this way." Too true, Izzy Ames thought, looking around at the mobile homes and a few houses lining unpaved streets beneath the dike that separated broken town from toxic sea. *It didn't always used to be this way.* And it would not be this way forever.

Izzy watched Cyrus Rivera stand from a crouch where he'd been fingering the soil he'd hauled to Bombay Beach in his Chevy Silverado. His jeans slid down over the waistband of his boxers, and he hitched his thumbs through his belt loops and turned to face her. The steep intelligence of his brow, his powerful nose and cheekbones, the stubble on his chin, a mouth that brooded, even in a smile, over a lawless array of teeth. And his eyes—irises the color of seaweed hid behind his shades. She'd once read that true hazel is rare, derived from a combination of pigments. Eumelanin. Pheomelanin.

Cyrus reached for his canteen, tilted it to lips fuller than Izzy's— sometimes it felt as if his lips could swallow hers whole when they kissed. His Adam's apple flexed, and muscles moved animal-like under the inked skin of his chest and arms. Rose, serpent, panther, falcon, and skull tattoos twined, pawed, and flew, and, in the case of the skull, hovered like a reminder of the fate that is certain for everyone. The skull reminded Izzy of something else, too. Of the way that, sometimes, her love for Cyrus felt like a different kind of death: even after almost nine years together, she found herself slayed by the sight of him.

She wasn't the only one. A man that beautiful, that skilled, disturbed people somehow, especially out here in the desert where the beauty that existed was raw and harsh and often hidden. But Cyrus could build almost anything out of anything, could make almost anything grow. When you looked at him, you felt you could do these things, too. You might even start to glow like he did.

He nodded his head once at Izzy, his lips softening and peaking into a smile, and she dipped her chin in response, feeling her own lips lift and her nipples tingle. *I love you*, she mouthed. Not long till they'd be in bed again, their favorite pastime. But it wasn't just the sex Izzy yearned for. She felt their love manifested in sleep, as dreams, in the words they whispered to each other like handing a candle back and forth when the desert encroached darkly outside their shack. Now, her womb pinched with desire.

Izzy, Cyrus, and their friends Seth and Nephy White had gathered in Bombay Beach to tend the "three-sisters" community garden they'd planted. Cyrus had the idea—a gift for the children. He, Izzy, Seth, and Nephy came from Salton City, Slab City, and Salvation Mountain, not here. But no one had built any gardens for them.

They had—all four—grown up on the shores of the man-made lake where movie stars once played golf, water-skied, boat raced, and fished for artificially introduced croaker. Slowly, due to pollution, increased salinity, and an overgrowth of dead algae that cut off oxygen and produced hydrogen sulfide gas, the Salton Sea deteriorated into an anoxic cesspool surrounded by mountains where the military once conducted bombing test operations. Selenium, the poisonous trace mineral present in agricultural drainage, washed into the sea and ravaged the brains, beaks, hearts, livers, wings, legs, feet, and skeletons of aquatic birds and kidneys, ovaries, spines, heads, mouths, and fins of fish.

✳✳✳

Izzy, Cyrus, Seth, and Nephy made the garden in the dust. First, they mounded dirt that Cyrus had hauled in his Silverado, then hollowed out a shallow, moon-like crater and planted corn there. When the crop was at four inches, they sowed bean seeds around it, and in the spring, they planted pumpkins at the perimeter. The prickly pumpkin leaves protected the mulch and drove animals away, the beans wound through the pumpkins, tendrilled up the corn for support, pulling nitrogen from the air and binding the sisters together.

Today, while the others watered and weeded, Seth hammered the wooden slats that made up the fence around the three-sisters mound—a few slats had come loose. He was taller and thinner than Cyrus, with a shaved head, now bandanna-wrapped to protect it from the scorch, a goatee, and iron-shredded abs. His shoulders still bore traces of scars from the cigarette burns he used to give himself. Izzy remembered the first time she'd seen the marks on his shoulders, but she'd been too afraid to mention them that day. She'd assumed Seth's dad, Rick, had made the marks, and she was even more shocked when she learned about the self-harm. Thankfully, Seth outgrew that habit after he married Nephy.

They were all damaged, weren't they, in different ways? All traumatized by something—poverty, neglect, unstable or missing parents. Seth's mother had left when he was a baby, Nephy and Izzy had never felt like they belonged in their families, and Cyrus had been adopted. Seth cut himself; Nephy slept with everyone before she and Seth got together; Cyrus still jumped at loud noises; Izzy clung to him. She tried not to, did her best, but growing up in a trailer by the Salton Sea, with a crazy mother and an unpredictable father, she couldn't exactly call herself secure. At least she had Cyrus and Nephy and Seth. At least the four of them had each other now.

"You okay, queen?" Izzy asked Nephy. "Is it too hot out here?"

"My nails are frickin' wrecked." Nephy, who had somehow managed not to break a sweat, looked up from under her straw cowboy hat and held out hands tipped with white acrylic talons. Or— they had been. Most had broken off since morning. No matter; she'd replace them by tomorrow, Izzy knew.

Nephy's rounded belly protruded under her white tank top. "I popped," she'd said that morning, patting her small baby bump. Her breasts, and her ass in the cut-offs, were already fuller, too. Her hair and skin lusher. But her waist still appeared narrow as always above the bump; Seth liked to show how his hands could encircle her, with room to spare.

"And you, my queen?" Nephy said, checking her nails again.

Izzy said, "I'm good." She didn't like to complain. Wanted Cyrus to know she was up for this. She looked at her own hands then. The short nails ached with dirt. Seth's hammer rang out in the hot silence.

Just then a bell chimed and a red-haired girl came riding up on a pink bicycle, Mylar streamers tied to the handlebars. A little white basket entwined with fake pink flowers. She paused, watching the four people planting in the garden, and Izzy got up, wiping her hands on her black jeans. The streamers gleamed like water or a desert mirage.

"Hi, there," Izzy said. The girl seemed close to the age of the child Izzy and Cyrus would have had if she hadn't miscarried, and even though that was a long time ago, this thought still stung. "How are you today?"

The girl squinted. Her face was small, already old-looking, and covered with grime. She'd bitten off her nails. Izzy remembered how she'd bitten her own nails as a child, bitten her nails down to the quick. Maybe as a way to let people know things weren't okay at home. But no one seemed to notice.

"What are you doing?" the girl asked.

"We're tending the garden," Izzy said.

The child took it all in: the wooden beds, the damp patch of earth, the seedlings, the four strangers. Two women, both with long black hair, one curvy, one thin. Two men, one dark, one fair and burned.

"Flowers?" the girl asked. "Will there be flowers?"

"Next spring. Beans flower, so do pumpkins."

She seemed to find this satisfactory and began riding her bike in circles in the dust. "Hartebeest, monk seal. Great auk, ibex. Javan tiger," she said in what Izzy heard as an almost iambic singsong.

"What's that?" Izzy asked.

"Passenger pigeon, Pyrenean ibex, quagga, sea mink, Tasmanian tiger, Tecopa pupfish, West African black rhino."

What was she talking about? Izzy wondered. "I don't—"

"African elephant, Asian elephant, bald eagle, giant panda, orangutan, polar bear, rhinoceros." The girl stopped riding.

Okay. Extinct or endangered. Izzy wanted to cover her ears. Instead, she knelt down. "That's sad about those animals, huh?"

The girl peered up through red eyelashes, almost transparent in the sun, her eyes starting to water. Not tears, exactly. Izzy's eyes used to water like that when her father, Larry, told her ghost stories to scare her. The little girl swiped a hand across her face, and the dirt there smeared. "We are all sharing the earth's pain." Her voice had a slightly robotic tone, as if she were repeating something she'd been told.

Izzy shivered with the kind of cold that comes from within, and a shade lowered down in her mind. That was the only way she could describe it. Some kind of foreshadowing or just anxiety, she still wasn't sure. Though the first darkness had come when she was just a kid, sleeping on the scratchy trailer cot, not knowing that her new black kitten writhed and mewled on the clothesline outside, its sounds sucked away by a succubus wind.

"What'd you say, honey?" the girl asked. She set her gaze on Cyrus now. "We will stand around the glass box and cry, and our tears will turn into flowers," she said.

Then she turned and pedaled away, across the road toward a house painted a salt-corroded blue, with a roughhewn windmill fastened to the front. The windmill didn't move in the hot, still air. Did it ever move? Stopping her bicycle in the weeds that grew in front of the house, the child got off the bike and ran inside. Watching her go, Izzy had the strangely distinct feeling that somehow, impossibly, this was the child she and Cyrus had lost. The child that had been only blood.

"Freaky," said Nephy, and Seth laughed. Cyrus's face remained unchanged.

Izzy was used to strange things happening; her whole life had been strange. Growing up by a burping, sulfuric lake, an ossuary for the bones of a million rotted tilapia. Where dust storms turned a child's lungs into those of a fifty-year old smoker with chronic obstructed pulmonary disease. And a fungus in the soil, stirred by the wind and inhaled, caused desert fever—coccidioidomycosis. A place where, once, bombs from the marine base detonated regularly in the distance. All strange. But this little girl shook Izzy, somehow, in a different way.

❀❀❀

Later that afternoon, the four friends went for lunch at the Ski Inn— the only real eatery in town. The low, awninged, orange building served burgers, fries, and beer, mostly. Seth ordered all three, Cyrus had a burger, Nephy ate a grilled cheese sandwich, and Izzy picked at some French fries—her body craved the salt, but the grease coated her mouth unpleasantly. They all sat by the bar with the glasses hanging upside down from the ceiling and dollar bills papering every square inch of space.

"Tell me something beautiful and something strange," Cyrus said. It was a game he'd invented, an easy one for Izzy to play since almost everything seemed both beautiful and strange to her.

Seth put his hand on Nephy's belly. "Beautiful," he said. "And strange." He took a pull on his beer.

His wife laughed, a little nervously, Izzy thought. "The garden's beautiful," Nephy said. She raised her glass of ice water in a toast. "That little girl was strange."

Cyrus shrugged. "She's just finding ways to make it out here," he said. "You gotta start young."

"To make it out of here or make it out here?" Izzy said.

He leaned forward in his chair, put his hands on his knees, then leaned back so his hands slid up the length of his thighs. He didn't answer her.

"She reminds me of you," Seth told her. "When you were a kid. Making shit up all the time."

"She still does," Cyrus said. "Not shit. Beautiful and strange things." He leaned forward again, slung his arm around her shoulders and pulled her close so that she could smell the comforting, grassy scent of his sweat and feel the dampness through his cotton T-shirt. "Or I guess now you make it real." He was talking about the items she created. She found porcelain and ceramic figures at flea markets and thrift stores—Buddha, Aphrodite, the Virgin Mary, cherubs, and roses—and made silicone molds of them, then poured in beeswax for candles or organic chocolate with different flavorings—rose, lavender, and prickly pear, the cactus with the pulpy flesh and bloody juice like a human heart. The chocolates and candles, along with Izzy's part-time massage business, brought in cash to supplement Cyrus's landscaping and construction work.

Izzy leaned into the curve of his arm, where it felt as if her bony shoulders had permanently carved out a space. "What about you, babe?"

"You are beautiful," he said, looking down at her under the thick shade of his lashes. "I am strange."

Nephy smiled with baby-sized teeth. She leaned forward, revealing her even more-generous-than-usual cleavage. Izzy got a whiff of patchouli oil and jasmine. The patchouli conjured the pale pinkish-white deadnettle-family flowers from which, Izzy knew, the scent was derived. "Same," Nephy said. She beamed around the table. "We are all lucky to have each other."

They raised three glasses of water and a beer and clinked again.

"To the beautiful and the strange," Cyrus said.

Precious Things

That Halloween morning, Cyrus drove them to work at the 29 Palms Inn. Izzy opened the truck's passenger window and her hair blew around her head in a squall. Sand gritted her mouth like particles of splintered, macerated bone. When they came to a sudden stop, something skidded out from under the seat and hit the back of her foot. She bent to pick it up: an old-school cassette tape. On the front, Cyrus had scrawled the words "For You" in Sharpie. She showed it to him.

"That's where it went," he said, looking back at the road.

"Thank you." She pushed the cassette into the car stereo. Nineties music blasted. The brutal, beautiful sound of their love.

The hills lay crumpled like discarded animal pelts, and beneath the truck tires, streaks of red stained the road as if the eviscerated landscape had bled to death. Izzy didn't want to imagine what else the red stains might be. Billboards of the various Deadly Sins—the gluttony of fast food, the greed of gambling, the pride of plastic surgery, the lust of strip clubs advertised by baby-faced women. Other signs: "Child Molestation: It Doesn't Just Happen to Girls" with a picture of a sad young man. "Sex Trafficking? Get Help!" "Reward: $10,000. MURDERED. We will find you!"

Cyrus drove past the exits for Palm Desert, Palm Springs, Desert Hot Springs, Pioneertown, and then pulled off the highway and parked in the dusty lot of the 29 Palms Inn. He and Izzy walked past the lagoon where a red houseboat bobbed on algae-dark water. The twenty-nine date palms for which the inn had been named, one planted by the Serrano Indians for each baby boy born at the Oasis of Mara, seemed to lean in, listening for clues. The dates, gathering heat from the sun, fattened with sugar. Whole civilizations had depended on them for energy, Izzy knew. The dry palm fronds rattled softly as if bemoaning the invasion of long-dead prospectors who had come to use water from the Oasis and extract gold from the earth at the Anaconda, Lost Horse, and Desert Queen mines. Soon after the arrival of the miners, the Serrano and Chemehuevi Indians abandoned Mara.

Cyrus had some repair work at the inn, and Izzy had booked a massage client. "I'll see you at noon by the pool," he said, kissing her on the mouth. "Text me if you need me." It was what he always said when he left. He smelled like sage and American Spirit smoke and tasted like the tang of the almonds he pulverized every time he tried to quit tobacco. She liked to bury her face into his body, smell his scent, rub against him to make herself smell just like him. Sometimes, when he was away at work, she'd sniff his pillowcase, his T-shirts. It was weird, she knew. She depended on him too much—physically, emotionally, spiritually, financially—but he had rescued her in a way, just by moving to town when they were young. Cyrus made her feel safe.

"Okay, babe. Have a good morning. Can't wait for tonight," she said. Pumpkin stew, ice cream, trick-or-treaters, bed.

He kissed her again, and then she watched him saunter away, the slight, to-the-left lean of his wide shoulders, the almost disproportionately long legs that looked as if they were always about to take off in a gallop, the light that always seemed to radiate off of him.

❉❉❉

Her massage client lay beached on the massage table on the lawn by the outdoor stone fireplace that smelled of old ashes. A roadrunner streaked by with a clicking-clucking sound, but the man didn't flinch or look up. Green frond shadows swayed across his body as Izzy kneaded his back with her lavender-oiled hands.

"Hot today," he said.

"Yeah. Hot."

He was silent for a while, which was a relief; she didn't feel like chatting.

"You gotta love it. Do you love it?"

"What?" she asked.

"Hot. The heat."

"It's a little scary," she said. She normally wouldn't have shared so much, especially with a guy like this, but she'd been caught off guard, thinking of Cyrus and the night they'd planned.

"Scary, why scary? It's gorgeous. Where I come from, it's freezing right now."

"I mean because of climate change," Izzy said.

"Climate change?" He guffawed. "What climate change? Darlin' that's just a myth made to scare girls like you. Which, I guess it worked."

Sweat didn't bother her, it couldn't in her business, but his odor seemed toxic, even putrid. "No," she said. "No. Sorry. It's real." She dug her hands into the clammy meat of his shoulders, now slick with grease, and he groaned. "We have to do something about it, you think?"

"Anything you say," the man moaned as she knuckled his hairy calves. "Just keep doing what you're doing."

Izzy, dreaming of Cyrus, hardly heard him.

❉❉❉

When they got home that night, Izzy and Cyrus listened to *Nevermind* while they prepared the stew from the pumpkin, corn, and beans they grew in their own three-sisters garden. They rolled masa into balls, patted them, cut out circles with the rim of a water glass, and cooked the tortillas on the stovetop. They spooned the stew into the tortillas and ate their fill. After dinner they shared, with one spoon, a bowl of homemade rose petal ice cream. Izzy's creation. It tasted, she thought, like her love for him.

They had constructed the cradle-to-cradle-style shack in Salton City from environmentally sound scraps and recycled window glass on land he'd bought with money from his construction business. Cyrus designed the house, drew up the plans, then he and Izzy built it together. They laid the pink adobe tiles and set them with grout. Izzy planted peppermint, basil, rosemary, thyme, and marjoram in the window boxes. Cyrus installed the swamp cooler, an evaporative system that originated from ancient windcatchers that caught air and passed it over subterranean waters. He built her a bookcase and arranged her vintage encyclopedias, her homeopathy and law books by color and size. On top of the bookcase, Izzy placed flowers and her candles and the crystals that she liked to believe had healing properties—malachite, amethyst, and rose quartz. A shrine to her books. Reading, she'd told him, saved her life as a kid. She'd sneak out of her parents' trailer at night with her books and her flashlight. Fueled by this food and illumination, she believed she might escape.

Years would pass before she found her true escape: in the home of Cyrus's arms.

※ ※ ※

Only a few trick-or-treaters came by that night. Izzy and Cyrus answered the door in elaborate ghost costumes she'd sewn from panels of tulle, and they handed out Izzy's homemade chocolates.

One little girl, dressed as the front end of a cow, pointed to Izzy and Cyrus and said, "You aren't dead!" and they both laughed; kids always made them laugh, although the child's words chilled Izzy, too. Maybe she was morbid, but ever since childhood the mention of death sent her down a path of dark ruminations. Only Cyrus's touch could snap her out of it.

Perhaps he really could read her thoughts now because he pointed to the cow's swaying rump, operated by a second child, to make Izzy laugh. She wondered how the back of the cow could see? Clutching blindly to the little girl's waist, trusting her to lead him.

※※※

After the trick-or-treaters were gone, the candles and smudge stick burned out. Izzy and Cyrus lay on the futon, her head on the hill of his chest, his hands in her river of hair—the rush in a storm drain after a drought. Yard, Izzy's three-legged rescue tortoise, kept watch with somnolent eyes. She had read that you couldn't pick up a tortoise in the wild—it would void its bladder in fear and might die of dehydration—so when she'd found Yard, she'd contacted Animal Rescue and they'd come to get him. Once he'd been treated, she officially adopted him and called him Yard because of his three feet. It still made Cyrus laugh whenever she said the name.

The waning gibbous moon lay vanquished by clouds, and the shack hunkered far enough from the highway that no lights shone in through the repurposed windows. Only cold burned the glass. In the morning there would be jackrabbits and roadrunners and maybe a coyote or a deer, Izzy thought. Maybe, if their love-magic was strong enough, and the clouds gave way in the night, there'd be rain. Maybe a rainbow.

But now there was only silence and the creature comforts of each other's bodies.

He kissed her deep—a lotus opened within. *Nelumbo nucifera*. Water lily. Its seeds lived for years, she'd read. Up to one thousand three hundred years. She found herself thinking of Nephy's belly in the white tank top the other day, her fuller breasts. It was possible that Cyrus had noticed, but it was hard to tell behind his sunglasses. No, Izzy told herself. Cyrus never really looked at other women that way; he only looked that way at Izzy, and usually when they were alone.

"Let's have a baby," Izzy blurted. Most of the time she repressed the thought, but it was as if the beating of her heart had forced the words out of her.

"No, baby," he said, voice firm, and reached for a condom.

Ever since the miscarriage years ago, he avoided the subject when she brought it up. There was a list of reasons why he didn't want a child: the early loss, their finances, the Salton Sea, the state of the world. Sometimes she wondered if it had mostly to do with their own broken pasts, some perception of her as unstable, unfit to be a mother, but he never admitted to this.

Tonight, though, she couldn't contain herself. "Please, baby," she whispered, feeling, again, the pull of her womb.

His eyes swam away from her like two dark fish. "We got to get out of here before we even consider it, Iz," he said with finality. They'd been saving to move to Los Angeles and were getting close. It would be a new start, a real escape from their parents and the sea shored with bones. A better place to raise a child, too, though he hadn't made any promises about this. Maybe she could apply to UCLA again, he'd suggested. It wasn't too late. She'd gotten a full-ride scholarship but hadn't taken it, hadn't wanted to leave Cyrus.

One night, just before the caul of sleep enveloped him, he'd said, "You'll do massage and I'll work construction while we go to school, and we'll save up and eventually get a little house. Hike and read on our days off. Go to libraries and estate sales and see bands. Learn to surf."

"To swim." She'd laughed. Desert child to the bone, she'd never learned. The few pools in town were empty like the one in Seth and Nephy's backyard.

⁂

Izzy and Cyrus were sixteen and seventeen when they took his adoptive-brother Joe's motorcycle to Los Angeles for the first time.

Joe had pieced it together from boneyard bits, but the bike was ride-able, at least.

"'To live and die in LA,'" Cyrus had said, quoting the song.

She thought he was teasing her when he first told her they were going: "We need a yellow convertible." Like the singer in the video who'd taken a total of nine bullets over the course of his short life. "But you'll have to settle for the Rat Bike. With no tunes, except yours truly."

"Cyrus in the house," she said.

He had surprised her at her job at the sandwich shop, come up behind her so that she jumped, pressed his fingers into her rib cage, grazing the underside of her breasts. "We're going. I'm taking you. Tonight."

"What?" she threw her arms around him, pressed her damp cheek to his—they stuck and separated with a light suction. His laugh bestowed her with the gift of white teeth, gold crowns.

She didn't plan on telling her parents, Larry and Leanne, she was leaving. Just grabbed a backpack, threw in some extra underwear, a bar of soap, and sunscreen.

"Where are you going?" Leanne shouted, coming up the path with the laundry as Izzy jumped out of the Airstream trailer that smelled even more than usual of the resinous, varnish-like creosote.

"Camping," she said. "With friends." Her boots scuffed up clouds of dirt as she ran. The sky looked different, just as big but much less empty somehow, clouds silvering with a rain that would not fall.

Strands of Izzy's hair, emerging from under the helmet Cyrus had carefully strapped beneath her chin, tangled in the gusts as they rode north and west.

He'd told her about the carob pods that smelled sweet as chocolate when they cracked under your feet, the acacia and jacaranda trees with pink, purple, or yellow flowers. How petals covered the sidewalks so they looked painted. He hadn't been wrong.

They'd exited the freeway and driven up into the hills, past magnolia trees, thick as two bodies entwined.

"Look," Cyrus said, pointing to the thick, wax-white blooms flickering among the leaves. "They're like candles."

Later, she would make some magnolia blossom candles for him.

They drove up and up. It was a clear night. "Smells like flowers," Cyrus said. "And if you really concentrate, the Pacific Ocean, baby." He inhaled. "No dead fish, mama."

They wound past facades that bloomed surreally out of the shadows like the pale magnolia blossoms on the dark trees. Spanish adobes, Italianate villas, French Normandy-style palaces, Tudor farmhouses, Colonial and Neo-Classical mansions. Stone walls covered with Sleeping Beauty roses. Hedges revealing glimpses of Cinderella-fountained courtyards with sweeping stairs, small white lights in topiary bushes. A Hansel and Gretel cottage with turrets, gables, spun sugar windows.

Izzy and Cyrus read a book about Los Angeles that explained how it was built on sacred burial grounds, earthquake faults, quartz mines, swamplands, and pre-historic tar pits filled with the bones of saber tooth tigers. Even the streets were named for tar (La Brea) and swamplands, marshes (La Cienega).

"LA: the land of devils," Larry liked to say, sucking on smoke.

✤✤✤

We got to get out of here before we even consider it, Iz.

"Don't move to LA without me, okay?" Izzy hummed it with pleasure now, in the shack, not really afraid Cyrus ever would. Although, perhaps part of her was afraid.

Cyrus took her chin in his hand like he might hold one of the china molds from which she made her chocolates and candles and looked into her eyes again. "There is nothing to leave," he said. "You are me and I am you. Love don't die."

Those words stalked her when she woke the next morning to find him gone.

Jennifer's Body

Blood stained the sheets from her cycle that had come in the night, reminding her of how Cyrus had shaken his head and rolled the condom on. Outside the window, their love hadn't conjured rainbows, rain, or rabbits. The day was already hot and bright with wind.

"Morning, Sunshine," she called, waiting for him to say his usual, "Morning, Mama Dawn."

Silence.

Izzy sniffed the air for the pancakes he liked to make them on Sundays, but all she could smell was beeswax, sage, and the residue of their sex. She got up. His boots and the clothes he'd worn the day before, including his ID, weren't where he'd tossed them on the floor last night, but his phone was there, still charging. She knocked on the bathroom door. Unlocked. The room was empty, his towel not even damp with the water that had skimmed his skin. She went outside, barefoot, in her tank top and underpants. His Silverado was parked in its usual spot. When she peered inside the cab, everything looked normal.

He must have just gone for a walk.

But when she came back in, she saw that his black socks were strewn out, animal-like, on the floor under the bed by the slightly bloodied condom wrapper. So, he had left in a hurry, without telling her...

She had asked him to always tell her where he was going because of her attachment issues. In psychology, attachment referred to how children bonded to their parents—securely, anxiously, avoidant if they didn't bond. Izzy was anxiously attached; Cyrus was avoidant, but they kept trying to make up for it with each other. Izzy always told herself that if they had a baby, they'd do attachment right.

It seemed especially odd that he'd left his cell phone—Cyrus never went anywhere without it, in part to help make them both feel more secure. She picked up the phone; she knew the code—a combination of their birthdays: 113128—but she'd never had to use it before. When she entered the numbers, the phone remained locked.

Izzy pulled on jeans and jammed her bare feet into her Converse, pocketed her own phone, and went back outside. In the three-sisters garden, the pumpkins lolled like decapitated heads. And Cyrus had hung from the gate, among the orange and black skull lights and Dias de los Muertos masks, a black-caped ghoul holding its head in its arms. Izzy thought of a word she'd just learned—cephalophore—which referred to statues of saints carrying their decapitated heads this way. The ghoul's held head watched Izzy while she checked around in the dirt for footprints or tracks. Nothing. She took out her phone and texted Nephy and Seth, who didn't respond, then called Ted at the 29 Palms Inn.

"Hey, Ted, it's Izzy. You heard from Cyrus?"

"No, ma'am. Why?"

In the background, a woman's voice howled about Lucifer over the chords of a piano. Ted had turned Izzy and Cyrus on to the music they now loved. Their boss had been in bands in the eighties, his face powdered Kabuki-white, his eyes lined with black, hair bleached and teased. In one picture, he lay sprawled in a pile of men and women who looked just like him. In the nineties, he'd grown his hair out, sported a goatee, wore flannel, changed bands. He'd moved from LA to "escape the madness" and now ran the inn.

"He's not here," Izzy said.

"Probably went for a walk. Or to the store."

Not after the way we kissed last night, she thought, but didn't say. Cyrus would have slept in, made her some pancakes, melting butter in the pan and pouring batter into the shapes of animals, flowers, and sizzling hearts.

"Maybe he's at a site?"

"His truck's still here. And his phone. He always takes his phone." She didn't mention the socks.

"Did you check it?"

She didn't answer. Maybe she'd forgotten the code.

Ted's voice frowned through the phone. "Did anything happen?"

What could have happened? They'd listened to music, cooked, and eaten; they'd talked and made love. And made lotus love. Everything like always. But now Cyrus and his boots were gone. His clothes from the night before and the ID he kept in his jeans. The silver band he wore on his ring finger. All gone. His truck and keys and cell phone and socks—still there. And this weight repeatedly fell from her throat to her chest to her stomach.

"Maybe give it a few more hours and then check in?" Ted said.

She thanked him and hung up, then punched the security code into Cyrus's phone again. The six darkened circles on the screen emptied and shook. She tried it once more. Damn. Had he changed it? Why would he change it? If she tried again too many times, the phone would permanently lock.

Where could Cyrus have gone without telling her? What had happened between the dream of last night and this strange morning that could have made him leave? Or torn him from her? What if he had gotten into some kind of accident? Harmed himself? But he'd never do that.

She realized how few people she could go to. Cyrus hardly spoke to his parents, and Joe was incarcerated at Calipatria Prison. Izzy almost never saw her mom and dad. Seth and Nephy and Ted were Izzy and Cyrus's only friends. They hadn't needed anyone else; they had each other. Maybe that was part of the problem, she thought now.

###

Izzy had first met Cyrus in the house where Seth grew up with his dad, Rick; Seth's mom was never in the picture. The house was still painted that mica-glittered pink, with surfboards and the wreck of a sailboat moored in the sand out front—reminders of the Salton Sea's pleasure days. With its TV, stocked refrigerator, and empty backyard pool for skating, the Whites' had been the hangout for years, a kind of derelict palace for skaters and punks who mostly lived in mobile homes or shacks. When Izzy, Seth, and Nephy were kids, before Cyrus moved to town, a photographer had come to take portraits of the residents. Izzy's dad, Larry, said it was bullshit exploitation, but Izzy wanted to pose with Seth and Nephy in the helm of that boat. After Cyrus came, things like that mattered less. They discovered another ruined boat down by the shore and took pictures of each other standing in it, pretending it could sail them far away.

Nine years ago, Izzy sat huddled against the fence by the empty pool in the backyard, wearing a hoodie and jeans, in spite of the desert sun—at least her skin wouldn't burn, though the sweat had turned on every pore like a faucet—feeling the cement vibrating under her ass. Though the previous day's dust storm had subsided, her lungs still struggled as they had when she was a young child, plagued by asthma that had sent her to the emergency room more than once.

The skaters rode the pavement waves up and down, back and forth in the metallic-scented air. Seth's hair stuck out from under his helmet, the strands not unlike pale rodents' tails. He grinned at Izzy as he dropped in to the bowl and popped an ollie along the bank.

Then she had looked up, and Cyrus appeared.

He stood at the sidelines, leaning on the wall, his hands in his pockets, watching the older, shorter, barrel-chested boy he'd come with shred the bowl. Izzy held her hand over her eyes; even with her sunglasses on, Cyrus burned too bright for her to be able to comprehend his presence at first. It was as if she'd conjured him.

He came and sat beside her. Nephy skated past and Izzy saw her friend eye them from inside the cavern of her helmet before she did a kick flip that sent her braids flying and was gone.

"Hey," Cyrus said. "What's up?"

"Just watching," Izzy said.

"You skate?"

She pulled up one leg of her jeans and showed him the Frankenstein scars on her ankle from where she'd shattered it, heard the tibia and fibula bones crackle like broken china on either side. The doctor had opened her up, inserted two metal rods and a screw. "Not anymore. What about you?" His body had an alertness to it, a quick muscularity, but he didn't carry a board.

"Not like my brother, Ripper Joe over there."

Joe skated past and gave her a cold look over the top of his sunglasses before executing a perfect darkslide.

"What do you do then?" Izzy asked Cyrus.

He laughed. His teeth flashed crooked and white with a few gold fillings she could see as he tilted his head back. "I listen to music. And I build things."

"Like what?"

"Like places to live that I can escape to one day." He laughed again. "You?"

"I listen to music and read law books alone in a trailer from which I hope to escape to a place you've built one day," she said, surprising herself with the boldness. Well, if she couldn't skate like a badass fiend anymore, she could at least speak her mind.

"Law books?"

"Yeah. It interests me." Later she would explain the interest came from wanting to help kids like herself.

He stared straight ahead for a moment as if gathering his thoughts. Then he turned to her, took off his sunglasses, leveled his gaze with hers, and held out his hand. She shook it. His skin had the texture of firm warm fruit. "I'm Cyrus."

"Izzy."

"Your whole name?"

"Yes. Why?"

He looked at her for a long moment. "Dawn," was all he said.

And then Seth skidded up, popped his skateboard into his hands, stood over them, blocking the sun.

"Look," Seth said. "Two peas."

❀ ❀ ❀

After Seth's father died of lung cancer, Nephy moved into the ranch house and she and Seth married soon after. Now she ran a daycare facility out of the place. Plastic Halloween skeleton hands scrabbled their way out of the dirt next to wooden tombstones that read, "Died of Drain Bamage," "Blow-Dried Hair in Bathtub," and "Rest in Pieces." Seth must have made them in his workshop. A rubber monster mask hung on the front door, a plastic skeleton with a plastic spider fastened to its pelvis hung on the doorknob, and a jack-o'-lantern moldered in the sun.

No one answered when Izzy knocked, so she went around back.

Skateboard wheels on hot cement had the dirty-sweet smell of creosote in the rain. Sounded kind of like rain, too. But, of course, no rain. Not here. Kids, some practically babies, others older, dropped into the empty bowl of the pool, popped ollies along the bank, and carved away.

Nephy held court from a plastic chaise lounge in the shade, surrounded by a group of the littler kids eating their leftover Halloween candy. She looked up over the rim of her sunglasses, eyes lined with dark, like a wild cat's, lashes crisped with mascara. Izzy could see Nephy's naval poking out like the top of a finger pushing up from damp sand.

"Hey, queen," Nephy said. She moved her hands in the air like a mesmerist so her silver rings and fresh white-tipped acrylics caught sunlight.

Could the ethyl methacrylate and polymethacrylate in the acrylic formula harm a baby in the womb, Izzy found herself thinking. And did the baby have fingernails of its own by now?

"Have you seen Cyrus?" she asked, bringing herself back.

"Wait, what?"

"He wasn't there when I got up this morning."

"Did he go to Twentynine Palms?"

"No, he left his truck at home."

"That's crazy."

"Has Seth heard from him?"

"Seth's getting beer. We had that haunted house thing here for the kids last night. You can try to call him."

A kid—little kid, maybe ten—wiped out and Nephy got up and went to him. She kneeled and comforted the crying boy, wiping his nose on the hem of her T-shirt.

"I have to go," Izzy said.

Nephy glanced back over her oiled shoulder. "Call if you need us."

"Thanks," Izzy said.

"Of course. We're always here for you."

Izzy heard the kids in the pool grinding concrete like teeth or the bones of fish. When she got back into her car, she called Seth, but he didn't pick up. Then she forced herself to call the local hospitals and emergency rooms. "Twenty-seven-year-old man, six feet two inches, black hair, hazel eyes," she repeated. Nothing. Good, she told herself. That's good. He hasn't been hurt.

✤✤✤

Cyrus's parents, Del and Jody, sat on the dilapidated front porch of their house drinking soda. Izzy pulled up next to Del's rusted out truck. When Cyrus and his brother Joe were kids, Del, an ex-marine, set off bombs in the sand dunes for fun. Cyrus would cower under the kitchen table until Del forced him out. He could pick Cyrus up easily then, by the scruff of his neck, before Cyrus outgrew him by two inches. "Don't be a pussy," Del said. "It'll make you a man."

Izzy approached, kicking tumbleweeds that tried to catch witchily at her jeans and Converse. She wanted to take off her hoodie—it was getting hell of hot—but she'd hurried out of the house without a bra. Del stood, scowling past her from under his cowboy hat at Cyrus's truck.

"Where's Cyrus?" he asked.

"Hi, Iz," Jody said. She was freckled, auburn-haired-and-eyed, short and heavy-set, the complete opposite of Del and clearly not Cyrus's bio-mom, though you could see her in Joe. She'd tried her best to take care of both her kids, but it just wasn't enough. "Want a Coke?"

"No, thanks, Jody." Izzy stopped at the base of the porch. "I'm here 'cause I don't know where Cyrus is. I woke up this morning and he was gone."

"Gone?" Del sat back down, rubbed his head like it hurt. PTSD, Cyrus always said. Jody reached to hold onto his sleeve, but he batted her hand away.

Izzy walked up the steps and stood on the sagging floorboards. "I thought you might have heard from him."

"Hasn't come by in a while," Del said. "Figured he was too busy with his work and all." Did Izzy detect a snort?

"I hope Cyrus is okay," Jody said. She was clutching at her own sleeves now.

"Anyone been around asking after him? Like any of Joe's old friends or something?" Izzy realized she was imitating the rhythms and cadence of their speech. A survival mechanism learned in childhood, a way to blend in when she felt uncertain or afraid.

Del finished his Coke, tossed the can to the ground, and crushed it with his cowboy boot. "Joe's a good boy," Del said. "Cyrus, too. Joe just got in with the wrong crowd."

"I know," Izzy said. "That's why I was wondering—"

"We love our boys," Jody said. She looked like she might start crying. "We made some mistakes, but we love them. They're going to make something of themselves. Even Joe."

"Is there anyone you think I should talk to?" Izzy could feel her throat tighten.

"Maybe ask your mom and dad?" Jody said.

"Why them?" Izzy's parents and Cyrus avoided each other as much as possible. Larry had never approved of him, ever since he'd gotten Leanne's "little girl" pregnant. Izzy losing the baby hadn't helped; Leanne admitted later she'd wanted a grandchild. "But out here by the Sea, they all die," she'd mumbled, and then refused to explain what she meant.

"I think I saw him over there the other day," Jody said.

Izzy smelled selenium and phosphate wafting in from the cadaverous beach. "Let me know if you hear from him."

"You, too," said Jody. "We love our boys..."

❋❋❋

Slab City, or The Slabs, once a California Badlands marine base, was now abandoned. Slabbers like Larry and Leanne had turned their back on society, infiltrated the area, and set up camp. He had rigged running water, electricity, and a sewage system, though the area as a whole had none of these things. He believed in free land, free art, and anarchy, "which is by definition free." Although the area was considered "lawless," the community had its own kind of laws, and, overall, the vibe was mostly respectful. In spite of this, Izzy had been wanting to leave there from as far back as she could remember.

On the way to her parents' trailer, Izzy stopped at Alma's Trading Post, a kind of one-woman, outdoor flea market. Alma knew a lot about what went on around town. When Izzy arrived, she heard a whistle and looked up to see Alma perched in her tree house like a wizened bird.

"Is that Izzy?" Alma had already started down the rope ladder, spry for an oldster. She stomped across the yard full of car parts, broken furniture, chipped plates, and plastic toys, and she stood in front of Izzy, akimbo elbows piercing the dusty air.

"You haven't seen Cyrus, have you?" Izzy asked.

"Have you been to that Nephy's house?"

"Yes. I was just there."

"Just asking." Alma's eyes looked shrewd as a crow's eyes. "I know they are friends."

"We're all friends," Izzy said.

"All friends..." Alma said. "I saw him over there a few months ago."

"Saw Cyrus?"

"Yes."

She meant that time when Nephy had called crying because Seth was drunk, threatened her. Cyrus went over to check. "He was helping them out," Izzy said.

"Helping them out."

Shut up, old bird.

The cross-hatching of wrinkles reminded Izzy of the doll heads Leanne used to make out of dried apples with teeth from grains of rice. As the apples dried, they began to smell more and more of vinegar. Now, Alma's apple doll mouth opened, and Izzy almost expected to see rice teeth, but the teeth she saw weren't nearly that white. "You don't want to mess with that," Alma said.

"Mess with what?"

"Anything, these days. Strange things going on around here."

"What does that mean?"

"Rumors."

"What kind?"

"Some kind of Satist cult thing."

"Some kind of what?"

"A Satist cult."

Izzy almost laughed. "Like, sadist?"

"No, Satist. Satan."

"Satanic?" Izzy asked queasily, imagining headless chickens and pentagrams painted on boulders with blood. She'd forgotten how crazy Alma was.

"Yeah. Beware of cults! Practice safe *sects*."

Ha. Yeah. "What have you heard, Alma?"

"I don't know. Just things. Something afoot."

No wonder Cyrus didn't want to raise a kid out here. "What does that even mean, Alma? Seriously."

"Something's afoot. If you want to find someone, you have to put yourself in their shoes," Alma said, as if she had picked these words of wisdom from the empty blue sky. She chuckled at her joke and began to whistle. It was no use. Izzy wondered if the air out here made everyone crazy, or was it the water? But she, herself, had been raised on both.

❉ ❉ ❉

Izzy's mother kept rinsing dishes and puffing a cigarette when Izzy entered the trailer where she'd grown up. The cigarette smoke couldn't mask the smell of the jackrabbits Larry killed and skinned, or the resin of creosote—greasewood, he sometimes called it—that he picked to make teas and ointments.

Larry used to quiz her: *How old can a creosote plant live to be? That's right, ten thousand. I'd like to get me some of that. Maybe it will wear off in the picking. Describe the flowers. Yes, solitary, axillary. Fruits? Globose with five indehiscent one-seeded carpels covered by trichomes. Define axillary, globose, indehiscent, and trichomes.*

Izzy knew way too much about the plant. Larry had homeschooled her, along with Seth and Nephy, even though they were all a grade apart, and Izzy had learned to list facts, usually scientific ones, as a way to calm herself when she was anxious or afraid. Once Cyrus had asked her how she got so smart. She'd tried to laugh it off, but he persisted.

"It's just a coping mechanism," she said. "And Larry, I guess."

Cyrus had said, "It's those encyclopedias you read for fun. And just the way you look at things. Your dad didn't teach you that. That's who you are." Being adopted by parents like Jody and Del, Cyrus believed more in nature than nurture anyway.

"When'd you start that up?" Izzy asked, taking the butt from between Leanne's lips. Leanne, her hands in dishwater, didn't try to resist. Just kept staring through the lace curtains at the bottle cap wind chimes in the juniper tree outside.

"You should have told me you were coming." Leanne looked around the trailer. "I'd have cleaned up."

In spite of the smells, the place appeared orderly as ever—Leanne still dealt with her stress by cleaning. That was one thing Izzy had inherited from her.

"I'm looking for Cyrus. Jody says he was by the other day." Izzy snuffed out the cigarette on the sole of her shoe and tossed the butt in the trash.

Leanne gazed yearningly after the cigarette. "Tea party?"

"No, thanks." Izzy held up her canteen of water. She'd had enough of Leanne's secret fairy tea parties for one lifetime. "Did Cyrus stop by here recently?"

"Come outside and we can chat."

Izzy took a breath. On the way out of the trailer, she passed a framed photograph of herself with her parents on her thirteenth birthday. Larry had his arm around her a little too tightly, she thought now. Leanne's smile was almost a grimace. Larry—raw-boned, grizzled even then. Izzy stood between them, towering above her plump, fair mother, wearing a hoodie with too-short sleeves and a flowered sundress Leanne had made her. She had hated that dress and would start wearing all black a few months later. Her brow was furrowed with worry, her eyes anxious, shoulders tense, shirking from Larry's touch.

Now, she followed Leanne into the yard. Izzy's mother toddled along in socks and sandals. Everything with her took time and patience—neither of which Izzy felt she had at the moment.

A mannequin with a mermaid's tail lay in a child's swimming pool. Leanne stroked the mermaid's blonde wig under the intricate crown of tilapia bones she'd collected from the shores of the Salton Sea. Crazy as she was, it was hard to deny that Leanne was an artist in her way.

She picked up the plastic baby doll from a large chair upholstered with pale blue fabric. The chair looked surprisingly clean for something that lived outside, even though the elements had gutted it. Leanne sat and placed the doll in her lap.

"So, has Cyrus been by?" Izzy asked again. The air around her head felt ready to combust with heat, and when she sat, the plastic slats of the lawn chair ridged her thighs.

Leanne's mouth seemed to have caved in on itself, and Izzy wondered if she'd lost another tooth, poor thing. Izzy had tried to give her money for dental work, but Leanne wouldn't accept it—said one less tooth didn't matter. "Haven't seen him."

Nearby, under the juniper, Leanne had buried the china teacups she collected so that no one would find them. She'd hung the wind chimes on the juniper branches, along with a collection of mismatched shoes she'd found, including a few pairs of little girls' ballet slippers. The pleated pink leather had now turned gray.

Leanne saw Izzy looking. "Alma had a whole load of them down at the Post. They remind me of you. When you were little. Remember how you always wanted some?"

In a breeze, the leaves trembled silver like the tinsel Leanne draped around the mannequin at Christmas. Now the thing wore a witch's hat, and a broomstick was tied to its wrist with a band.

"I don't care about your shoes. Jody said she thought Cyrus was here."

Leanne patted her blonde hair as if it were a 1950s society lady's beehive. She opened a large book of fairy tales, the one she used to read to Izzy when she was a child, and set it in front of the doll. Handless maidens, eyeless princes, and decapitated heads singing in wells. Those tales frightened Izzy as much as Larry's ghost stories.

She remembered one tale from another book about a fisherman who falls in love with a mermaid, and to be with her, he has to give up his human soul. After he visits a witch in red-soled shoes and dances with her before a laconic devil, the fisherman cuts away his own soul shadow with a knife. The soul travels around the world and brings back stories of jeweled and bloodied gods that impart great wisdom, and of lush palaces where courtiers wear cloaks embroidered with seed pearls and iridescent beetle wings.

The fisherman rejects the soul's wisdom and riches for love. Then the soul offers him a girl who can dance with feet like white doves, and the fisherman is tempted. He leaves the mermaid, who can never dance on feet like doves, or any feet at all, and she dies. A priest buries them where no flowers grow but is proved wrong about souls and love when unknown flowers sprout on their single grave.

"Cyrus?" Leanne said. "Where'd he get to?"

Izzy forced herself to inhale, exhale a few times. "Where's Dad?" she finally asked.

"Probably out drinking again. I have no idea." Leanne stared out at the swirls of heat along the horizon. "Might be for the best."

"What is? Dad—"

"That Cyrus isn't coming back," Leanne said.

Her snake-words dug their fangs in. This was why Izzy rarely came to visit. She stood and brushed dust off her jeans as if she were brushing the words away with it. "I have to go."

Leanne raised the cracked teacup to her lips. It was too small, and she spilled some of the plain water she called tea down the front of her tie-dyed T-shirt. Then she tried to pour some water into the doll's mouth, and the liquid dribbled down its chin. Izzy found herself thinking: *At least Leanne hasn't taken to hanging baby dolls in the juniper tree.*

"Might be for the best," Leanne said again.

Had Leanne always been this crazy? It seemed to have gotten worse the last few years. Izzy's throat swelled with dust and frustration. She wanted Cyrus, here with her now, more than she wanted water. "Please don't talk like that," she said.

Leanne shrugged and patted the doll's head.

"Don't speak like that about him, okay?" Izzy repeated.

"I'm sorry, child. I don't care to see you hurt."

"It's too late. And Cyrus is not the one who did the hurting."

❀❀❀

Izzy couldn't get back in the truck fast enough.

The cab smelled of Cyrus's sunscreen and the pine air freshener he liked. Izzy banged the steering wheel with her palms. She'd already exhausted all likely possibilities, and even the unlikely ones.

What the hell, Cyrus? You making me talk to the cops?

She remembered going to the police once, as a kid, after Larry had pulled out his pocketknife. "You sure he wasn't just showing you the knife?" the officer asked. "You sure you didn't misread the situation, young lady?" Later she wondered if she'd overreacted, but she still vowed never to ask the cops for help again. Still, this time was different. And, of course, Cyrus and she had always known: she would go anywhere for him, even the Riverside County Sheriff-Coroner's Department.

❀❀❀

A sand-colored building flanked by electro-shocked palm trees. "Wanted" and "missing persons" posters lined the walls. The felons had eyes that didn't quite sit right in their heads, eyes that contained what appeared to be a clear vision of the future they intended to manifest. The missing persons posters showed men, women, and children with no hint of what might become of them. Their loved ones had chosen the best smiling pictures so that someone might feel pity, or even remorse, and try to help.

The officer's skin and eyes had a dull, fluorescent pallor. Sleepless nights, too much caffeine, and human roadkill. He sat her down.

His nametag read Decker. She hadn't realized her hands were shaking until she handed him the picture from her wallet.

She thought she saw the man's mouth twitch slightly.

"Cyrus Rivera," she said.

"Yes." *Yes, so...* She heard something in the officer's tone after she'd spoken Cyrus's name. Brushing her arm across her face to wipe the sweat from her brow, she could still smell the salt and musk of sex on her skin. It was a scent she'd come to think of not as Cyrus's or hers but as theirs combined.

"You say he just wasn't around when you got up this morning?"

"Yes. But his truck was outside."

"What about his ID?"

"He kept it in his jeans."

Skepticism edged the man's voice. "So, he might have gotten up, gotten dressed, gone outside with his ID. Seems pretty straightforward. What about footprints or tire tracks?"

"Nothing."

"What about his cell phone?

"He left it. Charging."

"You checked it?"

She didn't want to admit that she'd forgotten the passcode or, worse, that he'd changed it. Had he changed it? Why? She said, "He left his socks. Like he'd been in a rush."

"You been arguing?"

"No!" She thought of the exultant way Cyrus had touched her, looked into her face like she was made of light. Did him not wanting a baby constitute an argument? No. He'd said he loved her, hadn't he? He always said he loved her.

But he changed the passcode?

She saw the officer glance down at the silver band on her ring finger. "You two married?"

Might as well be. But she shook her head, no.

Was that a smirk on his face? "Signs of anything else out of the ordinary?" he asked.

Izzy bristled cat-like from the nape of her neck and all down her spine. "He wasn't there. His phone and socks and—"

"I understand. Other than that. How was his mood?"

His mood? How could she make this man see? "We've been together almost nine years." How could she explain what "together" meant—that they had seen each other exclusively all that time, even as kids; that they had, together, built a house with a doggy door for her tortoise. They were all going to move to LA together. Weren't they?

"Anyone that might have had a problem with him?" the officer asked.

She shook her head again. Cyrus wasn't close to a lot of people, but everyone he ever met seemed to fall in love with him. Except Joe, maybe. "He has a brother at CAL," she ventured.

"I'm aware," said Decker. So, that was what she'd seen on the man's face. Guilt by association. Or something more? "The Rivera brothers got themselves into some trouble growing up," he added, squinting at his computer screen.

"That was Joe." Joe's ex-girlfriend Selma had asked him to deliver a package. Joe insisted that he hadn't known about the drugs inside, but he'd been put away just the same.

The officer cleared his throat.

"Cyrus never—"

"Has your *husband*—Has Mr. Rivera," Decker corrected himself with a subtle but distinct flourish, and she wondered if he meant something by it, or was she just being paranoid? "Has Mr. Rivera ever taken off like this before?"

"No." She added, "Sir," and composed her face, hoping to encourage some more sympathy. Cyrus did check in always, right? The stress had slowed her mind.

"It happens," the officer said. "Sometimes people take off."

"But the truck," she said.

"There are other modes of transportation, Miss Ames."

She was losing ground here. "I'd like to file a report." They'd changed the law in California; you didn't have to wait anymore.

He drummed his fingers on the desk top. "This kind of thing happens all the time. Men leave."

"*Men* leave?" She could no longer play the part she thought the officer wanted. "He would never leave me. He would never."

Izzy saw the tightness in Decker's face, then—she'd irritated him, apparently.

"Look, lady, I don't know what to tell you. I know you're upset. But like I said, these things happen. Doesn't sound like a case of foul play." He stood up, jammed his thumbs into his belt loops, and thrust out his chest. His stance reminded her of the cop she'd talked to when Larry scared her with the knife.

Doesn't sound like a case of foul play.

She would have been grateful for that. If she believed it were true. You can't curse at the cops, though, she told herself, standing to leave. You might need them.

"Ms. Ames."

She stopped and turned around at the door.

"If he's not back in three days—if you find some evidence he didn't just walk out—come back around. But until then, there's really nothing we can do here."

✤ ✤ ✤

So, Izzy went home. But she regretted that she'd backed down. How many times would her past trauma cause her to capitulate? She couldn't do it this time. *Come back in three days? Doesn't sound like a case of foul play. Of foul play. Of foul play.* Denial had turned to pain had turned to anger. Fuck the cops and their insinuations. She'd write a report of her own.

She looked at the rumple of sheets on the futon, the neat stacks of cassette tapes and the boom box, the sewing machine and acoustic guitar. Her massage table folded in the corner. Her favorite law book, officially nicknamed the "Dog Book," with a picture of a St. Bernard and the words "Help is on The Way," across the cover, lay open on the floor. Cyrus had put a juice jar full of desert grasses on top of the bookcase he'd built. The candles had pooled into wax; ghosts of sage smoke now silvered the air.

The tortoise blinked at her, his eyelids closing from the bottom up in that odd way they did, and swung his head to the side. "You okay, little three feet?" she whispered, knowing he responded best to soft sounds—who didn't?

Izzy cut up some apple for Yard to eat, blinking slowly back at him. She'd read you could do this with cats, to connect with them, so she always blinked at the tortoise, just in case it worked. Then she stroked his shell to make him feel "at home" as the animal rescue people had instructed her to do daily. It was a brief respite for her, as well, a kind of meditation, imagining the sensitive nerve endings that she knew were embedded in the rough shell. But touching the tortoise now made her think of what Cyrus had told her when he'd first seen Yard: "Some people link them with death." "I thought it was eternal life," she'd said.

Now, Izzy searched "Cyrus Rivera" on her phone. There was nothing online except his construction website. Cyrus didn't use social media. But Izzy composed a notice for a missing persons site:

6'2", 175 lbs. black hair, hazel eyes. D.O.B. 1/28/1990. Distinguishing Features: Tattoo of red roses and black serpent on right shoulder. Tattoo of skull with red roses for eyes on left shoulder. Panther tattoo across upper back. Falcon tattoo on lower back. Tattoo across left side of chest: "Izzy Forever." Silver band on left ring finger.

On Monday, November 1, at about 7:00 a.m., Cyrus Rivera was discovered missing from his residence in Salton City, Imperial County, CA. Rivera's 1988 half-ton, black Chevrolet Silverado long-bed pickup truck remained in front of the residence. Rivera never returned home. He is most likely wearing Levi's 501 jeans, a black short-sleeved T-shirt, black Doc Martens boots, and NO SOCKS. Anyone with

any information please contact ~~the Morongo Basin Sheriff's station~~
Izzy Ames at—

Smiling pictures of the lost might make the viewer more sympathetic, but she couldn't bring herself to use the photo in her wallet, so Izzy took the wooden box out from under the bed. There wasn't much inside—most of the more current shots were on the computer, and neither Izzy nor Cyrus kept many family pictures. But there were a few photographs.

An elementary school portrait of Cyrus. Dimples. Missing teeth. Hair slicked back, a button-down shirt, even a tie. "I hated that tie, but now I see why Jody made me wear it. Damn, I looked like a little girl," he said, years later, laughing.

One high school picture with hair in his eyes, a Nirvana T-shirt, and a fierce scowl. "Such a tough guy," she teased.

Izzy and Cyrus at the waterfall oasis at 49 Palms. In spite of the drought, that day water had spilled over the rocks, pooling brightly among the rocks at their feet as they stood in the shade of the ragged palm trees after hiking for almost an hour.

Izzy and Cyrus at his West Shores High School graduation with their arms around each other's shoulders. As soon as the ceremony was over, he ripped off the gown and put the mortarboard on her head, called her "Professor."

Cyrus with his new Silverado. Both of them shining. He'd named the truck Plata. "We will travel the continent in her," he'd promised.

Cyrus, bare-chested, revealing the still-raw tattoo of her name. "My best ink ever."

Izzy and Cyrus in front of the shack they had built together. She wore overalls with the bib hanging down around her waist and a white tank top. He wore white painter's pants and a black T-shirt. They posed with a rake. "Desert Gothic," he titled the photo, but she called it "Home." When you grew up with parents like theirs, you were always looking for a place to feel safe.

A photo of Izzy and Cyrus on vacation at a little motel in Desert Hot Springs. The pool was encased in glass and filled with natural hot spring water. Izzy and Cyrus made love so often on that trip that she'd been sore and euphoric for a week or two after. "Someday we should get married here," he'd told her.

A few strips of black-and-white photo booth images of Izzy and Cyrus clowning around, kissing. The last image of one strip was of them, side by side with their eyes closed, faces like masks. They'd taken these at a roadside carnival. Cyrus had showed her a journal entry he'd written when he was a kid, when he kept records of things to help feel alive. He described a dream of riding a carnival Ferris wheel "with a beautiful woman with dark flowing hair." He and Izzy took it as a sign.

She shuffled through more pictures.

One had been taken the night she and Cyrus had met at Seth and Nephy's. Some girl on the yearbook staff had snapped it and given a copy to Izzy. The girl said, "It was crazy how much I could tell how into each other you were."

In the photo, Izzy and Cyrus sat on Seth's tattered, chartreuse damask couch. She could remember now: the television droned, music played, people laughed. Cigarette butts lay like squashed insects in a crudely made clay ashtray shaped like the Salton Sea. Izzy's fingers stuck to the surface of the coffee table where something sugary had spilled. The light from the television greened Cyrus's eyes, made the room look like they were inside an aquarium.

Izzy and Cyrus weren't touching in the photo, but you could tell how much they wanted to. Their heads leaning together. Their legs lined up, thigh-to-thigh. They both wore black T-shirts, black jeans, and black Converse. They both had the same skin tone, clearly golden even in the green light. They both had the same black hair—he hadn't cut his yet and the stubble hadn't grown in on his face.

For a second, she had the thought of showing the photo to Cyrus. No, no. It hit again like a fist knocking her back in her seat: he wasn't here. She put the photo away.

They'd stopped taking as many photographs in recent years but here was one: Cyrus, not smiling, but it didn't look like a mug shot either, and his brooding features tended toward that sometimes.

She set up a page on the missing persons site and signed up for local alerts from the SBPD. She used the picture and report to create a flyer. She was careful about the font she chose, the placement of his face on the page. Should she change "NO SOCKS" to lower case? Did it make her sound unhinged? Yes, better in lower case. Finally, she clicked on Missing Persons of America and submitted the same shot and the description. When she clicked through the photos, children's smiles needled ice to her heart.

Jennifer Lane, sixteen, was found stabbed to death in a rail car... If anyone has any information, please contact the Homicide Cold Case Team at the telephone number below.

Missing from Colorado. May have travelled to California.

He was last seen wearing a CSI T-shirt, black cargo pants, white socks, and well-worn Sketchers athletic shoes with orange trim.

Three teens missing for over 40 years found at bottom of lake.

Please.

Please.

Please.

One young man, Elijah Chan, had Cyrus's crow-black hair, long, the way it had been when he and Izzy had met, sun-burnished skin and full lips parted over charmingly pointed incisors. He posed with a beer in his hand, an eagle tattooed across his narrow chest. A beautiful child. Izzy tried to imagine his mother dreading every phone call. How could you go on after that?

A series of clicks and Izzy came to a page that featured artists' forensic reconstructions of unidentified "decedents." The artists, with compassion, had drawn these visages in a state of repose. Still, the eyes looked lost. Runaways, prostitutes, hitchhikers, migrant workers, all organized by state.

She found California.

Bodies raped, mutilated, dismembered, strangled, tortured, torched, left in ditches. Bodies that had never been claimed by anyone. The website said that dental X-rays, spinal injuries, and surgical implants were the only ways to identify the deceased if DNA was not an option. But artists could guess at some things from the remains, like the appearance of muscles and bones that shaped the face. Noses and mouths were more difficult, as was the skin. Though it could be surmised that older skin had more lines, less elasticity, that the eyes sank deeper in, the orifices enlarged. Ages could only be determined within a range of about fifteen years.

It all sounded so fucking cold.

Sometimes the Jane or John Does had no facial reconstruction to mark them—just a photo, perhaps, of personal effects remained—a tarnished nickel chain, a pair of turquoise earrings, boots with worn out soles, a belt with a Harley Davidson buckle. T-shirts with pictures and slogans that had meant something to them once—Hawaii, New York, a movie queen, a rock god: a dream of where they had been or wanted to go, an image of the person they lusted after or wanted to be. Izzy almost heard the objects keening.

Larry had told her that the term John Doe had come from an 1834 song about "Two Giants...who always travel hand in hand/ John Doe and Richard Roe/Their fee-faw-fum's an ancient plan/ To smell the purse of an Englishman."

Fee-fi-fo-fum. Jack and the Beanstalk. Yes, fairy tales were brutal. Eyes pecked out. Heads chopped off. Bodies burned. Cannibalism. Blood-sniffing giants. Clever girls. Leanne sometimes called Izzy "Clever Gretel."

"Gretel wore shoes with red soles." (Like the ones worn by the witch in the mermaid story, Izzy had thought). "She told her master's guest that master was planning to cut off guest's ears, so he ran away. Clever Gretel blamed him for the wine and chickens she'd eaten herself."

"Clever and cruel," Izzy told the Johns and the Janes. She didn't like this type of story.

Valentine Does had been found on February fourteenth; Lavender Does wore purple sweaters; there were some Baby Does. Princess, Precious. Izzy wondered who named them. Had the public or the investigators tried to show some compassion this way? There was one child who particularly haunted her. He was called "Box Boy," and it was believed that he had been kidnapped, sexually assaulted, murdered, and left in a cardboard box. His hair had been recently cut, and his ears had been pierced.

The Janes, the Johns, the Baby Does. They cleaved your heart in half. Cyrus was not among them.

She buried her face in the woven blanket on their bed, closed her eyes, and inhaled—almonds and smoke. The scent of her love for him.

With Cyrus gone, she might as well have been breathing cyanide.

It made no sense. People like Cyrus didn't just disappear from their homes in the night. Crazy people or elderly people with dementia or runaways; not strong, sane young men who were planning to move to LA with their lovers someday. Unless Cyrus didn't love her. Was he unhappy? After all this time? How could he have been with her all this time and then decided, with no warning, that it was over? Had she pushed him too hard about a baby? She hadn't pushed him, had she? He couldn't have stopped loving her that easily. But the alternative was worse, and she was afraid.

Bluebeard

The next morning, Izzy woke wet-eyed. She dragged the back of her hand across her face, feeling the cold metal of the silver ring against her hot skin. She would not let herself cry for him. She would not cry. It would mean he was really gone.

She checked her phone. Messages from Nephy and Seth asking if she'd heard from Cyrus, if she needed their help. She texted back saying she could use help putting up flyers, but they both had to work that day, so she told them she'd go on her own.

Come for dinner later, Nephy texted. *You really have to eat. I know you don't eat when you're stressed. And bring flyers!*

Izzy texted back *Thank you*, then picked up Cyrus's phone, considered entering some random numbers to try and unlock it but decided against this. She couldn't risk any extra tries without some clue. So, she got out of bed, grabbed the flyers, and left, wearing the same clothes she'd put on the morning before.

The temperature had crept up, over one hundred, and the truck seemed to simmer and fizz with heat—she had to sit on a towel and use a T-shirt to touch the steering wheel. *Burning like my love for him. Burning like the end of the world.*

❀❀❀

Izzy spent the day putting up more flyers—the post office, the liquor store, the mini-mart, the gas station, the bank, traffic lights, on the walls of a crumbling, abandoned, graffiti-strewn motel by the highway on the outskirts of town.

To try to calm herself, she stopped at Leonard Knight's Salvation Mountain monument. Beneath the cross and the words "God is Love," thick layers of pastel paint shone in the light of the setting sun, almost blinding. She climbed, slipping on paint, up and over. Below her lay the monument like bright fabric. Three young Japanese tourists, wearing polka-dot mini dresses, silk flower crowns, and flip-flops, changed into high heels and tottered out to pose for a photo shoot in the center of the painted quilt.

Izzy went back down the mountain and entered a grotto where the artist had painted blue and purple birds, pink and red roses, green and brown trees, white clouds and messages from the Bible on the plaster walls and columns. Inside the grotto was a shrine where people placed laminated photographs of their beloved deceased. An older white woman with a sweet smile and a Christmas sweater. A woman from Mexico with a wrinkle-stitched face. A middle-aged Asian man in a suit. A high school portrait of a girl with blonde hair. A young, bearded hiker. Izzy saw them all rising up in that grotto, after the sun had set, shambling out into the desert searching for their families. So much for finding solace here. She wasn't going to post a flyer in the grotto, this shrine to the dead, but she tacked up a few pictures of Cyrus by the roadside and left.

❀❀❀

Salvation Mountain wasn't too far from Head Hunters, so Izzy stopped to see if she could find Larry, since Leanne mentioned he'd been drinking again. The place was more like an outdoor campground with lights, beads, and fish net strung over a makeshift structure among some Airstreams. Tiki heads stared at her from the depths of their carved-out, humanoid eyes. Locals and a few tourists lounged around with their "bring your own" liquor. Larry was there all right.

She stood watching him for a moment before she approached. Izzy's father sat in a beach chair with some kind of fancy drink. Even had an umbrella. Although she was almost as tall as he was, Izzy hadn't fully outgrown the fear she had of him ever since she'd found the black kitten dangling from the clothesline.

"Looks like you," Leanne had said about the kitten when Izzy first bought the animal home from the dump where she'd found her. "We can have a tea party!"

Izzy draped the fern of the kitten's backbone against her chest, and the creature purred and purred. She never stopped. Even when she ate or drank, she purred. Izzy felt the thrum in her heart as she fell asleep.

The next morning, she went outside and saw the kitten hanging. Izzy began to scream and scream, Leanne rushed out and held her, and then Larry came and pinched the clothespins and let the tiny body collapse into the dirt.

He never admitted to anything. He said the cat must have gotten out, someone must have caught it and put it there.

That was when Izzy realized she'd had her first darkness, although she wouldn't name it that until years later when Ted played the song for her and Cyrus. He was the only person she'd ever told about the kitten and about the darkness that had perhaps tried to forewarn her of what was to come.

"I think I've felt that, too," he'd said, pulling her against his chest, into a different kind of darkness. One that shone like a sea at night.

That was all Cyrus would say.

"Greetings, wayward daughter," Larry said now. He grinned. The expression *long in the tooth* came to mind. "I heard what happened."

"You haven't seen him, have you?" she asked. Larry was more lucid than Leanne but even less trustworthy.

He scratched his whiskers—a few grays had sprouted among the dark hairs—with the tips of long fingers. "How could anyone leave you, daughter? That makes no sense. He been drinking?"

"Cyrus doesn't drink." She repeated what had happened, said she didn't think he would have just left her.

"Tied at the hip still?" Larry had never been a Cyrus fan, even before the pregnancy. Less so after. "I'm sure he'll come back. Stay and have a drink."

"You know I don't drink either." She swatted at a fly. "Jody said he came to see you."

"Jody Rivera? She's almost as crazy as your mom. Why don't you go ask that brother of his in the can? Maybe it has something to do with drugs."

"Fuck you," Izzy said, but under her breath. You never knew how Larry might react. There was no way Cyrus was involved with drugs, but what if Joe or the people he knew on the outside had something to do with Cyrus going missing? It would take a couple of weeks to get in to see Joe at CAL. She didn't feel she had two weeks to wait.

Izzy walked away from Larry and the tiki heads with their empty wooden sockets. "Didn't ask how I'm doing," Larry called after her. "But it's all good in paradise."

Her father was an optimist; she had to give him that. He said you had to be, in order to survive out here. Or anywhere.

❀❀❀

After she had dropped off some flyers with Leanne and Jody—not really expecting either of them, especially Leanne, to be of much help—Izzy went back to see Seth and Nephy at the house where Izzy and Cyrus had met almost a decade ago. The memory shimmered in her mind, as if the house had been lit up with candles and stocked with glass bottles of wine, the pool filled with water. But there had only been a lava lamp, cheap beer in tin cans, an empty concrete basin where people ashed their cigarettes and shattered their bones.

Nephy answered the door wearing a T-shirt that said "Lady of the House." Her belly stuck out over the top of her sweatpants; her hair scraped back off her face as if with the dull edge of a butter knife. She looked worried and tired, nothing like her usual bored, glamorous self. "Izzy," she said. "What can I do?"

Izzy shook her head. Nothing. No one could do anything. But she hadn't wanted to be alone. Now, seeing Nephy looking so different than she had just one day ago, obviously worried about Cyrus, Izzy felt herself crumbling, and Nephy reached out and led her over to the couch. The couch where at a party almost a decade ago she'd fallen in love. The swamp cooler hummed, chilling the air. A fever chill.

"Izzy?" Nephy said again, putting her arm around Izzy's trembling shoulders.

"I'm going to find him." Izzy's fingers plucked at some stuffing exploding from the couch's innards, then she tried to jam the white synthetic material back in. She swallowed the insect-sized lump in her throat and wouldn't look at Nephy.

"Izzy..." A perfect little vertical line formed between Nephy's brows. Izzy couldn't remember ever having seen it before.

"I'm going to go see everyone."

Nephy put her hands on her swelling belly, rubbing in circles. She stretched out her legs in front of her and pointed and flexed her feet with the French pedicure—shell-pink with a wider-than-natural white tip. Her big toe joints looked like distended knobs of bone from the toe-crushing, cartilage-destroying high-heeled shoes she liked to wear.

"Izzy," she repeated, a third time, staring at her feet, shaking her head. "You'll make yourself sick."

"I can't stop," she said.

###

Nephy made Izzy lie down and stroked her head until she fell asleep. When she woke from her nap, she smelled dinner cooking—cornbread and chili with pinto beans, hot peppers, and onions fried in olive oil. Izzy realized she hadn't had anything to eat since the night before.

Izzy and Seth sat at the Formica kitchen table with the blue-and-white-checked vinyl cloth while Nephy still futzed around in her chintz apron, skulls hidden among the cabbage roses. The three of them were like some messed up version of a suburban family, Izzy thought. Without Cyrus, Izzy became the child, the wayward overgrown daughter, staring blankly at her plate of food.

"You have to eat," Nephy said, joining them, tucking her butt into the chair.

Izzy didn't want to eat, but her mouth watered anyway. And she knew she needed her strength.

"Was there anything off you noticed about Cyrus in the last few weeks?" she asked after she'd had a few bites.

"He seemed fine. Just being Cyrus," Seth said.

Nephy nodded solemnly.

"What does that mean?"

"Kind of tight-lipped is all."

"Tight-lipped how?"

"Izzy, he never told me what was going on in that head of his. He never told anyone shit except you."

What had he told her? He had not told her the most important things—why he had left and where he had gone. She blinked hard and pressed a napkin to her eyes to catch any moisture, telling herself she wasn't crying, it was the residue from the fried onions in the air.

"Did Cyrus ever tell you about getting into trouble with the cops?"

Seth shrugged. "Like I said, never told me shit. Why?"

"The cop I went to made it sound that way."

"Cops." He looked like he was going to spit. Then he said, "When did you go to the cops?"

"Yesterday."

"What else did they say?"

"Nothing. As usual. Just tried to make it sound like Cyrus was trouble. Like Joe."

"Who wasn't trouble as a kid? They're useless, the cops. Did you call the hospitals?"

She nodded.

He cleared his throat. "I'm sorry to ask this, but you don't think he just took off?"

Nephy put a hand on Seth's arm and shook her head almost imperceptibly.

"No," Izzy said. "He wouldn't have left without an explanation." The words echoed in the hollow of her chest.

"I'll help," Seth said. "Nephy and me. We'll help. Leave some flyers and I'll make copies and post them around town."

✤✤✤

After they had cleared the table and washed and dried the dishes, the women quietly kissed goodbye. Izzy thanked Nephy and left. Seth was sitting on the deck of the boat out front, reading a paperback book in the dying light and smoking a cigarette. He looked a lot older than his wife. All that sun and smoke and booze. All that harm. You'd think if your dad died of lung cancer, you'd quit. Izzy remembered going fishing at the Salton Sea as a kid with Nephy and Seth. They'd stood on a rock as the sun set and the sea blistered red as the cherry of Seth's cigarette. The fish they caught were too toxic to eat.

Seth had poked a gelid orb with his fingertip. "At least it doesn't have three eyes."

"Don't," she had said, and he'd laughed. His own eyes had looked barnacle-hard, she remembered.

"Heading home?" he said now.

She told him yes.

He began to pick at the blue paint peeling off the boat like bark. She saw the scars on his shoulders and remembered the iguana with the burns at the rescue center where she'd brought Yard to be evaluated. Seth had told her about the center—he liked to go there to look at the animals—and the burned iguana. He couldn't stop talking about it, almost obsessively, a strange gleam in his eye. Someone had burned that creature for fun. Izzy had wanted to take the iguana home, but he hadn't been available yet and when she went back, he was gone.

"Izzy."

She waited.

"He'll turn up," Seth said. "It's not like he never did this before."

"What do you mean?"

"I mean there were times when you called over here asking about him."

"Not for years." She could hardly even remember though. She wanted to go home, crawl into bed.

Seth bit at his lower lip, lengthening his chin, running a hand over his stubble—tinted blue in the evening light—to his neck with the prominent Adam's apple. "Like I said, Nephy and me will help."

"Thanks, Seth." She felt a wave of exhaustion and steadied herself against the boat.

"You okay, there? Need anything?"

"I'm okay. Just got to get home. Thank you."

She started to leave, looked back. Seth had leaned against the boat again and a tide of evening shadows lapped his feet. But it was Izzy who found herself floating away into darkness.

❋❋❋

By the time she got to the shack, her head felt as if someone had been battering her with dirty shoes like the ones hanging in Leanne's tree. Izzy fell into bed and gathered Cyrus's pillows into her arms. Together the pillows formed an effigy of a man.

Except for the odd job that kept him away, she had slept with Cyrus beside her for seven years; they had slept together on and off—in camp sites, abandoned buildings, or the back of his truck—for two before that. How could she ever sleep again without him?

Heart-Shaped Box

In Twentynine Palms, Izzy headed for the vegetable beds but found them deserted. The virid leaves; a blush creeping up the faces of the tomatoes and peppers. For a moment she thought, with a pain in her chest as if someone had squeezed her heart like a fruit: Cyrus must have been here to water early this morning. But—she caught herself—of course, that wasn't true.

Izzy opened the gate. The surface of the swimming pool lay smooth as tinted glass. Twin palm trees whispered to each other. How long had they stood there, like lovers? Years and years. The café rested under its awning. Cool inside air made the sweat on Izzy's skin congeal.

Ted squinted up at her from behind his round, wire-rimmed glasses and rubbed his chin. "Hey, Izzy. Did he show up yet?"

"Not yet." Izzy stared blankly at the yellow X-eyed smiley face on Ted's T-shirt.

The first night Izzy and Cyrus spent together, they listened to *Nevermind* on a boom box he'd found at a garage sale. They lay on a rock, their legs spread out in front of them. Their legs, almost the same length from hipbone to ankle. Their hands almost exactly the same size, too, palm to palm. The wind howled and tried to force its way through their woven blankets and under their clothes, but Cyrus had lit a fire and wrapped her in his arms.

"I don't think he was murdered," Cyrus had said.

Izzy had pushed a black lock of hair off his forehead. "Me either."

"That note they found. Calling himself names. Emasculated, infantile, unappreciative, erratic."

Sometimes Izzy thought she and Cyrus not only had the same legs and hands but the same mind. "Death," she said. "He called himself a death rocker. Didn't want his daughter to become that."

"Yes."

"And he loved them," Cyrus said. "His wife and kid. He loved them. He called his wife a goddess." He ran a finger over her eyebrow, down the side of her face, across her lips. Tingling, Izzy thought of smears of red lipsticks, the tear of white satin, bleach, tiaras, cigarette smoke. "He used the word altar."

"I'll worship at your altar," they said together. The singer had misspelled the word, Izzy remembered. Maybe he'd done it on purpose. *I'll worship at your alter*-ego? He'd also called himself "Jesus Man."

"Opiates in his blood stream," Cyrus said. "He did it himself."

That shiny boy full of songs, stomach burning and roiling with pain. In one picture, his wife balanced their baby on her white satin hip while she held his right hand. In his left, he dandled a baby bottle as if it were his. Then, just a short time later, gun to the head. Killing the music.

But Cyrus was happy. He was happy with her.

Now, Ted came around from the back of the bar to greet her. "You okay? I wanted to come see you, but it's been busy."

I am lost, I am lost, Izzy thought.

"Have you been eating?" Ted asked her.

In answer, she only held up the flyers. "Can I leave some?"

"Of course." He went back around the bar, washed his hands, took two slices of whole wheat bread and laid them on a plate on the counter. "I've been asking around, too. Still no word?"

"Nothing."

Ted spread the homemade prickly pear jam on one slice of bread. "Did anything happen that night? On Halloween? With the two of you?" When she didn't answer, he looked up and saw her expression. "Sorry," he said, opening a jar of almond butter.

"It's okay, thank you." She sat, almost catatonic, watching Ted make her an ice coffee, black.

"What else? What are you going to do?" He slid the cup and plate with the sandwich toward her, but she still couldn't eat, just drank the coffee down. "Izzy?"

"I'm going to keep looking for him," she said. "I'm waiting to get in to see his brother Joe at CAL."

"You're going to CAL. By yourself?"

"Yes."

Rubbing vigorously at an invisible stain on the curved wood bar, Ted said, "I don't want to overstep, but is it possible he just took off—"

Why did everyone seem to think this?

"He wouldn't—" *fall out of love with me just like that.* "He wouldn't just leave me without saying anything. He wouldn't leave his truck."

Izzy's boss nodded. *Humoring me? Was he?*

She realized how odd she sounded, as if the truck was more important to Cyrus than she was. What if he'd left the truck to make it look like something other than the truth—that he was done with her? None of it made any sense.

Ted looked out over her shoulder, through the glass to where the swimming pool now flashed with sun, like a fish before it's caught, unaware of any danger.

No more reassurances: "Be careful," he said.

❀ ❀ ❀

Barren desert, train tracks, and fields of alfalfa lined the highway. Irrigated water from the canals emptied out into the Salton Sea, making it even more fetid. Because of the constant sunshine and irrigation systems, the Imperial Valley farms stayed in operation almost all year. Groves of date palms stretched off into the distance behind an ornate iron gate, like a portal to fairyland or a desert Gothic novel.

Izzy turned off the highway. Beside a scruffy, stunted palm a sign read, "Welcome to Bombay Beach." She took a dirt road past the fire station and the Ski Inn. Like *skin*, Izzy thought for the first time, though she knew it was named for the water skiing that took place during the Salton Sea's pleasure days.

"You are beautiful," Cyrus had said, that last day at the Ski Inn. "I am strange."

Had any of this occurred, Izzy wondered? Or had it been a dream from which she awoke, only to find him gone?

✿✿✿

Izzy stopped at Ms. Aqua's Chow and Market, a brick box with iron bars at the single window and almost nothing on the shelves, just some candy bars in boxes and a bucket full of ice with water bottles.

"Lovely day," the storeowner said, playing with the cross around her neck. "How are you on this fine day?"

"I'm looking for someone." Izzy handed her the flyer. "We did some work around here."

"Handsome fellow," the woman said, looking at Cyrus's picture. "He's your man?"

Izzy nodded. She put two water bottles and some cash on the counter. "Do you recognize him?"

"I try not to get involved."

"But does he look—"

"I put it all in the hands of the Lord," the woman said. "You can always go poking around yourself."

That was that then.

✿✿✿

Izzy drove past a bombed-out looking building tagged with a list of names—Valentine, Bunny, Google, Stretch—and a skull and cross bones. Someone had set up a drive-in with three rows of ruined cars facing the side of a truck where movies were projected at night. Across the road from this squatted a little building with a sign that read "Silverlight Cinema" and a silhouette of a man in a hat and trench coat. The Bombay Beach Opera House, painted blue to blend to sky. A building painted dirty pink like sunset sand—the Seaside Baptist Church. A few fat black and white rabbits hopped along the cracked cement road—someone's oblivious dinner—and a dog barked behind a chain link fence, but otherwise the streets slept, deserted in the heavy heat. The selenium-filled wind stank stronger here.

She found the three-sister's garden, already withering. What had made her and Cyrus think they could be of any help by trying to plant vegetables?

Across the road, stood the windmill house.

A group of children, including the red-haired girl on the bike, played in the dirt behind a fence. Izzy thought she heard them chanting, "Gather the wheat, gather the clover. Green Man, Green Man, let Osiris come over."

They froze and fell silent when they saw her. All but four of the children, the bike-girl, another older red-haired girl, and two red-haired boys—hopped the fence and ran off. The littlest girl adjusted a broken tiara on her head. It looked as if it had been made from twisted wire and bottle caps.

Izzy's water from the market tasted like plastic when she took a sip. The chemicals in most heated plastic might cause breast cancer, she'd heard. Bisphenol A.

"Hi." She waved. "Can I ask you something?" She fished for cash in her jeans' pockets, but they were empty.

The children all lined up in a row holding hands by the fence and just stared up at her as if they'd been told to do this—like something out of the horror movies Cyrus used to watch. The one with the demon kids standing in a cornfield.

Izzy held out the flyer. "Does this man look familiar?"

Still holding hands, the children stepped nearer, but no one spoke.

She smiled at the littlest girl. "I met you before, remember? We came to plant the vegetables."

The girl sucked on her lower lip with her two front teeth.

"This man was with me. And two friends. Do you remember?"

The girl nodded. She turned to the others.

The taller girl started to chant softly, "Bubal hartebeest, Caribbean monk seal, great auk, ibex, Javan tiger."

Shit. Not again.

"Passenger pigeon, Pyrenean ibex, quagga, sea mink, Tasmanian tiger, Tecopa pupfish, West African black rhino," both girls said.

"Wow, you know a lot about animals. They're all endangered, right? Or extinct?" The girls didn't respond. "I'm Izzy. What are your names?"

The kids looked at each other now.

"It's okay." She reached out her hand to the taller boy. He looked at her for a while before he shook her hand, limply. "Give me a grip, buddy," she said, and the boy tightened his grasp. "Nice to meet you."

Silence.

"Can you help me? I need to find him."

The girls started up once more. "African elephant, Asian elephant, bald eagle, giant panda, orangutan, polar bear, rhinoceros."

Who were these children? More lost than even she had been at that age. Maybe the garden had been a stupid idea, but what else could she and Cyrus have done for them?

The first girl said, "We are all sharing the earth's pain."

Fuck.

The children looked at each other again. The taller boy shrugged. His eyelashes were pale red, almost transparent in the sunshine.

Izzy handed him the flyer. "Please call this number if you see or hear anything," she said. "Okay?"

Then the smallest girl walked over. "When he dies, we will stand around the glass box and cry, and our tears will turn into roses and lotus flowers," she said.

❀❀❀

On the way back home, Izzy couldn't breathe. Stench and silt were in her lungs. So, she pulled over at Mecca Beach. A sign read, "Salton Sea State Recreation Area." No one at the booth, so she just drove up and parked, got out. No one anywhere. A strange apocalyptic light. Caustic, as if it had burned those fish to death right through the water.

"Come on," she told herself. "Get some fresh air." She laughed grimly. The breeze—so slight it hardly ruffled the surface of the lake—stank of rotten fish.

The sponge-and-crunch beneath Izzy's feet felt lunar—crumbled tilapia bones and hollow-eyed carcasses. The sea stretched out to the horizon, opaque in the sun like a dead eye.

This place is so fucked up. It never seemed so fucked up to me before.

She bent over, trying to catch her breath again. Trying not to vomit. Her skin like a cloak of a thousand clams. What had just happened?

Extinct animals. A glass box. Flowers made of tears.

Where was Cyrus? Izzy walked back to the truck feeling the sickening crunch, the gaze of hollow eyes at her feet. Dead fish had been piled up in the center of a circle of carefully placed carcasses— as if done with intention.

The sun had started to set over the water.

She turned away from the mandala of fish bones. The eye sockets seemed to be looking southwest, the jawbones gaping in that direction. Maybe there was a clue somewhere closer to home.

❀❀❀

Izzy stood in the doorway, surveying the shack. Yard peeked up at her, then disappeared into his shell, as if he knew what she was about to do. He didn't like too much noise or movement. Well, it couldn't be helped.

"At least it doesn't smell like dead fish here," she said aloud. At least there weren't dead fish bones arranged in a hellish circle on the floor. But she had to face Cyrus's clothing, and the sense of loss they might stir up frightened her, too.

Izzy opened the closet. She took out all of Cyrus's clothes and placed them on the bed. Each item old and worn but clean. The red and black plaid wool flannel that smelled like a wet dog when it rained; the black polished cotton button-down dress shirt; the short-sleeved, pale green plaid button-down he wore in the summer, the fabric thinning slightly at the shoulders. The Levi's denim jacket, the khaki Dickies jacket, the down parka, the black hoodie, the black gabardine suit he'd found at the Goodwill. He could lock his phone but not his pockets. She went through each one; all of the pockets were empty.

She opened his dresser drawer and took out his jeans and T-shirts. Unlike her clothes, that tended to get easily tumbled about when she searched for something, his all stayed neatly folded. She shook out his black and white cotton, short-sleeved T-shirts and his long-sleeved winter thermals. She slid her fingers into the pockets of his jeans. When she poked a finger into the little front pocket, she felt a twinge of desire, remembering how she liked to touch him that way, pretending to be searching for things—change, a missing key. He'd laugh and say, "I feel something here," placing her hand on his fly and she'd unzip him, take him out—No, no time for that now.

She opened his underwear and sock drawer and placed everything on the bed, shook each item out and refolded it, putting it back where it had come from. A few small burrs clung viciously to one of the socks, and she pried the prickled balls loose with the tips of her fingers and threw them in the trash. His boxers looked tattered and faded, and she found herself not aroused but only saddened at the sight of them; she'd planned to buy him new ones for Christmas.

Lastly, she took all of his shoes out of the bottom of the closet and lined them up by the bed. Converse, running shoes, work boots, one pair of worn black Doc Martens dress shoes similar to the boots he'd been wearing the day he vanished. Cyrus was more fashion-and-brand-conscious than Izzy was; he scoured thrift stores for the exact right thing. He'd been so happy to find two pairs of Docs in his size.

I'm not going to cry about his shoes, she told herself. Just shoes, that's all.

Izzy picked up Cyrus's phone. She typed in 199092. Their birthday years. Nothing.

She looked at the blank phone screen, a little glass box like the one the red-haired girl had mentioned. Izzy thought of the gasping carcasses of fish bones. For the first time since the morning Cyrus had disappeared, she felt the full weight of dread leadening her bones.

Common Disaster

CAL, the Imperial Valley prison, reeked of cow dung for miles around. Birds fried daily on the electrified fence that had been constructed to kill prisoners in an instant. The place blended into the landscape, like a pockmarked gray building might look on the moon. Nothing as far as a dry eye could see. A blue-clad prisoner, trying to escape, would be easy to pluck off that wasted land.

When she finally got her appointment, two weeks after Cyrus disappeared, Izzy dressed in the appropriate attire. No blue jeans or chambray work shirts, the website said; nothing too similar to what the prisoners wore. Luckily, she only owned black clothes. In all black, she drove through that moonscape. Braved the breathless isolation of the metal detector to see Cyrus's brother.

❋❋❋

Joe sat hunched, vulturine, wearing the blue shirt and jeans. Looked a lot thinner than when he'd been put away. More tattoo ink blackened his neck and arms in spirals and lines; she could see when his sleeves rode up.

"Damn, girl, it's been a while. Brought me some candy?"

She'd tried to bring a bag of fun size chocolate bars the first time she and Cyrus had come to see his brother at CAL, but food wasn't allowed, and she'd had to throw it away in the bin outside. Should have known better. "Sorry, Joe."

"Damn. Sucks. I'm jonesing for some sugar."

"All I got are questions," she said. Jody had let Joe know Cyrus was missing.

"And I don't have answers." He scrutinized her face. "You don't look so good."

It was true. She hadn't been sleeping, the thin skin under her eyes stamped with inky circles. Her cheekbones protruded. Her hair had tangled so much that when she combed it the little snarls only seemed to get worse, and she'd snipped some out. Her pants sagged on her waist and hips.

"Yeah, I'm not doing so good."

"Yeah."

"This couldn't have anything to do with you," she continued, getting to it. "Him going missing?"

Joe grimaced. "You still think I'm a tweaker."

"I never said that." Though it had crossed her mind in the past. Even if Selma had fucked Joe over, he wasn't exactly an angel, either. "I have to check everything. Maybe someone out there...angry at you, I don't know."

Now Joe just laughed. "No one on the outside gives a shit about me."

"Can you tell me anything? Please. What if—"

"You check his phone?"

"I don't know the code. Joe, can you think of anything weird that happened? Anything messed up?"

"Since when? PTS-Dad? My girl gets me thrown in here like a piece of bad meat? Nah, nothing weird at all."

"But Cyrus. Did you ever think he would—" She made herself say it: "hurt himself?"

His eyes lost their carrion sheen for a moment, and he lowered his voice. "Not for a long time."

"What does that mean?"

"When something pissed him off, Cyrus used to talk about going down into one of those mine shafts and never coming back up."

Izzy covered her eyes with her palms, pressed until a mosaic of colors danced. When she removed her hands, Joe smirked and said, "But then he met the love of his life."

She tried to hold it together. "Please, Joe. I woke up and he was gone. It's been two weeks."

He shook his head like a bull's, as if it weighed too much for his tatted neck. Watched her closely, thinking—she could see by the way his pupils tick-tocked, back and forth.

"The cop made it sound like maybe Cyrus got into trouble as a kid," she continued. "Maybe drugs or something..." Like Larry had said. Izzy was willing to consider it now.

"Saint Cyrus? All peace and love since the social worker dropped him off at our door? Won't even crack a beer or smoke weed." Joe inhaled sharply and closed his eyes like he could taste the marijuana. "Yeah, I don't know. Maybe Cyrus wasn't as much of a saint as he seemed."

Desperation clawed up Izzy's throat and formed words from raw tissue. She felt the congestion in the corner of her eyes, at the excrescence of the red caruncles, and blinked back tears, no longer trying to manipulate the situation; this was for real. "You need to tell me if you hear anything."

The guard approached.

"I need to do nothing," Joe said. "Except get the hell out of here. And you should, too. Since you can."

She didn't want to hear any more. She stood to leave. Joe was right; at least she could leave, and he would still be there. Maybe that was why he couldn't bring himself to help...

❀❀❀

When she got to the truck, Izzy took out Cyrus's phone and typed in a different combination of their birthdays, 128113. No. Then 012890. His birthday, not hers, not theirs. The numbers jumped and settled. 011990? The phone remained locked. She only had three more attempts left before she'd be locked out permanently.

Did he think she'd try to check his phone behind his back? How could he think that?

In the desert heat, her heart burned like a bird on a wire.

✸✸✸

"No word yet?" Jody asked.

She and Del sat on the porch drinking beers, as if they'd never left. But this time they both stood when they saw Cyrus's truck. Del spat in the sand, maybe because he realized it was just Izzy at the wheel. The crevices in his face looked deeper somehow.

"No word," she said, then asked "You?" though she knew the answer.

They both shook their heads. "Haven't heard anything," Jody said. At least Jody hadn't given Izzy that look—the one that said, *he took off and left.* But every time Izzy had that thought, the alternative loomed even worse.

Del handed Izzy a beer, and she took it without thinking. "I saw Joe today."

Jody frowned at the mention of her older son, her thin freckled skin crinkling like tissue paper, and asked how he was doing.

"Not too upset about Cyrus. He wanted candy."

"Drink your beer," Del said.

Izzy needed something, so she popped the can and took a sip. It tasted metallic. But cold. Like she'd reminded Larry, she and Cyrus never drank, except maybe a glass of sparkling wine on New Year's Eve. Maybe a little out of vanity, but also for practical purposes, Cyrus kept his system clean and kept out of trouble—there was always so much work to be done. Though Larry and Joe and the cops had implied otherwise.

"Did Cyrus ever have problems with the cops?" Izzy asked.

Jody and Del turned their heads at the same moment and looked at each other, then away. Jody said, "We thought he was heading that direction. Hanging out with Selma and all."

"Till she got her hands on Joe," Del said.

"Wait, what? Selma? Joe's Selma?"

"It was before he met you," Jody said, as if that was some consolation.

Del scowled at his boots and remained silent.

"What kind of trouble was he heading for?" Izzy asked Jody. "Something with drugs?"

Jody said, "The drugs were all Selma. My boys are good boys."

The grime of CAL still clung to Izzy's skin, the beer roiled in her stomach, and the thought of Selma made her sick, but Izzy knew she'd have to go see her now.

❀ ❀ ❀

Izzy found Selma Jenkins at the Range, an outdoor de facto stage where bands performed, and where sometimes the locals showed up in dresses and tuxes from a communal collection reserved for the Slab City "prom." "For people who never went to one," Izzy had been told. She had to admit there was something about this practice she liked; she and Cyrus and Seth and Nephy hadn't gone to the prom since all of them except Cyrus had been homeschooled, but once, a few years ago, they'd strung up some Christmas lights in the White's backyard, played some nineties music, and danced in their own thrift store finery.

Selma—tattooed and pierced and wearing a tattered pink satin dress over her jeans—was doing a sound check when Izzy approached. Ink diamonds dripped down her face and across her chest arced the words, "Fool's Errand." Had she gotten that tattoo before or after Joe? Brutal.

Selma didn't see Izzy at first, but a man, tall and brick-shouldered as Frankenstein's monster and preternaturally pale, even under that desert sun, crouched in the dirt by the stage and watched both women. Izzy felt an explosion of beetles along her spine.

When she finally noticed Izzy, Selma tapped the microphone and glared out across the torn-up couches to where the other woman stood. "Izzy Ames," she said, her vocal cords scratchy from cigarettes. "I heard you lost your man."

"I heard you lost yours, too," Izzy said, in spite of herself. "I just saw him at CAL."

Selma knelt, put one hand on the stage and leveraged herself to the ground. Izzy spotted a pair of small feathered wings attached to her back, but they did nothing to lighten Selma's heavy gait.

"How's old Joe doing?" she asked.

"Not too good."

Selma scratched at her bicep with the pinup tattoo and the words "Daddy's Girl" scrawled underneath. Izzy had heard that Selma wandered into Slab City one day and started hanging out with a crowd of bikers. No one knew where she came from—where did any of the lost kids come from?—but she said she'd seen a documentary about the Salton Sea once and knew it was home. Better than whatever home she'd left, apparently.

"And you're here looking for Cyrus," she said.

"Have you seen him?" Izzy asked staring through the hole of the Totonac ear plug stretching Selma's lobe.

"I'd have liked to see a lot more of Cyrus. Who wouldn't? But I guess you're the one who got him, huh?"

Izzy wanted to punch those sharp little teeth. "You hung out with him when you were kids?"

"He was a pretty boy, that Cyrus. I always wanted to put barrettes in that hair. Maybe a little eye shadow—"

"He's missing, Selma. He could have hurt himself. Or someone could have—"

Selma shimmied her shoulders so the wings fluttered. "I'm sorry, man. I really am."

"What do you know?" Izzy almost shouted.

Frankenstein shook his head as if he had a bug in his ear and made a moaning sound. Izzy wondered if Selma would sic him on her.

"I know shit," Selma said in her cigarette-scratched voice, her eyes frozen on Izzy, un-melting even in the flammable heat. "Except this: your ego drives you. I suggest you go home and lock yourself in the darkest closet. See if you can find yourself first." And though she was the one in the wings and the too-small satin dress and the tattoos that spoke of a harsher past than Izzy wanted to contemplate, her eyes looked, Izzy had to admit, clear as desert sky.

❋❋❋

When Izzy got home, she stripped off her dirty T-shirt, her pants, her underpants, leaving on only her socks. She went into the closet and took out Cyrus's black suit. She buried her face in the fabric. It smelled slightly of mothballs—the chemicals naphthalene or paradichlorobenzene—under his sage and smoke scent.

Izzy slipped on the jacket over her bare skin. The fragile silk lining had been torn in places so she was careful not to rip it further. She stepped into the trousers and zipped them up, careful not to snag the zipper on the small patch of her pubic hair, ignoring the arousal she felt at the sensation. She rolled up the cuffs of the pants and stepped into the black dress shoes, remembering something Alma had said the day Cyrus went missing. *If you want to find someone, you have to put yourself in their shoes.*

I suggest you go home and lock yourself in the darkest closet, Selma had said.

Why was Izzy listening to crazy people?

Because.

Because who else was there?

She looked at herself in the narrow full-length mirror on the inside of the closet door.

Someday, she and Cyrus had planned to get married. He would have worn this suit. She would have worn a vintage white satin slip from a thrift store with white combat boots, or, if she were lucky enough to find one in good condition, a woman's white crepe designer pantsuit with satin trim, like she'd seen an actress from the 1970s wear at her wedding to a rock god. Izzy could tailor the suit to fit and dye it with tea if it was stained. White roses in her hair. None of it mattered now. He was gone. Izzy's fingers felt into the pockets of the suit jacket again. Where the lining had torn, another small opening had formed. Something met her searching fingers. A small slip of paper.

"Miracle Manor," the paper said. The place she and Cyrus had gone. For a moment she thought, I read his mind! He was thinking of wearing this suit, thinking of our wedding! But there was a date on the receipt. Four months and twelve days ago. A weekend Cyrus had stayed overnight at the inn for a construction job. Izzy had not been with him to the motel for five years.

Atomic Dog

She waited until the next morning to drive to Desert Hot Springs. Yesterday had been long—and painful. Again. She didn't have the stamina to face what she might find at the motel.

But, when she woke, she coaxed Yard from his shell with some kale leaves, dandelion greens, and water, forced some coffee down her throat, and got into the truck—the small piece of paper she'd found in the lining of Cyrus's jacket sweating ink into her clenched palm.

She took the 86 North and the I-10 West from Salton City to Desert Hot Springs. The town had been built on a sub-basin containing a hot water aquifer, and at one time the town featured forty-three spas with geothermally heated mineral pools. Izzy had read that the same grinding of the tectonic plates beneath the earth's outer crust that caused earthquakes also heated the mineral springs to soaking perfection. There was something strange about that, she thought—the same source providing the threat of violence and the promise of comfort (although sometimes the mineral springs were too hot, scalding, and had to be cooled for soaking purposes). If there was a personal metaphor for her here, she chose not to examine it.

Miracle Manor had been built in 1949 on sacred Native Cahuilla land renamed Miracle Hill, and although the motel had been sold twice and upgraded, it still felt like a place from the past, with its nine small bungalow rooms curved in a horseshoe shape around two mineral pools, one encased in a glass conservatory and both offering the benefits of sulfates, bio-carbonates, carbonates, iron, and magnesium. The San Jacinto mountains glowed purple in the distance; Izzy had read that mountain ranges looked this color from far away because of the scattering of distant light. Across the street from Miracle Manor, an early settler named Cabot Yerxa had built his rendition of a Hopi house from recycled lumber, nails, and railroad ties. He'd lived there alone with a donkey named Merry Christmas.

Izzy thought of the shack she'd helped Cyrus build from all those recycled materials. For the first time, she realized: if Cyrus did not come back, she might lose the house. It was in Cyrus's name. And she didn't have enough money to pay for it on her own. Where would she go? Back with Larry and Leanne in the trailer? She'd sooner die. And Seth and Nephy had no room for her. She didn't want to live with them, anyway. She imagined lying on the stuffing-vomiting chartreuse couch listening to them fucking through the walls. Listening to a baby cry.

Miracle Manor on Miracle Hill. It had once felt, to Izzy, as magical as its name, but now the sight of the little green-and-white sign made her heart swing like a pendulum in her chest.

✦✦✦

When Izzy showed the two women at the desk the missing person flyer and the receipt from Cyrus's jacket, they only shook their neatly shorn heads in unison.

"We have to be discreet," the gray-haired woman said. Her voice was soft and articulate. She wasn't from around here.

Izzy tried to control her voice. "He's missing."

"The police aren't investigating?"

"They've done nothing."

The other woman leaned over her partner's shoulder and squinted at the flyer. "Why?"

"Who knows? I don't know. They think he's some kind of delinquent. People out where I live see you the way they see you." She found herself wanting to confide in these sophisticated women with their contrasting skin and matching haircuts. "It's why I've always wanted to leave."

The gray-haired woman said, "We thought the desert let you forget your past. That's why we came."

"I guess it depends on where you were born," Izzy said.

The dark-haired woman looked up from the flyer, looked at Izzy, back at the flyer, back at Izzy. "I remember him. But he came here with you."

"That was five years ago," Izzy said.

"I remember. You were a striking couple."

"What about this?" Izzy pointed to the receipt again.

The gray-haired woman stared at Izzy for a moment. Then she typed something into her computer. She nodded. "He was here."

"Alone?" she managed.

"It's just under his name." She hesitated, looked at the other woman. Something intimate and tender passed between them. "But the bill looks like food and drinks for two. It's hard to say."

"I just remember him with you," the dark-haired woman said again.

Izzy turned away to gather herself.

The first woman said, "I'm sorry for your loss." She added, "If Lois were here, she could maybe help you."

"Lois?"

The woman explained. The second owner of the place, a naturopath and mystic named Lois Black Hill, who'd been trained by healers in Brazil and India, had presided over the place with a black poodle named Andre at her side. She had come to the desert after a career as a singer, fashion model, designer, and club owner in New York, Paris, and Morocco respectively. Lois communed with a spirit named Omra and showed her guests videos of psychic surgery in which the surgeon reached inside their patients and removed strings of black substances with their hands.

"Where's Lois?" Izzy asked.

"She died in '96."

"Oh."

Some wind chimes tinkled like ice in a liquor glass, and Izzy rubbed at the goose bumps on her upper arms. The woman had said, "I'm sorry for your loss." Was Cyrus lost? Or had he chosen to leave her? Was the piece of paper in her pocket the thing that would save her from grief (he was not dead, nothing nefarious had occurred) or plunge her into despair (he had left her, which was its own kind of death)? At this point, she believed it was the latter.

"You know, that makes me think—" The woman typed something into the computer. "Yes, there was something going on that weekend. The Heart House. Or something. Sometimes they have their retreats here." She typed some more. "The House of Hearts," she said, wrote it down on a piece of paper and handed it to Izzy who pocketed it, robotically, without even looking.

"You can leave some flyers," the woman said, but Izzy was already half gone.

If Cyrus had stayed here without her, had he stayed here alone? Why wouldn't he have mentioned it unless he'd been hiding something? Someone? And if Cyrus had left her, why? Because he'd met someone and had been too much of a coward to come out and say it? He'd chosen instead to make her think he'd harmed himself or been harmed in some unspeakable way? Because by leaving his truck and his keys, of course he'd known she'd think that. And what about the fact that without him she didn't have the money to make it on her own? She'd have to give up the shack. Where would she go? How would she support herself? Was this other person the reason Cyrus hadn't wanted to have a child with Izzy? Rage swept through her like a sulfurous wind off the shores of the Salton Sea.

⊕⊕⊕

Izzy stopped for gas along I-10. Still adrenalized with anger, she got out and swiped her card, uncapped the tank, and jammed in the nozzle. The heat of the day, the gasoline fumes, and the lack of sleep dizzied her. The sky looked too vast, too blue. Clouds moved fast, as if in time-lapse, their images impossible to decode.

While she watched the numbers tick, she saw what looked like a small black horse lolloping long-leggedly toward her. Bony, starveling. Sweet skull face that came up level with her waist. He rubbed against her hip, then planted his boxy head against her stomach and the knot of anger loosened. His ears curved at the top like delicate horns.

"Where've I been all your life, huh, boy?" She wondered how the dog could even walk on that asphalt. Must have been hot as hell, even this late in the day. Singeing those footpads. She knelt and pressed her palm against the ground. *Too hot.* She tried to touch his feet, and the dog pranced a little distance away.

Izzy walked up to the cashier. The dog followed her.

"Who's this?" she asked the guy behind the glass.

"He's a beauty, huh? Might be pure Great Dane. We call him Dog. Original, huh?"

"Yours?"

"He showed up about two weeks ago, and we've been taking care of him, but we were going to call Animal Control today."

"Two weeks? Like since Halloween?"

"Yeah, I think. Something like that."

The dog began to whine softly. It sounded almost like a high human whistle.

"I'll take him," Izzy said. She bent down and looked into Dog's eyes. They had a familiar greenish cast or maybe it was just a trick of the light. Dog. Dog Gone, she thought.

"I see you and I hear you, Dog Gone." She rubbed his ear between her thumb and forefinger the way one might touch a rose petal to coax out its sweetness. Someone or something had taken a precise bite out of the side of the ear. Dog stopped whining and leaned in to lick her face. Even the whiff of warm dog breath didn't lessen the charm. "You and him both got gone at the same time? It's better I have you instead."

Dog sat with his head in Izzy's lap on the way to the grocery store. The animal's square jaw lay heavy, comforting, against her thigh.

She bought the biggest bag of dog food she could find, realizing it wouldn't be cheap to care for this boy. She bought bottled water, and also eggs, milk, cheese, peanut butter, honey, bread, and vegetables, although she didn't like the idea of spending so much, and she still wasn't hungry. But now she had not one but two other creatures to care for. And she needed fuel for her mission. Though she wasn't exactly sure what it was anymore.

Maybe her mission now was just to grieve the Cyrus she'd thought she'd known.

❀ ❀ ❀

When they got home, Dog nosed Yard who retreated—three feet and a head—into his shell until Izzy called Dog off and offered Yard some shredded kale. She fed Dog, too, and forced herself to eat a spinach omelet. Then she bathed Dog in the bathtub, dried him off with a towel, and made him a bed out of more towels. Yard, emboldened, would have none of this and, with a combination of elephantine lumber and duck-like waddle that Dog seemed to find quite fascinating, pushed his way onto the makeshift bed. Her tortoise had changed, Izzy thought. Maybe they'd both changed. In response to Yard's advances, Dog wriggled off the pile of towels, and eventually climbed onto the futon where he managed to curl his entire body into the crook of Izzy's legs. The warm weight of him kept her from getting up and shattering glass.

Fuck Miracle Manor. Fuck Cyrus.

Fuck. Cyrus.

Dog and Yard were her only miracles now.

Part II

California Love

Dog batted gently at Izzy's arm with articulate paw-hands, and she opened her eyes, feeling half-dead, poisoned with yesterday's adrenalin. But Dog needed to run. And maybe running would make Izzy stronger, sharper, more alert. Maybe it would move the anger out through her body. So, she got up and pulled on sweatpants, put on a sports bra under her tank top, smeared on sunscreen without bothering to wash her face. Added a cap and sunglasses. Called for Dog. They walked outside, the sun bright as glass shards in her eyes even behind dark lenses.

She inserted her headphones, tapped the music icon on her screen, and she and Dog took off running. He heeled naturally, long legs keeping pace with hers, his jowls and ears flapping. A woman's voice sang about a man crashing and burning in Malibu. About rescuing him. But what if he did not need or want to be rescued? The song had such a happy, jangling sound Izzy had thought; later, when she interpreted the lyrics a little, they shocked her. Tears flecked her cheeks, and then the wind brushed them away. She picked up her pace until her breath seared her chest.

It was not until she got back to the shack that Izzy remembered the piece of paper in her jeans' pocket, the piece of the paper from the woman at Miracle Manor. "The House of Hearts Retreat Center: Heal from Grief and Childhood Trauma with Sky Larkin L.S.W." And an address in Joshua Tree.

Izzy typed the information into her computer. A picture of a woman came up. She had tan skin and long, dark hair with bangs, wore lots of silver jewelry. It was hard to tell her age from the photograph, but she was probably in her forties, maybe older though her skin was unlined. Melissa "Sky" Larkin L.S.W. Grief and Childhood Trauma. There was an upcoming date for a meeting. "Everyone welcome."

"Heal from Grief and Childhood Trauma." Well, Izzy needed help with grief and trauma herself now. And even though she'd told herself she'd given up on trying to find Cyrus, had accepted the fact that he'd left her, a part of her still needed to know why. What had changed? Why hadn't he told her? And, of course, the question remained— whom had he brought with him? Maybe if she knew these things, then she could begin to heal.

Izzy stroked Dog's head and gently pried a nugget of crust from the corner of his eye. He let her groom him manually this way, without flinching, as if they had done this a thousand times.

"I guess we're going on a road trip," she told him.

※※※

A dead dog—brindled—lay on the side of the road, its entrails strewn around it like ripped red flowers.

"Don't look, Dog," Izzy said.

Telephone poles lined the highway, irrigation ditches pumped water through the desert, bales of hay were stacked like a wall, smokestacks billowed clouds into the air. Citrus and date groves and tented crops of corn. Human attempts at trying to make a wasteland livable. The mountains multicolored—purples, blues, pinks, striated layers in the distance. *The colors of my love for—No.*

No.

No.

On the other side—railroad tracks that seemed to lead nowhere. The air permeated with the stench of putrefied water from the Salton Sea.

※※※

Izzy and Dog got to Joshua Tree by late morning. They drove down the Twentynine Palms Highway, past the rows and rows of oddly shaped yucca brevifolia, or izote de desierto, "desert dagger." How weird that Joshua Trees were a type of lily—they looked so fierce and primitive. Hunched and stunted, but fierce. A different kind of annunciation.

She turned onto a side road leading to the retreat center and kept driving. The building sat back from the road behind a row of palm trees and a thick white plaster wall. Izzy parked, got out, stretched her legs, and let Dog pee. He side-eyed her, as if for reassurance, and she met his gaze. *It's okay.* Antlered branches and palm tree debris like strips of dried meat blocked the way here and there, and she kicked them aside. The air was unusually still, holding its breath, as if awaiting the heat of the day.

Izzy, with Dog following neatly at her heels—someone had trained him; how could such a beautiful, well-trained dog have been abandoned at a gas station?—walked through the entrance and into a small terra-cotta-tiled courtyard. Coral and magenta bougainvillea flowered the façade of the house and arborescent saguaros beckoned visitors toward the wooden door. It was open, and a sign read, "Retreat Center. Welcome."

Steps led down from the entry room into an inner, pillared courtyard with a rectangular stone fountain surrounded by potted palm trees under a rectangular skylight. People mingled about, making conversation. Hippies, hikers, bikers, a few touristy types, as well as yoga babes and some skeezy-looking older dudes. One overbaked man with a depraved droop to his mouth and a camera around his neck chatted up a blonde woman with large breasts and floral tattoo sleeves. A little boy, his hair like a dandelion floret, sat cross-legged at her feet, playing with a small wooden pig on wheels.

Another man, wearing a gauze shirt, jeans, and sandals, approached Izzy. The man's hair and beard curled like leaves, and bushy brows like vines shaded his eyes. She thought she detected a faint red dot, like a fading tattoo, in the center of his forehead. Forehead tattoos—not a good sign.

"Welcome," he said. He took Izzy's hands in his own—cool and long-fingered—and she quickly drew her hands away.

"Gorgeous creature." The man smiled down at Dog, who had pressed up against Izzy's leg, but didn't touch him. "Therapy dog, I assume. You're here for the meeting?

"Yes."

"And you are?"

"Aurora," she said, without thinking. It was what Cyrus had called her sometimes. Aurora for dawn, her favorite time of day. Mama Dawn. Pink Sky. She regretted choosing this fake name, this name that reminded her of Cyrus, but it was too late. And at least she hadn't given her own name. It seemed unwise to do so based on the forehead tattoo alone.

"Jeb Bauer. Call me Jeb." He led her and Dog through the house and out into a large backyard with a stone grotto among palm trees. The water cascaded over the rocks into the pool, cooling the air. A few people soaked in a hot tub. Under the palm trees nestled chicken coops, a vegetable garden, and a pen with a miniature black, pink-snouted pot-bellied pig. The pig snuffled wetly at Izzy's hand through the slats of the pen, the ring in its ear catching the light like a small crescent moon, and Dog whined.

"You're just in time for yoga class," Jeb said. "Go grab a mat."

Oh, great. Just what I felt like doing. But she didn't want to draw attention to herself by refusing.

Under a white canopy, a table draped in white linen held a crystal pitcher of water and a stack of towels. More guests stretched on yoga mats. Izzy reluctantly took a mat and placed it in the back of the class. Dog sat down beside her.

"Done this before, Down Dog?" she asked him.

Jeb stood under a palm tree, hands clasped in front of his groin, face eerily serene. A woman with long black hair cut in bangs came out of the house and walked toward him. The woman Izzy had seen online. She was tall, her soft curves and long limbs clothed in blue gauze. Her eyes dark, with a hint of green, glittered unnaturally like the rings on her fingers when she removed her oversized sunglasses. *At least she didn't have a forehead tattoo*, Izzy thought.

"Welcome to this Kundalini class," she said. "Please get settled on your mats. Sit up straight and tall with your legs crossed." Everyone took their places and the woman went on. "Put one hand on your belly. Breathe in through your nostrils, into your belly, expanding it, then contract it and release with a gust of air back through your nostrils. This is called Breath of Fire or Skull-luster. Let's all try it."

Izzy tried to breathe in, but her breath felt shallow, the air catching inside between her collarbones. What was she doing? Why was she even here?

The woman walked among the guests, lightly trailing her fingers across their shoulders and backs. Izzy saw the silver chains that connected the woman's many rings to the bracelets on her wrists, and another thin chain strung from nostril to ear. When she reached Izzy, she put her hand on Izzy's abdomen and Izzy flinched. *Get your hands off.* But she couldn't say anything in front of all these people.

"Fill your belly up like a balloon. Just follow along." The woman continued to walk up and down between the mats. "According to the Kundalini system, our bodies contain seven sacred centers, or chakras, traveling from our groins, or root chakra, up along our spine to just above our heads—the crown chakra."

She touched herself with the side of her hand, a flat blade pressed below her navel, then moving upward as she spoke. "The first, or root chakra. The second chakra, the chakra of emotion, sensuality, creativity, and sexuality. The third, or solar plexus chakra. All three of these chakras relate to our animal nature.

"The fourth chakra, the heart chakra, is important because it is through the heart that our animal nature, the energy of the first three chakras, can be controlled."

A soft sound rose. Maybe it was a sudden breeze moving through the palm fronds? Or a sigh from the enamored crowd. They were eating this up.

"The fifth chakra is the throat chakra, and we can associate this with self-expression, the need to tell our own story."

The woman was watching Izzy, almost too intently.

"The sixth chakra is the nexus of love and wisdom, the means by which evil and chaos may be overcome."

Izzy reflexively put a hand to her belly, where the woman had touched her, and she cringed, trying to push away a wave of the darkness hovering at the periphery of her mind.

❀❀❀

After the class was over, Jeb and the woman approached.

"This is Sky," Jeb said. "Sky, this is Aurora."

The scent of flowers mixed with warm resin as Sky put her arms around Izzy, pressing her breasts against Izzy's chest. Without looking at Dog, Sky patted the top of his head. The animal shrank slightly from the woman's touch.

"What brings you here?" she said. The combined glow of her unlined skin and white smile had an almost blinding effect.

"I'm looking for this man." Izzy pulled a flyer from her backpack and showed Sky the paper.

"Handsome. He seems a bit familiar. But we see a lot of people." Sky met Izzy's eyes.

Izzy wanted to snatch the flyer back, crumple it in her hand. Why couldn't she be done with that? Done searching. Done with that handsome face. Done. But she wasn't. "He went to your retreat. In Desert Hot Springs. With a woman."

She felt vulnerable, like she'd said too much.

Sky watched Izzy for a moment. Reading her? "I think I understand. I'm so sorry, darling," she said.

Darling? What a load of crap. *You understand nothing,* Izzy thought.

Sky glanced at Jeb, who nodded. She turned back to Izzy, "You've come to the right place. I'd really like to help you. Your distress is more than understandable. Why don't you have some food with us and then stay for our little meeting."

Izzy just wanted to leave.

But then: "Who knows?" Sky said. "He does look slightly familiar. He might show up."

❀ ❀ ❀

Would you like a drink? Barley beer? Date palm wine?" Jeb asked.

They had all moved back into the central courtyard of the house.

A young man with a shaved head and a slightly receding chin appeared holding a tray of drinks. He watched mutely as Izzy took a beer. She sipped it—frothy and fresh.

A buffet—black beans, rice, corn, whole wheat bread loaves, green salad with pomegranates and figs, and individual saffron-colored cakes—was set up on a long table. Izzy, suddenly wildly hungry, heaped a pale-blue ceramic plate with food.

The woman with the tattoo sleeves approached, her son pulling the wheeled wooden pig on a string behind him, and introduced herself as Amanda Flowers. "And this is Kurt John Martin Flowers." The little boy clung to her leg, and she stroked his head. Izzy imagined blowing on the dandelion flower hair, watching the seedpods becoming wind borne, making a wish. Though she wasn't sure what she would wish for anymore. For Cyrus to return? For Cyrus never to have left? Or perhaps: to never to have met him? Where would she be then? In Los Angeles with a degree and a job, maybe a family?

Dog got up and sat in front of the child.

"Is he friendly?" Amanda asked. Her eyes had a floating quality because of the large, pale irises, the small specks of pupils. "He's huge! Like a horse. Or a person."

Izzy nodded but kept a strong hold on the leash just in case, and the little boy reached up to pat the animal's flank. Dog sat very still and let the child pet him. Kurt smiled gummily at Izzy.

"He likes you," Izzy told him.

Amanda knelt to stroke Dog's bony head. How did she even move in those skintight jeans? It was hard not to stare down into the white V-neck T-shirt at her cleavage. The flowers sleeving her arms made Izzy think of Cyrus's tattoos. Roses. Serpent. Panther. Falcon. Skull. Her name.

Not my name. Not anymore.

"Where are you two from?" Amanda asked.

"Salton Sea."

"That's some serious psychic energy over there, too. What do you do by the Salton Sea, Miss Aurora?"

"I make and sell things. Candles and chocolate. I work as a massage therapist." It sounded odd already. The reminder that she'd once done things beside search for Cyrus. She'd need to get back to these things now, figure out something else, too, in order to support the animals and herself, in order to keep the house.

"Really? I could use a good massage." Amanda tilted her head to the side, and she rubbed at her neck muscles. "I'm a doula and an exotic dancer, which is why my body's wacked most of the time. Plus, I'm still nursing so there's that—"

"You're nursing?" The words had slipped out in a judge-y voice, unchecked, but Amanda didn't seem to mind.

"Oh, yes." She beamed. "He's getting a little old, but we both like it. Although, I'm always leaking on everything."

Izzy tried to imagine her own breasts expressing milk. She'd thought of it, imagined her breasts swelling, her nipples drawing and then letting go. Now her body felt hard like a boy's, rigid with focus, determined.

"Do you live out here?" Izzy asked.

"No, I'm visiting. We're in LA. Culver City, actually, if you've heard of it. I grew up by Ballona Creek." Amanda explained that the creek was a natural waterway, once lined with sycamores, willows, Montezuma cypress, and filled with swamp and rainwater. The Gabrielino-Tongva people lived there; they farmed castor beans and used board boats waterproofed with asphaltum from the La Brea tar pits. The flooding left silt deposits that enriched the soil. "Like the Nile," Amanda said. Until a big flood in 1934 that made farming impossible.

Izzy wasn't sure why Amanda was telling her all this, but anything about LA interested her, especially now that she needed to think about starting a new life. "So, you came here for the meeting?"

"Oh, yes. The work they do is really powerful. They helped me so much. You'll see."

"Can I ask how?"

Amanda's aqua eyes flitted and lit on Jeb surrounded by a gaggle of young women. Sky sat alone, cross-legged by the waterfall, eyes closed, meditating.

"With my grief," Amanda said.

Grief, yes. Everyone had so much grief.

Izzy nodded and brought out another flyer. "I wanted to ask you... Does this man look familiar?"

"No, but he looks a little like that guy over there."

Izzy turned.

A tall man, shoulders so broad they further narrowed his waist and hips. His black hair had been slicked back wetly from his wide face with its dark eyes, and he wore a long-sleeved black hoodie and black jeans. Black Converse. Her breath caught and her heart lifted, then fell in her chest. He reminded her of Cyrus. Maybe too much. Why hadn't she noticed him before? Had he just arrived?

He nodded his head at her.

Maybe she would stay a little longer.

❀❀❀

Evening came, pink, then blue. The house had been lit with white tapers and votive candles, and the guests sat around on cushions, facing Sky. Izzy and Dog, with his head on her thigh, sat beside Amanda, who had left her child upstairs with a nanny. The man who resembled Cyrus stood behind them, leaning against the wall. Izzy imagined she could feel his eyes on the back of her neck—a warm sensation, not unpleasant.

"Tonight we are going to discuss chaos," Sky said. "Our whole world is a tomb ravened by chaos. Think of global warming, ice floes melting, the destruction of coral reefs and the extinct or near-extinct species. We've become so out of touch with the earth, with anything of meaning."

Izzy remembered, with a twinge of anxiety, the words of the red-haired horror movie children at Bombay Beach: *Passenger pigeon, Pyrenean ibex, Tasmanian tiger, Tecopa pupfish, West African rhino.*

"Even these recent fires scorching the earth, burning the paws off of bears, killing horses and mountain lions, destroying everything in the wake of the flame." Sky shut her eyes and winced. "I mean, the president says there's no such thing as global warming! Have you seen those fires? They've had to evacuate.

"Think of the horrors of war, violence, poverty, and disease," Sky went on. "Sixty-five million displaced people around the globe. Nuclear proliferation. A man without conscience or humanity who denies these travesties running this country."

The night he'd been elected, Izzy and Cyrus went through all the stages of grief. And then they had gone through these stages again and again with each new political development, until Cyrus's vanishing obliterated everything else. How had he not realized that his leaving—his *betrayal*—would obliterate everything? That she would feel a grief worse than any she had ever known? Maybe he had realized...

"These are facts of our times, and we can't ignore them," Sky went on. "We must acknowledge chaos. You've all heard of the idea of embracing the Shadow? He can't be neglected."

She moved her hands when she talked, and Izzy saw the quiver of silver chains between Sky's rings and the bracelets on her wrists.

"The word paradise. It means an enclosed garden." Sky gestured around now with her glittering fingers, as if writing invisible symbols in the air. "This is where our attraction to courtyards might originally come from. The enclosed garden, the courtyard, the womb.

"But we can't remain in that enclosed space forever," Sky said, turning her head as if speaking directly to Izzy. "If we never leave the womb, it becomes a tomb."

Is that what I had with Cyrus? Was our relationship a tomb?

"Only after our surrender to chaos can we be reborn, anointed with wine, water, and salt, reassembled and fully reunited with the Beloved. And in this way, the world can also be reborn." Sky paused as if for effect. "We need to wander actively out into the world, out of the womb, to search for ourselves. We must embrace and accept our shadow selves."

Izzy thought, *Yes, yes, this is right. But how does one do that? What exactly does it even mean? And why am I agreeing with her?*

"But to wander out into the world and find ourselves, we need first to attach securely to the source. So tonight, in order to heal, we will pick a partner and try to create an attachment."

What if that man with the tattoo, that Jeb, approached her, Izzy thought? Horrible. She had to leave. But she couldn't get up right now with everyone watching. Maybe she could slip out in a moment.

"Look around the room and pick the person with whom you have the most karma to clear," Sky said. "It will be apparent to both of you, trust me. Gender, age, nothing should be an impediment. It might be the person who turns away from you. In fact, that might be the clearest sign you should partner up."

Oh, just fucking great.

Some chuckles from the group. "If you are the one turning away, take a breath, turn around, and confront your truth."

Grinning wolfishly, the tan man with the camera went and took Amanda's hand. She gazed starrily up at him in a way that gave Izzy the creeps almost as much as the man himself did.

Sky's voice assumed a more business-like tone.

"However, both partners must agree to work together. Please do not feel obligated to say yes to someone just because they ask. We want you all to feel completely comfortable!"

Izzy jumped when someone brushed against her, and a man's voice said, "Sorry."

Not Jeb, thank God.

It was the man who looked like Cyrus.

The man let Dog sniff his hand, then crouched to pat the animal's head firmly but gently.

"Is this your dog?"

She nodded.

"Of course he is. Beautiful dog."

Dog nosed the man's leg. Izzy hadn't seen Dog do that with anyone but her. She just stared at the two of them. When the man stood up again, his jeans slid down so she could see the elastic waistband of his boxers.

Sky came over and put her hand on the man's arm. "Have you two met? Ever, this is Aurora. Aurora, Ever."

He took Izzy's hand, engulfing it in his own warm hand, meeting her eyes.

Sky walked away. "Please sit on a mat facing your partner," she announced.

"This is weird, yeah?" the man said, releasing her hand. His voice sounded kind, warm like a fire kindled his throat. *Kind kindled, kindling, the kindling of kindness*, Izzy thought. The same warmth he exuded through his hands when he'd touched her. Her own hand felt suddenly so cold.

"Definitely weird."

"I've never done this before," he said.

"Me either."

"It's not really my scene."

"Same."

"Like, a little too culty." Ever nodded in Jeb's direction, lightly touched a finger to the center of his own forehead and quirked his mouth.

"You think?" Izzy recalled Alma's joke about safe sects but refrained from telling him.

"Do you want to try anyway?" the man asked Izzy. "You know, karma." He laughed softly.

"Okay," she found herself saying.

"Once you've settled on your mat, sit facing each other and try to maintain eye contact," Sky said to the group.

Izzy sat cross-legged facing Ever. Dog sat next to her. She and Ever looked at each other awkwardly.

"You may feel the desire to cry or laugh," Sky said. You may feel panic, or vestiges of rage, or you may feel peaceful. Try to stay calm but conscious and follow the images that come to mind. By seeing and being seen, we can face who we really are. We can surrender, receive. This is how transformation can occur."

Some whispering: a few giggles.

"Just look at each other," Sky said. "Don't speak."

Izzy tried to look into Ever's eyes. She felt the pressure of tears and willed herself not to cry.

###

After the exercise ended, Izzy excused herself, and Dog followed her up some stairs to a restroom on the second floor. She looked at her reflection in the mirror, glad she hadn't worn mascara, since even though she hadn't let tears flow, some drops had leaked out. Then she took a breath and rinsed her face with cool water in the pale chalkblue ceramic sink, dried herself with one of the many fluffy white hand towels.

A row of pinky-finger-sized glass bottles of scented oils marked with the fragrance and corresponding chakra from one to seven— red amber, musk, jasmine, rose, amber kashmir, sandalwood, lotus— lined the counter. Izzy un-stoppered the lotus fragrance and touched her finger to her temples. She opened the bathroom cabinets—a habit she'd gotten into as a kid when she went to other people's houses. Lots of homeopathic remedies and lotions and potions made with natural ingredients. That was something else Izzy had once done, in what felt like another life—created concoctions of coconut oil and aloe, honey, and lavender. She'd given Cyrus some sandalwood skin cream she'd mixed with real gold she'd saved up for a year to buy. For a year! He'd said it was girly but used it all up, the gold particles glistening. She told him that *he* was the girl. She'd always seen his vanity but not his selfishness, not his betrayal.

But what was she supposed to do now, without him? Was she supposed to curl up and die? Maybe.

Or maybe not.

Izzy sprayed some rose water on her face and plucked a leaf from an aloe plant on the windowsill. She split the fleshy leaf and squeezed the gel onto her fingers, then rubbed it into her skin. The aloe had a dirty, medicinal scent.

She stepped out into a hallway lined with doors, one of which was open, and she and Dog went inside the white room; Izzy closed the door behind them. Gauze draped a large white bed, and black lacquer furniture with gold lions' feet looked ready to dance away. Inside the open closet, Izzy saw clothing organized by color—pale blue, white, cream, metallic silver, and gold. Silks, satins, velvets. Even Izzy, who knew little about fashion, could tell this shit cost. She picked up a pair of high-heeled shoes posing coyly on a low shelf and examined them; the soles were a bright, glossy red. Like Clever Gretel's shoes, Izzy thought, and put them down.

She went over to a bedside table and opened the drawer—a couple of state-of-the-art sex toys, lube, condoms.

Izzy opened the top drawer of a black lacquer bureau. Jumbled, underthings, pricey-looking; she ran her hand over the garments, creamy as fondant. A pair of black lace panties decorated with pink satin roses; the tags were still on. She had never owned anything remotely like this lingerie. Had the woman Cyrus—she made herself think it—*fucked* owned things like this?

Izzy balled the piece of lace in her fist and then slipped it into her pocket. There was something else in the drawer, too. Something hard and cool. She recoiled for a second but then fished it out. A small stone statue of a woman, all breasts and cleft. Hands pulling herself open for all to see. Sheela na gigs, Izzy knew, were grotesques, also called hunky punks, carved figures squatting erotically on the facades of medieval churches to ward off death, or the dangers of lust. Izzy pocketed the figure.

She'd stolen things before when she was younger—nail polish or lipstick or candy. Sometimes she still poached little soaps and shampoo bottles, tea bags or honey from the 29 Palms Inn when she went to work with Cyrus—she knew Ted would look the other way. She would have stolen books from the library, but she needed to be able to go back there all the time and get more. Besides, books were sacred. But this stuff wasn't sacred. This place felt somehow like an affront, like the stone woman's body.

Izzy went into the bathroom again, ripped the tags off the stolen panties and put them on, throwing her old, black cotton underwear with the loosened elastic into the trash. Then she and Dog went back downstairs and outside.

###

The upcoming November full moon was called Beaver because this was the month when Native American tribes and European settlers set traps for the animals whose pelts would provide furs for the winter. But this humpbacked gibbous looked more like the so-called Cold Moon of December. The lit-up hot tub shimmered, green and vitreous as an eye. A fire burned in a pit, filling the air with wood smoke tang, and somewhere someone played a hand drum. Izzy could hear the slap of palms and fingers on taut leather.

Ever stood there, in the shadows, holding two beers. "There you are," he said, handing one bottle to her and then stroking Dog's ear with his free hand. "I thought you two left."

She thanked him and took a sip of the beer.

"That was intense," he said. "I'm not sure what it was, exactly."

"Do you know much about them?" she asked him. "This House of Hearts or whatever it's called."

"The ad said it's for healing. That's all I really know."

Dog went and situated himself decidedly on top of Ever's feet. "Therapy dog," Izzy said.

Ever smoothed his thumb along the bony ridge between Dog's eyes. "No doubt. You don't need much healing with him around."

She nodded. "Not too much."

"Where are you from?" he asked her.

"Slab City. But I live in Salton City now. You?"

"Joshua Tree, but I'm from LA."

"I've always wanted to live there," Izzy said.

Los Angeles.

The city that had been populated by those seeking wealth through gold, oil, land, or water, fame through the movies, or freedom from oppression. And these settlers had created their own oppression. Haciendas and then bungalows had replaced orange groves, and, in turn, mansions and manor houses, towers of limestone, copper and glass, and highways of asphalt had replaced bungalows. Rock and punk music had erupted in suburban garages or canyon dwellings, then blown by Santa Ana winds through the streets and into the clubs along the Sunset Strip. Graffiti twined up and along freeway underpasses where a growing homeless population slept.

Gangs torched and looted, while mountain lions, bears, bobcat, mule deer, skunks, raccoons, and opossums still fought for their own territory in the wild.

To live and die in LA.

To live and die without Cyrus.

"Why did you move?" she asked Ever.

"I thought it would be better to get out of the city. Better air. And there was a good doctor in Palm Springs. So, I opened a recording studio out here."

A doctor, a need for healing. She wanted to ask him more, but a kind of unspoken agreement then passed between them. It all felt like too much, these thoughts of loss, so she took another sip of beer and asked about his work instead. He told her he played instrumental covers of nineties bands but with a funk twist. He told her more about his band, ze Monsta. And Izzy listened, glad of the distraction.

She did not miss the reference—his band shared the name of one of her favorite songs. Cyrus had heard there was a place to watch, or at least hear, concerts in LA for free. After the ride on Joe's bike and a long hike in the beam of his flashlight, toward the sound of the music that had begun down in the amphitheater, they found what looked like a small campground among the pine trees. Oddly, no one had gathered there yet; maybe they'd come later, the "tree people" as the singers from the theater called them. Cyrus opened his backpack and took out almonds, apples, cheese, crackers, and a canteen of water. He and Izzy sat on flattened beer can cartons and ate and drank and listened; it was hard to really see anything beyond the pines. But the singer's wail reached Izzy; she felt it in her sternum and scapula and coxal bones. She closed her eyes and saw a video she'd watched of the singer on an outdoor stage at a music festival in England. The singer wore pale-blue eye shadow, an intricately laced white satin dress that just grazed the top of her forearm-slim thighs, and high black boots. She held her guitar over her pelvis and strummed with a ferocity that never reached her placid face.

"Dance with me, baby," Cyrus had said as the singer returned to the stage for an encore. He stood and held out his arms for Izzy to join him, his head cocked to the side so his hair fell into his smiling face.

"I don't dance," she said, but she stood anyway, her limbs longer and more awkward than ever.

He put his hands on her hips, and she draped her arms around his shoulders and leaned her face into the base of his neck where she could feel his pulse beating with the rhythm of the music below them and the stars in the amphitheater above. Cyrus and Izzy swayed like that, among the pine trees, in the distant light of the city where they had vowed to someday return.

"I worship at your altar," Cyrus whispered.

As he kissed Izzy, she felt a chill run through her like wind under the door of the desert shack on the coldest of nights. The chill was not simply from his kiss or from the singer's voice. That bucolic summer evening in the trees above the amphitheater, in the city they both dreamed of as their sanctuary, their escape, Izzy experienced the distinct sensation that someone was watching them from the trees. But no one ever appeared and she realized it was just the darkness inside her that followed her everywhere, even to this city she loved.

Later, Izzy had seen an image on the internet of the singer taken from the stage below. It was probably a doctored image, but it intrigued Izzy just the same. The fearlessness of the woman, naked beneath her dress. An apotropaic symbol warding off death and evil, a talisman to enter another world. Sheela na gig like the stone woman, heavy and cool in Izzy's pocket.

But that magic hadn't protected Izzy from Cyrus's leaving. Maybe she shouldn't have ignored the darkness she'd felt that night in LA. Maybe it was trying to tell her something, even then. But it was too late now.

She turned her focus on Ever again. "I listen to a lot of nineties music," she told him. "Our friend Ted turned us on to it. My friend," she corrected herself.

"Music is life."

"I agree. But why, do you think?" She'd asked Cyrus this once, lying on a rock, still warm from the day, looking up at the stars.

He had said, "It drowns out the sound of bombs going off in my head," before taking her into an embrace as warm as the stone on which they lay.

"It combats oblivion," Ever said now. "Also, it proves to me that souls exist."

"How?"

"Because when I listen, or when I play, I can feel my soul in my body," Ever said.

Sex does that, too, she thought.

Ever shifted slightly, and she could see, almost feel, the musculature under his shirt. He gestured to a small stone bench with lion's claw feet. "Do you want to sit?"

She joined him, and they sat staring out into the garden. Even at a distance, the heat from the flames in the fire pit warmed Izzy's skin.

"Why did you come?" he asked. "I mean, I guess I'm supposed to know just by looking into your eyes for half an hour."

He didn't seem like the rest of these people, although she wasn't a hundred percent sure she could trust her judgment. Still. "My boyfriend went missing," she told Ever. "I thought something really bad—but it looks like he just took off. And I found out that a few months ago he went to one of these retreats in Desert Hot Springs. So, I came here."

"To find him?"

She brushed her fingers along her throat, trying to swallow down the lump there. "I don't know what I'm doing anymore."

"Grief fucks with you," Ever said.

She nodded. They turned and looked at each other. He put down his beer and leaned forward, elbows on knees, and tapped his lips with one finger. Cyrus had done that sometimes, and she felt her heart stutter, and the breathless gap that followed.

But this was not Cyrus. She wished she hadn't come. Izzy's eyes filled again. Her tears blinded her for a moment and she wiped them away—*No crying, no more crying*—gazing into the green lights surrounding the pool.

"Want another beer?" Ever asked.

No, he was not Cyrus. But he looked like Cyrus. And his hands were warm.

She forced a smile and the muscles in her face felt stiff, as if she hadn't smiled in weeks. Maybe she hadn't. She heard her own voice say: "Only if you want to carry me home."

He brought them both another bottle, but neither of them drank a sip. They sat and talked about nothing for a while.

"What happened to you?" Izzy asked then because the unspoken agreement had dissolved as the shadows inside them spilled and merged with the shadows around them. "What's the very worst thing?"

"Why do you want to know?"

"Because you know mine."

He looked at her for a long time, considering. Then: "My girlfriend and I moved out to Joshua Tree together," he said.

She waited.

He went on: "Because she was sick. Leukemia."

So that was what the move to Joshua Tree was about. "I'm so sorry."

He hunched his shoulders and looked at his hands.

"What's her name?"

"Emma Lee," he said. "She passed recently."

"I'm sorry," she repeated. "What's the best thing that ever happened to you?" she asked, maybe too quickly, wanting to soften the pain.

"Emma Lee. Was he yours?"

"Yes. We met as kids. It felt like the end of the world where I lived. I had books and music, a couple of friends, but he was—" She stopped herself.

"I think I understand."

"I was going to move away, be a social worker."

"That's cool," Ever said.

"But then I met him. I didn't have money for college. I got my certificate and started giving massages, and Cyrus did landscaping, construction. We were thinking of moving to LA when we saved up enough money."

"Why there?"

"I got into UCLA, but I didn't go." She'd said this proudly, she realized. She was proud to share it with him. "And we thought it would be a better place to raise a kid than where we're from."

Ever watched her for a moment, as if debating something in his mind. Then he said, "Emma didn't want kids. Later she told me it was because she'd 'intuited'—that was the word she used." He stopped. "That she wasn't going to be...that she'd get sick."

"I'm sorry," she said again. "So, you wanted children?"

"Yes." He looked away, folded his hands together, his fingers locking into a perfect puzzle, and stretched his arms in front of him. "Moving feels like it makes sense, when things are hard where you are."

She nodded, drew breath.

Then she said, "You remind me of him. Physically I mean. It's almost uncanny."

"That might not be a good thing," he said. "But. You remind me of Emma." He leaned closer, and she smelled mint and cedar wood on his skin—coolness and warmth, both at once.

That was when she wanted to grab him, claw at him. Tear off his clothes to see his tattoos. Roses. Serpent. Panther. Falcon. Skull. Her name.

No, no, that was not what she would find. Cyrus was gone. He had left. He had left her.

But Ever was solidly here.

And she was here. Somehow the betrayal hadn't killed her the way she had thought it would.

She looked up at him.

It was decided, then, between them.

"Remember you said you'd carry me home?" Izzy asked.

"I'm not sure I actually said that."

"I believe the exact words were, 'Only if you want to carry me home.'"
He leaned in. "I believe those were your exact words."

"Exactly. But you answered by bringing me another beer."

"True. True," he said. Neither of them mentioned that she hadn't
even had a sip.

"Do you live around here?" She laughed out loud, but it sounded
more like a gasp of hurt. "Listen to me."

"Yes, I do," he said. "And I am. In that order."

"I'm so confused."

"Apparently we have karma to clear," he said, smiling.

"And we've created an attachment," said Izzy.

"I have a cat, though. Does your therapy dog like cats?"

"I don't know," she said.

"Well, I guess we will find out. Come on."

They walked out together, with Dog, through the house, out the
front door. Ever's black Ram truck was parked near Plata. *Even his
truck is similar.* Izzy thought of the missing persons flyers still in
her bag. In the picture, Cyrus's eyes looked pixilated, hundreds of
tiny dark dots. Were those eyes watching her from inside the bag,
watching her get into her truck and follow a stranger home? Part of
her hoped Cyrus's eyes were watching.

✤✤✤

Ever signaled for a long time, alerting her, before he turned off the
highway. The two black trucks passed a handwritten sign that read,
"Dark Road," and Izzy wondered if the name bothered Ever. Probably
not. She could see his smile in her mind like the distant lights at the
end of the dirt road.

The road led to a gate with a metal sign of a crescent moon
and the words "Rancho de la Rosa." Behind a garden of rocks and
succulents, a low porch ran the length of the ranch house. A metal

peacock and an old-fashioned framed still life of overblown roses hung on the outer wall of the house above an outdoor couch covered in a woven blue and pink Mexican blanket like one Izzy and Cyrus had on their bed. Blue glass wind chimes spun and clinked. A pair of large desert boots slouched by the door.

Beyond, across the highway, lay the monument. Ever and Izzy parked on the pavers and then walked up to the door with Dog. The large room, lit fuzzily by candles and strands of white lights that gave everything a gauzy radiance, housed a home recording studio with a computer, microphones, monitors, cables, a large set of keyboards, a drum set, guitars, and bass. Also: two worn green velvet armchairs, a brown leather couch, an emerald green Moroccan rug covered with red and blue birds and flowers on brown branches, a wooden coffee table with mugs, ashtrays, incense burners, and candles oozing vanilla scent with each drip of wax. On the wall hung photos of famous musicians posed in front of the studio, stern as cacti and casting long shadows in stark desert sunlight.

Izzy collapsed onto the couch. Shifting shadows became a black cat with green eyes.

"Oh," Izzy said, tugging on Dog's leash, but he just lay on the carpet, and the cat stalked over, sniffed him a bit, then glided into her lap.

She closed her eyes, twirling the long, solid tail with her fingers. The cat purred and pressed his head to her stomach. "I'm so tired," she said.

"Why don't you rest?"

Suddenly, her head felt chasmal. Pain was there but at the periphery. The cat curled into a ball in her lap, reverberating against her full belly. She tried not to think of the kitten she'd had as a child.

"Trout loves you," Ever said. She glimpsed a flash of dimples for the first time. The cat's name almost made her smile, too. "Maybe he knew you in another life."

"Was I a cat?" she asked the animal. He brought his nose to hers. "Or were you human?"

"Maybe you were both both."

"Do you believe in other lives?"

"Maybe." Ever crouched down near her, watching her face. His knees strained his jeans—the fabric would tear.

"I'm so tired," she said again.

She and Ever looked at each other. Then he reached out and touched her cheek with one finger. It was what Cyrus would have done.

"Sleep here," Ever said.

She wrapped her arms around herself, pressing her fingers into the notches of her rib cage, and closed her eyes tight to shut everything out.

✢✢✢

She woke in the night, leaned on her elbow, and watched him asleep beside Dog on the floor at her side. As if he'd sensed her gaze, he opened his eyes. Something glimmered in the dark between them.

"Can you come over here?" she whispered. It almost felt like she was dreaming.

She heard the sound of his smile. "There's not much room."

"Then I'll come down there."

His sleeping bag smelled clean and warm—like lavender and camp fires. She lay beside him on the floor, staring at the ceiling, Ever's hands folded on his chest, his legs crossed at the ankles. Dog jumped onto the couch and curled up, turning his back away, which made them both laugh.

"May I touch you?" she asked after a while.

"Yes."

So, she laid her hands on him, one part of him at a time. And as she touched him, she asked him questions.

"Tell me about your eyes."

He turned a little toward her, reached to brush a strand of hair off her forehead. "They like what they see."

"Tell me a story about your mouth."

She brushed her fingers across his lips. "I wanted to be a lead singer, but I can't sing, so I learned to play guitar."

"Tell me about your nose." She ran her pinky finger down the little bump on the bridge.

"Kind of jacked. I broke it playing ball when I was twelve."

She lifted his T-shirt and ran her fingers over his pecs. Almost hairless. No tattoos. A few faded acne scars shadowed the place where his chest subtly dipped.

"I have a heart in there," he said. "What's left of one."

"Same," she said. "Stomach."

"I work on these abs, but—" he pinched a small bit of gut.

"I might need a microscope to see that." She put her hand on his bicep. "Your arms."

He flexed. "I work these arms."

"Your legs."

"Too skinny. But fast. Stronger than they look."

"Your feet."

"Kind of jacked, too. And big. I can't find shoes that fit."

"I like them."

She took his hand in hers and examined it. The fingers were tapered, calloused from guitar strings, the lines so deep she could have read his palms by Braille.

"I broke that, too," he said, moving his wrist in a circle, their fingers still interlocked. "Got a pin in it."

"Me, too." She held up her ankle and he let go of her fingers, sat up, and took her foot in his hands, ran a finger over the scars, massaged the back of her calf. "Does it still hurt?"

"No, it was a long time ago. Gets stiff sometimes. Does yours?"

"Sometimes. Luckily it's my right."

"You're a lefty?"

He nodded, lay back down, and looked into her eyes, and she held his wrist, trying to sense the pain under the surface of his skin. Everyone had so much hidden pain; it made them more beautiful, she thought. Ever sighed and then, without thinking, she moved her hand between his legs. Her fingers grazed thick denim.

"Not much to tell about that part. I met a girl. We were eighteen. Together eight years. Haven't been with anybody since."

Izzy closed her eyes and laid her head on his chest. She could feel his heart beating—yes, it was still there. And now she felt his hands touching her eyelids with a tenderness that she'd already almost forgotten existed at all.

"Your turn," he said.

She moved her hand from between his legs, and he touched her hair, her temples, the bridge of her nose. Now he touched her chin, ran a finger over her lips. He caressed her throat and her clavicle bones and her shoulders. Ran a finger down the inner flesh of her arm to her wrist, so that she prickled all over. He laid a palm flat on her belly. The desire writhed, then.

Now he was lifting her T-shirt, gently exposing her breasts. His other hand moved toward her jeans, tugged at the waistband, tugged them off of her without unbuttoning them—she'd lost that much weight in the last few weeks. Izzy had a brief thought—she was glad she'd stolen the underwear—before Ever's fingers slid beneath the waistband of the lace covered with tight, satin knots of pink roses.

Meet ze Monsta

Izzy heard a key in a lock and opened her eyes, trying to remember where she was. Light poured in through a panel of glass in the beamed roof. Dog had jumped up and managed to fit himself against the curve of her back, his legs dangling off the side of the couch. He lifted his head heavily and blinked sideways at the door.

Ever eased in with a canvas bag of groceries in one arm, and Dog unfolded himself and ran to Ever, tail wagging. "You okay?" Ever asked her. "Know where you are?"

She sat up, rubbing her eyes and trying to nod her head, but her neck and back were so stiff. Where was she? She was with him, this man she had just met.

He began to take the food from the bag—eggs, butter, cheese, spinach, onions, berries. "Omelet?"

Eggs comforted her. "Thank you," she said.

"I make a cruel omelet."

"Cruel?"

"Sorry. Bad old joke. So old I don't even notice when I say it."

She got up and pulled on her underpants and jeans. The small stone woman she'd stolen from the retreat center had fallen to the floor, and she put it on the coffee table and went into the kitchen with

Trout now at her side, coiling his tail around her ankles. Ever had shaved, and she could see the smooth line of his jaw, could smell— when he kissed her cheek, so naturally, as if they had done this many times before—the sandalwood of his soap mixed with the nag champa and coffee.

Izzy put on her shoes and went out to the truck for the extra food she'd stashed there for Dog. While she fed him, Ever took out some onions, heated oil in a pan.

"I'll chop the onions," Izzy said. She couldn't remember the last time she'd felt like cooking. Yes, she could. On Halloween.

After they'd eaten, mostly in a gentle silence, Dog waiting patiently at their feet for scraps, the sun through the skylight catching afire dust motes in the air, Ever asked if she wanted to shower.

"I need one," she said. When had she last showered?

"You need one not at all. I just thought you might want to."

"I don't have a change of clothes."

Ever went to a closet, neatly stocked, and handed her a clean towel and a black T-shirt.

Izzy thanked him and showered in a bathroom hardly big enough for her to fit, let alone for Ever; he must have to hunch over in the stall. Scrubbing at her skin with a washcloth, rubbing between her legs, feeling the prickle of nerves there, she thought of last night. She stepped out, toweled off, and put on her jeans and his shirt, leaving her rinsed underwear to dry on the towel bar. The clean towel even smelled of coffee, sandalwood, fireplace. She opened the medicine cabinet: toothbrushes, aspirin, bandages, gauze, hydrogen peroxide. She opened a drawer and rummaged around. There was a tube of toothpaste, which she used, squeezing some onto a wet finger and rubbing her teeth. There was floss in the drawer, a gold tube of lipstick, bobby pins, a few still trailing strands of dark hair. This made her shiver, and she shut the drawer.

"You should stay for a while," Ever told her when she emerged. "My band's coming to rehearse."

She didn't really want to go home, so she called Nephy and left a message saying she was out of town, asking her to check in on Yard. They hadn't talked in a few days, ever since Miracle Manor. Izzy didn't want to talk about what she'd discovered in Cyrus's jacket. She wanted only to forget.

###

Monsta: Word (guitar), Quinn (bass), and Robert (drums). Three tall men who resembled angels more than monsters. They all seemed a little surprised when they saw Izzy, but they didn't say much.

While the band rehearsed in the studio, she and Dog went out through the screen door. Under a honey mesquite tree, lounge chairs surrounded a hot tub with a fire pit nearby. Izzy looked past a low brick wall to the monument and listened to the music floating out of the house. She remembered what Ever had said to her about souls. Music as proof that the soul existed.

###

She fell asleep and woke later. Ever stood over her. The sun was setting behind him, limning his body, making him glow.

"You hungry?"

She blinked up at him. Something flashed between them like a mirror in the sun.

"We're going to make dinner," he said.

She smelled chlorine, the ghost of smoldering coals, the citronella of insect repellent. Ever took a lighter from his pocket and crouched down on his heels over the fire pit. He flicked the lighter, holding the flame to the kindling until it ignited. He, Izzy, and the band wrapped corncobs, veggie burgers, and buns in foil and laid everything on the grill. No one said much, and Izzy was grateful for that. She ate a plate full of food and drank a beer. After dinner, they roasted marshmallows. Ever pulled one off the stake and let it cool before he handed it to her. The sweet goo melted into her mouth, but the char of burnt sugar grazed her tongue almost painfully.

"You two met online?" Word asked. He was leaning over the fire with the marshmallow on a stake. He had a perfect Afro, and both his ears were pierced.

"What?" Ever asked.

Quinn picked up an acoustic guitar and began to strum it. Robert reached for a hand drum and rubbed the skin lightly—a sibilant, hushing sound. His braids hung down over his face. Both men seemed to be trying to put an end to the conversation.

"Well, the resemblance is kind of uncanny," Word said.

Ever's body tensed.

Word went on: "I figured you had to try hard to find someone who looks that much like her, am I right?"

"Just kind of happened," Ever said.

"Have you seen Emma?" Word asked Izzy, not looking at her still.

"Hey, man."

"Relax, Everado. I just think she should know."

"She knows."

"I know," Izzy said, bristling, although Ever hadn't told her that she and his girlfriend looked alike, only that Izzy reminded him of her. "And he looks a lot like my—like Cyrus."

"Like who?"

Ever gave Word a hard stare.

Quinn studied them through his Buddy Holly glasses. "I'm sorry," he said. Then he added, "That's some cosmic shit there, though."

###

After Word, Quinn, and Robert had left, Izzy went into the tiny bathroom and looked at her reflection. The food, beer, and fire had flushed her face. She took off her jeans, put on her now-dry underwear, put on her jeans again. She opened the drawer and picked up the tube of lipstick; it felt heavy in her hand. Izzy never wore lipstick; it would be stupid to wear it now, but she opened the gold tube, leaned in to the mirror and dabbed the waxy substance to her lips. It had belonged to Emma Lee, she was pretty sure.

Izzy wiped the lipstick off with the back of her hand and looked at the red stain on her skin. *Have you seen Emma? I just think she should know. She knows. Yes, she knows. That's some cosmic shit there.* Then she pocketed the tube in her jeans and left the room.

###

Ever led her up a ladder onto the roof of the studio. He'd laid out sleeping bags and blankets, and he and Izzy sat and had another beer. They looked out over the desert, up at the firmament. The sky canopied her star-filled belly over the earth. Izzy closed her eyes and for a moment she forgot how and why she was here, where she had come from, who she had been, and what she had lost.

Without even touching him, Izzy felt the heat radiating through Ever's flannel. She wanted him to fuck her, make her warm from inside, make everything go away except that warmth.

"Sorry about Word," Ever said.

"It's okay."

"You don't need any attitude thrown at you."

She didn't say anything.

Without looking at her, as if, she thought, he was trying to protect her, Ever asked quietly, "Did you report it to the police? Him leaving?"

"Yes. The police won't do shit."

"What makes you say that?"

"The way they acted when I told them. It's like they didn't take it seriously."

"I don't get it," he said. "I mean, even if he just left, they should rule anything else out."

"You didn't grow up where we did."

"Meaning...?"

"A lot of cops don't care about Slabbers."

Ever shook his head and frowned.

"That was one reason I wanted to get my degree: help some kids. Social work. Or law. Cyrus's brother Joe is still in the pen for driving drugs. His girlfriend gave him a package, didn't tell him what it was. One guy I knew growing up, they put him in prison. Said he died from falling and hitting his head. But his wife and kids knew the cops beat him. They couldn't afford the autopsy."

"I see what you mean." There was a pause, and then Ever asked, "I hope this is okay to ask, but do you suspect anyone?"

"Everyone loved Cyrus," Izzy said. "Except my parents, but they don't count."

"Why not?"

"Leanne's crazy. Certified. Larry's just—" She stopped herself; there was enough pain here without exposing her childhood wounds.

Ever didn't press her. "So, you're sure he left?"

"I found a receipt in his pocket from the motel where we used to go. Drinks for two. He never told me. And I've been trying to crack the code on his phone. For some reason he changed it—" She trailed off, still ashamed of this fact, confused by it, and she was grateful that Ever didn't ask any further questions. They sat in silence for a while.

Then he pointed above their heads at the ejaculating night sky. She closed her eyes to wish on a star. But, as she'd wondered the night before, what could she wish for now?

Ever kissed her, lightly at first, and for a long time, then ran his hands over her head, slid them down her neck and across the bone necklace of her clavicles. "It's called the beauty bone," he said. She could hear his breath grow ragged. He eased her onto the pile of sleeping bags, still kissing her, moving his fingers over her breasts— the aureoles felt tender, the nipples rose to meet him. She was already wet, had been since they'd come up here on the rooftop. What was this desire she felt for this man, this stranger? It ached in the dark loam of her like a seed, and spread its roots through her limbs, into her fingertips, toes. It was almost like someone else's body had overtaken her.

"Is this all right?" he asked.

She nodded against his jaw, already scratchy again with stubble.

He slid down and nuzzled her with his whole face—the angled thrust of his nose and cheekbones and chin, the soft of his eyelids and lips—drew her thighs together so that the sensation of fullness intensified, then with his nose pushed the small piece of cloth aside and slid his tongue over the patch of hair, parting her vulva and finding her clitoris.

"I want to make you come," he said.

"What about you?"

"Just you first. Relax."

She couldn't remember Cyrus having ever said this to her.

"And then I'm going to press down on you just right and make you come again while I'm inside of you," Ever said as she dissolved into concentric rings of pleasure, like a stone thrown into a pool of still water.

✳✳✳

Izzy woke naked, draped across Ever's warm expanse of chest. They'd gone back down the ladder into the house, to his bed, and fallen asleep there. Her mouth tasted like someone had been trying to stuff her T-shirt down her throat. She disentangled her limbs from his, hoisted herself up, dragged on her jeans, and put on her shoes.

As Izzy reached for her backpack, she saw a framed photo on a table by the bed. The woman had hair that swept darkly above wide cheekbones. Her body appeared lanky and strong, limbs a little too long for her jeans and flannel so that oddly small wrists and ankles showed. It was true: she resembled Izzy in an almost uncanny way.

The best thing that ever happened to you. Emma Lee.

This man and her, they were both only in search of ghosts.

Maybe they were ghosts themselves.

Or monsters, thought Izzy. *Meet ze monstas.*

Izzy fastened Dog's leash and opened the front door to leave. The black cat sat there in the dark, mewling, watching her and Dog with virescent eyes. A gray mouse lay curled on the step, spilling its insides, an offering.

###

Sitting in the truck, Izzy looked up Ever online, entering his first name and ze Monsta, and found his personal page. It wasn't private. Everado Fontana. A photo of his face in dark sunglasses, hard to make out. A cover photo of him and the band in the desert. She clicked back through more pictures. Requisite guitar shots from below the stage, a few artsy studio shots, selfies in the same dark sunglasses, pictures of the black cat, Trout. Pictures of famous guitarists. The black-and-white portrait of three of Izzy's favorite female singers leaning into each other dreamily, as if conjoined. Some political posts about the environment and the president's immigration policies, health care, police brutality. Izzy remembered a time when she had posted things like that, when she and Cyrus discussed these things, a time when the outside world mattered—

Izzy found a picture from a year back of Ever and his cat and the woman whose photo Izzy had seen. But now the woman's hair was shaved. Emma Lee Reed.

Izzy clicked on the name.

Ever's love, Emma Lee, had used the same picture as her profile shot. On her page: a series of memorial messages.

I miss you!

I think of you every day, beautiful Emma.

I still can't believe you're gone, my darling sister, my best friend.

Under the profile shot—hundreds of comments. The last one was from Ever, dated a few months ago.

The moon now is just as it was that night. It feels as if it's tearing something loose. I cannot cure myself, can't face the truth. Eclipse within my chest obscures the light.

Izzy and Ever both loved someone else; maybe they had made love to someone else last night. But it didn't matter. Even if she never saw Ever again, Izzy felt changed, somehow. Her purpose now was to begin to find herself.

Long Snake Moan

The text came just a few nights later, sending a toxic pang of adrenalin through Izzy's body. She'd signed up for local alerts right after he'd gone missing, telling herself it was because she wanted to make sure she didn't miss anything about Cyrus:

Advisory:
#SBCSD Homicide Investigates Discovery of Poss.
Human Remains, San Bernardino County

San Bernardino County Sheriff's Department homicide detectives are continuing their investigation into the circumstances surrounding found partial human skeletal remains discovered by an environmental study crew Thursday at approximately 11:23 am, in the Red Sand Gold Mine's 100-foot vertical mine shaft southeast of Twentynine Palms. The abandoned gold mine was last worked on in the 1970s.

Homicide detectives and San Bernardino County Department of Medical Examiner-Coroner personnel have concluded a search for additional human remains and recovery efforts.

What is believed to be an adult male vertebral column was found and recovered in the cave. Investigators collected and transported the remains to the San Bernardino County Department of Medical

Examiner-Coroner's office, where they will be examined to determine
if they are human and for possible identification of the deceased.

There is no further information at this time.

Anyone with information about this incident is encouraged
to contact the San Bernardino County Sheriff's Department's
Homicide Bureau.

Izzy's whole body seized with a pang of adrenalin like those
death-throe rabbits that Larry used to slice through both jugulars
for dinner.

Even if the remains were not Cyrus's, even if he had gone to
Miracle Manor with someone else, something inside her now knew
with a wave of that old, familiar darkness, that she had mostly fought
off until now—he had not simply left her. And even if he had betrayed
her, he had loved her. He had loved her once.

Cyrus, my Cyrus. Why did I give up on you?

Once, she'd read about a psychic, although he didn't like that
word—he called himself an intuitive—who helped police with
murder cases. Walking past a concrete wall, he started to feel sick,
queasy, started to sweat. He examined the wall and thought he saw
the jagged shape of a tooth in the concrete. The police tore out the
wall but found nothing. The intuitive received a message, something
about jewels. This led him to the murderer—an ex-detective, who
was fired for pawning stolen jewelry and now owned a construction
company, had ground up his victim into the cement.

Izzy knew she had to trust her premonitions now, though she
would rather have run from them—screaming. She stayed up the rest
of the night searching for more information about the advisory online.
In the morning, she called the police and asked about the remains.
The officer she spoke to said the body had not yet been identified, but
she would certainly be notified if there was a connection to her case.

"When?" she said, trying not to shriek like a lunatic. "When will
you identify them?"

"We'll let you know."

She hung up. When she and Cyrus and Seth and Nephy were younger, they had hung out in mineshafts sometimes. Joe had said that Cyrus talked about going down into those mines and not coming back up. Should she go down into those mines now? Maybe she needed to do this as some kind of penance. For giving up on Cyrus so easily, for sleeping with a man she didn't even know. And maybe she'd find something important underground.

She took from a drawer the scissors with which she had trimmed Cyrus's hair. She yanked her own hair into a ponytail. This hair, so thick, had protected Izzy her whole life—from the sun, from the cold; it shielded her face from the eyes of men. At the same time, it made her vulnerable. As a child she'd wanted to cut it, but Larry hadn't let her. "I don't want you looking like a boy." Now, Izzy tugged the ponytail to the side and sawed it off as if it were a live thing.

Like a warrior. More like Cyrus. And I'll be less encumbered in order to look for him.

Part of my penance.

Izzy picked up Cyrus's electric razor. It still had remnants of his hair caught in the blade. Seeing the little strands of black hair made her gasp with fresh pain.

She put the razor down.

She picked up the scissors again and hacked her hair shorter, short as she could. Long black strands lay strewn in the sink, like a shredded fright wig. Without hair she looked ugly, she thought, naked and small.

Then she took the razor dusted with Cyrus's cells to her head. And she buzzed.

###

"**What a nice** surprise." Larry shambled out of the trailer, followed by Leanne. Larry's lips shone from what Izzy guessed was rabbit grease. His belt buckle was in the shape of an eagle, and Izzy thought of the kid on the Missing Persons of America website who resembled Cyrus, the one with the long hair and the tattoo on his chest. That beautiful lost boy. "But you look like shit," Larry said.

"What happened to your hair?" Leanne asked. "You're different."

"Maybe that's a good thing."

They both surveyed her as if she were a barren plot of land or an empty hen house.

"Have you heard anything?" Izzy almost barked at them.

Larry shook his head no. "You?"

"Leanne, can you make some tea, please?" she asked.

Leanne shot Larry a look, and he nodded. She headed toward the juniper tree where she kept the teacups hidden in a wooden box.

"They found some remains," Izzy said.

"What-now?"

"Human remains. At an abandoned mine site."

"So what?"

"He's been gone three weeks now, Larry." She showed him the text on her phone.

"You think that was him? That ain't him."

Izzy tried to gulp down the sand dune in her throat. "I'm going to look," she said.

"Look where?"

"The mines."

"You have any idea how many mines there are out there?"

"Over three hundred. You have that old map anymore?"

"I don't like the idea of you running around out there by yourself. Did you hear about that couple that got lost?" Larry made a face like he'd tasted dirt. "Lost. They just found them, skeletons hanging on to each other. He'd shot her first, then himself."

Izzy had heard. So messed up. But then what wasn't?

"Desert plays tricks on the mind," Larry said. "You should know as well as anyone."

She looked at him the way she had as a child when she wanted something. "I'm going. With or without your damn map."

"Hang on," he said now. He went back into the trailer, passing Leanne who placed the teacups out one by one.

"Tea?" Leanne asked, pouring some water into a cup. Izzy knew the conversation with Larry was over. She couldn't ask him more with her mother around.

Leanne began to drone on about the thirty-one elements of the folk tale. Izzy tried to breathe away the frustration tightening her jaw.

"Think about these story elements in terms of your life," Leanne said. "It might help! Have you ever violated an interdiction? You've left home and faced a difficult task. Then asked yourself, why am I doing this? Why am I devoting myself to this thing that might ultimately destroy me?"

She looked at Izzy, who shivered with a preternatural cold. "But you go on anyway. Have you received a magical agent? Performed a reconnaissance mission? And what about branding?

"What about transfiguration?" Leanne went on. "Have you ever been broken?" She fixed her eyes on Izzy. "Have you been made whole?"

"Stop," Izzy said.

Leanne smiled, beneficent. "Oh, I got you a present. Well, Alma gave him to me. I almost forgot." Newly energized, she scampered off behind the trailer and came back hauling a large mannequin like the one under the juniper tree. But this one was male.

"I thought you'd like him," Leanne said.

Izzy almost gagged on her own spit. She knew she'd have to take the thing with her to appease her mother.

And there was another gift, too.

Larry came out of the trailer holding a wrinkled map of the Joshua Tree mines in his hand and carrying a smaller canvas bag on his shoulder. "You might need it out there," he said. He glared at the mannequin. "More than that piece of shit."

She felt the heft, the weight, the L-shaped coldness through the fabric. Before she took it out, she already knew: Larry had given her a gun.

"Why?"

"Like I said, you might need it."

"So, you think I'm right?"

"About the trouble he's likely in? I think every one of us out here is in deep shit," Larry said. "But, yeah, it can't hurt."

She hated guns. But she wasn't about to give it back. Not yet. Maybe she was going crazy like Leanne, like Alma; maybe Izzy had already gone the way of those desert women. Or like that couple that died in each other's arms.

But in the morning, she'd begin searching every mine she could.

###

The approximately three hundred abandoned mining sites that littered the Joshua Tree landscape had been built during the gold rush, but silver, copper, and other minerals—green-banded malachite, black pyrolusite, azurite, and turquoise—were also prospected. The mines consisted of various adits and shafts going down into the earth and scattered waste piles of tailings, the residue of ore. Larry liked to tell Izzy about the mines, some five-hundred-feet deep, the search for gold in the quartz veinlets. He'd taught her all the terminology including that word—veinlets—pressing his fingers to her wrist where the blue threads ran beneath the skin. He called her eyes malachite. Once, when she was nine, he'd even taken her underground. He did like to scare her.

Going into that mine as a teenager with Cyrus, Seth, and Nephy made it better, made Izzy see that it wasn't so bad down there—a hangout, a hidden world. Cigarettes and beer and a stick to draw their names in the dirt. *Izzy and Cyrus 4Ever.* Maybe her presence made it better for Cyrus, too. If she went down there now without him, it would be like going underground as a child again. Worse.

It's not him, it's not him, Izzy told herself, running to the bathroom. But he could still be down in one of those mines, and she was going to find him. Maybe he was hiding for some reason? Maybe he'd been injured or...her stomach heaved viscously, then dispensed bile into the toilet. But the darkness stayed inside.

When she thought of the mines, it struck her, for the first time, how many entrances there were to hell.

And she would search every one.

#&#

In the morning, Izzy checked her phone—texts from Nephy and Ted—and the page she'd made and Missing Persons of America. A few people had left messages praying for her.

One private message was from Everado Fontana:

Is this Aurora? Where'd you go? I don't have your phone number. Here's mine. Please call me some time—Ever

Izzy and Cyrus 4Ever. The irony of this didn't escape her.

Not now, Izzy thought. I can't. There would be no more drinking, no more hooking up. Only searching. It would give her something to do at least.

She fed the animals, apologized to them, let Dog out to pee in the cool-blue-dark.

After Izzy had eaten oatmeal with ground flax seeds and blueberries, she packed a canteen of water and some dried fruit and almonds, sunscreen, a compass, a flashlight, and gloves, and, from the shed, a pick ax, rope, and Cyrus's goggles and construction helmet. She also packed Larry's map and .38 revolver. The sun had just begun to rise. Good. Maybe she'd beat the heat by at least an hour.

#&#

By the time Izzy got to the first mine site, the one where she, Cyrus, Seth, and Nephy used to go, the sky already burned like sheet metal. The truck bumped over the uneven surface. Izzy parked and got out. A tarantula ran over her boot. She thought of the vinegarroons, carnivorous arachnids that used to terrify her as a child. They were rumored, when threatened, to release a vinegar scent so strong you could taste it at the back of your throat. The proper name,

Thelyphonida, meant murderess. But vinegarroons were the least of Izzy's worries. There were hundreds of mines beneath the desert floor.

The narrow path led up into the distance among Joshua trees, yucca blooms, and desert grasses under the barbarous sky. A wrecked tractor and the rust-covered dinosaur bones of other mining equipment marked the site. The air tasted silty, metallic with sand and with heat.

Izzy walked up to a sign that read:

Danger
Unsafe Mine Opening and High Walls
Deadly Gas and Lack of Oxygen
Cave-ins and Decayed Timber
Unsafe Ladders and Rotten Structures
Unstable Explosives
Stay Out, Stay Alive

A skull-and-crossbones presaged the final warning. A dilapidated door hung off its hinges at the entrance to a cave in a rock that resembled a humanoid skull or a deformed octopus. A seat ripped from the innards of a dead car stood sentry at the entrance like a throne for a chthonic god.

The area had been cordoned off with yellow crime scene tape. *Stay Out, Stay Alive.*

She would not stay out, though. No.

❊ ❊ ❊

She managed to search three more mines that day—the Rose of Peru, the Gold Standard, and the Brooklyn Mine. The road in was easy at first, then got rocky, and the truck tires slipped. The Rose of Peru Mine, active between 1939-1941, was where, about a hundred and forty feet down, the body of a pregnant nineteen-year-old had been found by a team of rescuers a few years before. Nineteen. Pregnant. Dead in a mine. How did these things even happen? But no one was searching for Cyrus yet, except Izzy. Tire marks and bullet casings had given the young woman's killer away, but Izzy saw no signs of these things now.

She exited the mine, hiked past some abandoned cabins, climbed a few small hills, and went about a hundred yards in to the Gold Standard. The hill to the entrance rose, steep, and gravel crunched under the teeth of her boots. She stuck to the road along the left side of the canyon for a few hundred yards and entered at the main adit, followed the air lines that ran along the top and bottom of the tunnel to a split in the path, took the left branch that dead-ended in what felt like at least a hundred and fifty yards, then tried the other side. A vertical shaft dropped about thirty feet, bridged only by cross-sticks of timber wood. Shining the moon of her flashlight down, she stepped carefully onto the planks, and they shifted slightly, so she jumped across the rest of the way. Nothing there, either. Just the dank air, caved-in littered tracks, rocky walls, and low ceiling of another deserted mineshaft.

Izzy surfaced and followed the road about a quarter of a mile farther to the Brooklyn Mine Camp. Rotten carcasses of cabins, one strung with a strand of broken light bulbs, huddled in the sun. Pink mud piles in the distance indicated cyanide, she knew, the substance to leach the gold out of the ore. You had to be careful breathing here. Although part of her wanted that cyanide in her lungs, could she sacrifice herself to find him?

This shaft, fifty or sixty feet deep, yawned near the entrance of the mine. A perfect place to dispose of bodies, but it looked empty. She entered the mine and followed the ore cart tracks, but someone had filled in the adit. How easy for some sick fuck to do that, she thought. Just bury someone, pour some concrete. She ran doubled over—through the tunnel.

When she emerged, she stopped and stared up at the sky. Night was coming. A perigee moon, weighty and white.

"It's not safe in those mineshafts," Ted had said when he'd called to check up on her. "You know that, right?"

Nothing. Nothing was safe.

###

She returned home by nightfall. Dog raised himself up, strutted over to her, swinging his head back and forth like a dejected lantern. One of Cyrus's black Converse lay half-chewed on the floor. Both dog and tortoise regarded her sadly.

"Okay, okay, I get it. You're mad I left."

She let Dog out, fed him and Yard, took a quick shower with the homemade lavender soap she had once made for Cyrus, and then got in bed, checking the missing persons page on her phone.

To Whom It May Concern:

I am the broken-hearted mother of twenty-two-year-old Regina Smith seeking help in finding the someone or something that took not only my precious child's life but also her eyes, heart, lungs, liver, and kidneys. Her empty body was discovered in the Mojave Desert. Please contact me with any information leading to justice for my daughter!

The marine's wife's body was discovered in a deserted mineshaft near Joshua Tree National Park.

A human jawbone that was found was determined to be that of a man who was reported missing nineteen years previously. The discovery was made when a group of four hikers stumbled upon the mandible near an abandoned mine shaft. Deputies responded and took a photo and sent it to the coroner's division, who later determined it was, in fact, a human bone.

The head of an unidentified male was found in a backpack in the Joshua Tree area. The decedent is thought to be a Caucasian male between 14 and 19 years of age. He had straight, light brown hair, numerous fillings, and had received high-quality dental care during his life. The reconstruction featured above is an artist's rendering of what the John Doe may have looked like. Anyone with information should contact the San Bernardino County Sheriff-Coroner.

Bad shit happened in the desert. So much agony, everywhere you looked.

Izzy clicked on a link to a video of still photos—people just before they'd disappeared. One little girl, seated on a rock, seemed to be laughing, revealing her missing front teeth, but—the video offered— she might have been grimacing in terror. A young boy who'd vanished on his paper route supposedly appeared to his mother late one night many years later and told her he was in fear for his life and had to keep his identity secret. A surveillance camera had caught the image of a man with hair styled into a pompadour, so perfect it resembled a wig, like the killer in a story Izzy once read. The bars of a metal fence hid his face as he walked away from an apartment building where a woman was later found in a pool of her own blood.

The robotic voice that narrated the video echoed inside Izzy as if she herself were made of tin.

Hollow as she was, she had no appetite. Except for these tales of horror. Had she been feeding on them to help deflect her own pain?

Izzy picked up Cyrus's phone. She typed in a random series of numbers.

Nothing. A waste of a precious chance. She should have at least made an educated guess.

Nephy texted her, then: *Meet me & Seth @ Alamo 4 breakfast 2morrow...worried*

\#\#\#

Izzy agreed to see Nephy and Seth early that day, before her search. She needed to eat, and maybe seeing her friends would do her good. But even just the photographs of margaritas, shrimp, tacos, and rare meat decorating the pale blue, red-trimmed façade of the little Mexican place made her stomach queasy, especially this early in the day.

A short time after she'd been seated, Seth's truck pulled up outside. He and Nephy got out. She wore her hair in braids under her straw cowboy hat. Her leg muscles gleamed with oil between the cut-offs and cowboy boots, and her belly seemed to have popped out some more. Inside of her, a baby swam.

Seth walked in ahead, his gait stiff. He held the door open behind him for Nephy, like an afterthought. Instead of the usual goatee, he wore a full beard, and without his bandana Izzy could tell, for the first time, really, that his hairline had begun to recede. But it was, of course, her hair that became a subject for discussion. She touched her head; it felt bumpy, boyish, and small.

"Izzy," Nephy said when they saw her. "What did you do?"

Izzy shrugged.

The waitress came to take their order—huevos rancheros all around, although Izzy, getting a whiff of the eggs, chilis, and oil, doubted she'd be able to eat much. She looked at Nephy across the table. Something was different about her, too. Makeup. She had makeup on her face. Nephy wore mascara, eyeliner, eye shadow, lipstick—never base makeup. A bruise showed underneath, a faint stain on her cheek.

"What happened to your face?" Izzy asked.

"Oh, it's nothing," Nephy said. "I fell." She glanced quickly at Seth, and then away.

"You're pregnant. You have to be careful."

Nephy pursed her lips in distaste and touched her hair with her acrylic-tipped fingers. "Seriously, why'd you cut your hair?" she asked.

Izzy said, "It would get in the way."

"In the way?"

"I've been searching the mines."

Nephy and Seth exchanged a look. "What mines?" Seth asked.

"In Joshua Tree. They found something in one." She made herself say it: "Remains."

"Remains? Human remains? Shit, Izzy, you hear how you sound?" Seth pushed up his shirtsleeves, agitated, and Izzy saw the old burns, still visible there, under his tan. The smell of cigarettes wafted off of him.

"I know how I sound. I don't have a choice. Someone has to do something—"

Nephy said, "I know this has been hard for you—"

"It's okay," Seth said. "Let her finish."

Izzy noticed that his eyes were bloodshot; he was on edge. Had he been drinking already this morning? And what was with Nephy's bruise? He couldn't have hit her...

"Go on," Seth told Izzy.

"Someone has to look for him. The police aren't doing shit."

"But the mines?" Seth said. "There's no reason to think—"

"What am I supposed to do? Sit at home waiting for him? Getting my nails done like you?"

Nephy skewered Izzy with her eyes. "I understand how upset you are," she said. "But this is getting really fucked."

"What's fucked? That I'm looking for him? Or that he's fucking missing, Nephy? That he might have killed himself? Or that someone else might have—"

They all sat in silence, staring at each other.

It seemed long ago now that she and Nephy had been close; hell, a long time since the four of them—Cyrus and Izzy and Nephy and Seth—had been close. Though they'd never verbalized it, Izzy knew that when they were younger, they all envisioned themselves as pseudo-stars of their own dark teen movie, in a way, walking in a line through town, dominating with their height, their impervious expressions; if Izzy were forced to admit it: dominating with their sexuality, too. People envied the way they had bonded to each other, as couples and a group.

There was an abandoned bait shop down on the shores of the Salton Sea where Seth once shot a film of Izzy and Nephy dancing, silhouetted against the setting sun while Cyrus sat with his back to them, fishing, tossing the poisoned tilapia and pupfish back into the water.

"Just let it go, Izzy," Seth said. She wasn't sure, for a moment, if he meant the memory of the past—as if he'd read her mind—or the search or the argument with Nephy. Leanne and Joe had told Izzy something similar—to let everything go. And she had, for a while. But why were they all telling her this? Seth's snake eyes rolled back in his head for a second. And then, in a softer voice, Izzy thought she heard: "It's all unfolding."

"What was that? What did you say?" She might have screamed the words; she wasn't sure.

Seth blinked at her, lizard-like.

"What did you say?" she repeated.

"We're all upset."

"That's not what you said."

He continued to stare at her with his hard, bloodshot eyes. Nephy touched the bruise on her face. In that moment, Izzy hated them both.

"Fuck this," she mumbled. She threw some bills on the table, got up, and walked out, the door chiming blithely behind her as if it didn't understand either: she had work to do.

⸙⸙⸙

When she arrived home from the mines that night, she checked her webpage and Missing Persons of America again. She stared at the bright screen until it seemed to move like water. The missing people drowning there. Dog hauled his massive head onto her lap, and she could feel the brush of his whiskers and his eyelids fluttering against her hand. She rubbed his ear, the one with the bite taken out.

"I'm sorry, I know. I get you and then I leave you," she told him. "I understand." But although she could empathize, she told herself she didn't really understand abandonment, at least not the way Cyrus had. Izzy's parents were unpredictable, but they had always been there. And it was likely, now, she realized, that Cyrus had not abandoned her.

She checked the SBPD website. The words rang in her head, as if read by the automated, uncanny valley voice from the video she'd watched.

The victim was discovered in the backyard of an abandoned home.
Manner of Death: Homicide.

State of Remains: Charred/Burned.

Estimated Age: 12-18 years old.

Approximate Height and Weight: 5' 4", 110 lbs.

Clothing: There was a small amount of charred T-shirt and a small amount of a sock.

Dentals: Available. #1,16 Unerupted.

Fingerprints: Available. Fingerprints submitted to San Bernardino County Sheriff.

DNA: Samples submitted—tests not complete.

Body had been burned over 95% of body (charred and unidentifiable).

Identity may be confirmed by fingerprints, dental X-rays, or DNA.

The body of John Doe was discovered in an open-topped rail car. Based on the condition of the body, it is believed he had been deceased less than 24 hours at time of discovery. He is believed to have been in his mid-late teenage years, had dark hair and scars on both arms. He was found wearing blue jeans with a black belt, a gold belt buckle skull with wings, a white shirt with an apple and silhouette of New York City, and black cowboy boots. The reconstruction featured above is an artist's rendering of what the John Doe may have looked like. The additional photo has been enhanced to aid in visual identification and may not reflect the original case file image.

She was walking home from her job at the beauty salon. The next day, the 23-year-old was found shot to death and partially nude in the desert. A student walking to school discovered her body. Accounts of the murder and investigation at the time reported one person was detained for—

Not him. Not him. But still. Each of these people was someone's child, perhaps someone's lover. Secretly suspicious that she was indulging some ever-growing appetite for other people's pain to distract her from her own, Izzy shut the computer, but the tinny voice still ricocheted around her head. If the Colt Army Special Larry had given her could talk, it might sound like that voice.

She put her hand on the gun in her backpack. Larry had taken her out to kill jackrabbits when she was a kid. The same type of rabbits that hopped like sentries around the shack. They were brown as the hills at twilight, quicker than tumbleweeds. Izzy had refused to fire at the animals, she hated guns, but now she was glad he'd taught her to shoot.

The mannequin watched, eyeless, from the corner of the room.

###

Perhaps she had cried out in her sleep because she woke to Dog licking her cheek. The warm, soft tongue. The dog-eyes always watching. She looked around at the Cyrus-less room with that sinking-stone feeling: throat-chest-belly.

The spine in the desert had still not been identified. Ted had called Izzy, apologetic, and told her he'd had to hire someone else, but she hadn't been able to bring herself to look for other work. She still felt compelled to spend her time in the mines, as if nothing else could distract her, at least temporarily, from the helplessness and pain that dogged her. She'd have to make the savings last for now.

Izzy's birthday had passed without her having noticed. Neither Nephy nor Seth had texted her since their meeting at the restaurant. Fuck them. Cyrus was as gone as ever; his phone was still locked.

Izzy got up, checked her own phone, let Dog out, fed him and Yard. She choked down two hard-boiled eggs and an apple, drank some coffee. She dressed, gathered the supplies she'd packed the night before, including the gun. She stroked Yard's shell and blinked at him, kissed the soft divot between Dog's eyes and told him to be good. Then she drove back out into the desert.

###

Deep among the Joshua trees and yucca and desert grasses and sand banks and boulders, Izzy closed her eyes and tried to sense where to go next.

"Cyrus," she said. "Tell me where to go."

She opened her eyes and walked toward the nearest base, the ball mill where the miners processed ore. Beside the ramshackle wooden ore bin was a large piece of yellow machinery with the words "Compressor Reciprocating Power Drive: Property of US Marine Corps." stamped on the side. There was also a table with a bowl of rusted nails, a bottle that said "Marvel Mystery Oil" in old-fashioned script, and another large bottle labeled "Cyanide Powder."

She followed a set of metal tracks that led from an ore dump, a midden of debris that could have been animal, vegetable, mineral, or human, to the mine itself.

Among an outcropping of tan and gray boulders, Izzy found the lower portal. She felt a mild gust of air, ensuring there was oxygen down below. Larry had taught her this. A cable fitted with wheels for transporting buckets of ore ran on a tram from the portal to a deep vertical shaft in the distance.

Izzy closed her eyes, took a breath, and entered the portal. Using her flashlight, she walked, stooped over, along the narrow dirt passage to her left, among the rocks and the discarded gobbing. A lone bat slept snuggled in the rock crevices, kitten-furred and that small. She almost wanted to touch it with her finger, but she'd known a kid who died of rabies from a bat bite.

The mine had been active in the seventies, abandoned in the eighties, she'd read. Along the path of ore cart track crossties, usually removed but still in place after all this time, she found a vinyl kitchen chair, empty bottles of bleach and oil filters in a box, and brown paper bags labeled "Anionic Polymer," the substance used to help avoid clumping of the ore. Bundled up yellow ventilation tubing the color of crime scene tape. A small metal machine that resembled a torture device. Two white helmets hanging on the wall just like skulls.

The passage she'd chosen led to a collapse, so she turned, went back to the junction, and ventured in the other direction. This passage was steeper, took her farther down.

She came to a wooden ore bin with a rickety ladder that stopped partway up. A hangman's rope on a pulley led to the chute gate through which the ore would tumble out into a waiting, now broken cart. The chute was marked with the number three, scrawled in red.

Izzy shone her flashlight into a shaft that might have gone one hundred and fifty feet deep. This ladder resembled a rib cage. Darkness lay at the base.

Eventually the tunnel she traversed opened out into a larger square-set chamber with timbers made of tree trunks supporting the roof. Someone had constructed the chamber in a cathedral-like fashion. Remnants of ore carts littered the space, but the area was now broad and open enough that she could venture around the carts and down the wooden stopes.

From here she moved into a narrower passage. So narrow that to see what lay ahead she had to lie flat and wiggle through. Izzy chose her stomach so she would be able to see and shimmied down the opening. The gravel cut into the flesh of her breasts and belly. She felt pressure against her ribs as if invisible hands squeezed the bones together.

The way it would feel to be crushed to death.

She shone her flashlight into the darkness.

And that was when Izzy saw the hand.

A human hand is easily recognizable, even with the flesh and skin eroded away. A hand is what makes us a primate, with its five digits; its muscles, ligaments, tendons, sheaths, arteries, and nerves; its twenty-seven bones. The fingers contain fourteen of those bones, the phalanges—distal, middle, and proximal—in each finger except for the thumb that has only two—the distal and proximal—and the most nerve endings in the body. That is, when the human attached to the hand is alive to feel.

This was a big hand. It was a hand with a silver ring still clinging to one finger.

❊❊❊

By the time Izzy had reached the exit, running from the thing she'd seen, her gut erupted.

She wiped her mouth on the sleeve of her hoodie and fell to her knees.

Izzy saw herself, walking through the desert with outstretched hands. In them, she held something, a gift of some kind. Whether to give or receive, she did not know. A coyote howled the blues. Or was it the devil himself singing? The sun came up, blood-ing her face, her hands, the gift. Dawn. Now even the morning light had become a terrible thing.

❊❊❊

There in a white room, blinded by sun through a window, Izzy saw a man hovering at her bedside, and she cried out for Cyrus.

It did not matter if she was dead. Cyrus was there. He had come back to her.

The sea, too, had come back. The cloudy, skinned water cleared, like a lasered eye, of the selenium that caused embryonic deformities in aquatic birds and fish. Pelicans, double-crested cormorants, egrets, ibis, ducks, geese, stilts, dowitchers, and avocets gathered at the shores. Alfalfa, Bermuda, and Sudan grass grew in abundance where there had once been only fields of white salt. The dust storms had subsided, the sulfuric stench of death been replaced by the sweet sugar beets; the bomb ghosts now rested in peace.

He stepped closer—shaved head and a beard.

This man was not Cyrus.

Cyrus had vanished.

"You scared us there," Seth said, distantly.

She blinked her eyes at him. He gestured to a vase of sunflowers on the counter. "Hope you like."

"What about Cyrus?" The sunflowers smelled bitter and the water was already sour with decay.

"You rest now."

"How long have I been here?"

"Three days. Leanne told us what happened. Nephy sends her love."

"What happened? Where's my phone? Wait. What about Dog and Yard?"

"Your mom has them," Seth said. He wasn't looking at her but away, out the window. "Very, very big dog. Didn't like me. He's okay, though."

Izzy called out for Cyrus again, repeating his name, and the nurse came and told Seth to leave.

❋❋❋

When Izzy woke, Leanne was there, peering myopically into her eyes over a large stuffed black cat. It resembled, in a perverse way, the kitten Izzy had rescued from the dump as a child. The one that she'd found hanging dead on the clothesline the next morning.

"You still alive, girl?"

Izzy wasn't so sure. She noticed that the sunflowers were gone. How long had she slept? Had Seth really been there at all?

"I brought tea." Leanne gestured to a bedside table set with three chipped china cups and a broken teapot. "For us and Kitty."

"Thanks." Izzy wanted that thing gone. It looked unsanitary. How had Leanne even gotten it in here?

Leanne poured some water from the teapot, added a straw, and held out the cup to Izzy. She tried to sit up but everything hurt. "I have to go find him. Where's my phone?"

Leanne wrinkled her forehead. "You can't go anywhere; you have to heal. The doctor said you could scar real bad." Izzy's mother had a mirror, a round one with a plastic handle that looked like bone, and she held it up for Izzy to see. A person she didn't recognize looked back at her. One eye was black with coagulated blood, the upper lip swollen. A large bandage covered the nose and one side of the face.

"You fell and hit your head outside the mine shaft. Hurt your ankle, too. A ranger found you. Your dog's okay. And that tortoise you like. Foot."

"What about Cyrus?" Izzy asked again. Then: "I found something. I found—"

Leanne poured water into the third teacup and set it down in front of the stuffed cat. Some water had spilled—the teacup spout had broken off. When Leanne looked up at Izzy, her eyes were red, and she sounded more lucid than Izzy had ever heard her. "What you found—they said it could be him. They're not sure."

It was him. His hand. His ring. It was him.

Izzy opened her mouth, but no sound came out.

Instead, the desert whirled its sands and shook dry leaves with woe. Dead sea waters moaned. Jackrabbits and roadrunners screamed in pain. Cracking fault lines rummaged deeper through the earth. Leanne's mermaid mannequin sobbed, lonely in her dried-up plastic pool.

To Bring You My Love

Izzy could not remember much of what happened next. She'd talked
to the police, who'd taken a report. Someone—Izzy wasn't sure
who—had confirmed that there would be an investigation, a forensics
report, that the thing she'd found was a man's severed hand; she had
bent over and retched in the dirt. Dismembered. The horror of it
struck her again like a blow to the throat. Like that blow to her head
when she'd fallen outside the mine.

She had been released from the hospital, and now Nephy was
bringing her home. A small crowd had gathered around Cyrus's truck.
Izzy got out and began to limp inside, leaning on Nephy for support.

Alma from Slab City took off her straw hat and wiped sweat from
her brow with a bandanna. "Are you all right?"

"What can we do?" someone else asked.

"So awful about Cyrus."

"It's effed up is what."

"Something's afoot," Alma said. She grimaced, showing her
small, brown teeth.

Nephy asked them to leave.

A woman with plastic curlers in her hair came toward Izzy then,
pushing an empty stroller. The woman's face looked swollen and

blotchy. "Nothing's changed," she said, grabbing Izzy's arm. "It was all for nothing."

"Get the hell away!" Nephy said.

"If he was going to die, at least we could see the change."

###

Nephy opened the front door of the shack, and Dog ran to Izzy, began rubbing frantically against her. She could not find the strength even to touch him. Instead, she stood there, frozen, looking around the room. Cyrus's chewed-up black sneaker was gone. Izzy hadn't been able to touch it. Someone—probably Nephy, maybe Leanne—had cleaned for her.

"I'm sorry. I'm so, so sorry." Nephy's eyelids, usually smooth, maybe slicked with gold or silver shadow, looked red and puffy. Strands of black hair, long, the way Izzy's had once been, hung disheveled around Nephy's face. The bruise on her cheek still showed, somewhat paled now, not hidden with makeup.

She put her arms around Izzy. Nephy's skin pulsed, warm and smooth, and her hair, scented with coconut oil, tickled Izzy's skin. She could sense Nephy's baby sleeping like a cherished secret between them, and Izzy closed her eyes. Then the two of them were crying. It sounds like birds, Izzy thought, more like avian shrieks than human cries.

"Shhh. Rest now, my queen," Nephy said, finally, stroking Izzy's head. "You have to rest."

Before she fell asleep, she saw the two of them—Nephy and herself—circling above the desert on tapered wings.

Beneath them stretched an uncanny valley of decedent-sketch zombies. They stared up empty-eyed, and waved their hands above their heads as if they had no shoulder or elbow joints. They wore the clothes they'd been found in—the bathing suits, flowered dresses, jeans, boots, belts with heavy buckles, T-shirts with pictures of New York and Los Angeles. Their hands were full of chunks of minerals, green and blue as Cyrus's eyes, black as his hair, gold as his skin.

✤ ✤ ✤

She didn't wake until late the next afternoon, Dog nosing her neck, licking her cheek. Nephy had left a note saying she'd check in later. Izzy got up and looked in the mirror, gingerly removed the bandage from her face. The reflection in the mirror did not disturb her, not really, in spite of the small, round artifact of the head, the black eye, the raised and painful gash across the bridge of the nose and the cheek. The scar was only a reflection of her inner cicatrix. This was the mark that branded her as the one who had lost her beloved.

Izzy had been raised in a dead place, found Cyrus, devoted her life to him. She had awakened one morning to find him gone. She'd searched for him, given up, and found a dog and a man who looked like him. She'd returned and shaved her head like a warrior, like a penitent, and entered the mines alone. Down in those mines, she'd feared that Cyrus was dead. But even still, she'd refused to accept that he was really gone.

Her lover, her companion, the man who had rescued her from her childhood, had been murdered. The man with whom she had conceived and then lost a child. The man with whom she had hoped to conceive a child once again. A child with Cyrus's deep eyes and full mouth and deft hands.

Hands.

Cyrus's hand.

That had built things. That had fixed things. That had touched her with love.

But now there was no Cyrus; there would be no child. Even if he had loved someone else, there was now no chance of reconciliation. The loss had changed her into someone else. Though she knew even then that it would take her a long time to fully exhume the person she had become.

She popped a Percocet and left the bathroom, almost stumbling over Yard who looked up at her beadily, as if to say, *What now*? Ignoring him and Dog, too weak to even reach down and stroke the tortoise's shell or the dog's smooth, bony back, Izzy stood blinking around the room. Her eyes rested on the mannequin Leanne had given her.

Izzy lit some white candles. She stoppered the tin bathtub and filled it with water from the pipes Cyrus had installed. She took the mannequin and lowered him into the tub, arranged the stiff limbs so that they fit. She ran the water over the plastic body with its strange planes and flat beige curves, then rinsed it away.

What was she doing? She didn't know. But she felt she must not stop.

Izzy took the mannequin out of the tub and dried it with Cyrus's bath towel, which she had not touched since he left. It smelled vaguely of mildew but also—still, when she pressed it to her face—of sage and of smoke. Or at least she imagined it smelled of these things.

She carried the mannequin to the bed and laid it on a sheet. The hard head, the flat chest, the weirdly blank pubis, the jointed legs and arms, the awkward, useless feet. The thing was not like Cyrus at all.

Cyrus's head: the high forehead, the thick hawkish eyebrows and cheekbones, the deep-set eyes.

Cyrus's generous shoulders and chest that she'd often rubbed with coconut oil. His tapered waist. His muscled arms, full of his blood. The way the veins stood out like the venation of leaves in his forearms. The V of muscles pointing toward his groin—

Cyrus's legs, smooth, almost hairless, and narrow in proportion to the rest of him, but long like his arms. She'd rubbed out the knots that formed there after he ran.

Cyrus's large feet with the long second toe. She'd bathed those feet at night in salt water strewn with rose petals.

She remembered the ever-surprising softness of his skin, the warmth penetrating through fabric. The flowered and winged flesh of his back and chest.

She remembered his hands.

She poured some acrylic paints—red, green, black, blue—into cups, added water and painted Cyrus's tattoos as best she could onto the mannequin's shoulders and chest. The roses, the serpent, the skull, her name. She sat beside the mannequin and closed her eyes and tried to breathe while the paint dried. Then she turned the mannequin over and painted a primitive-looking panther and falcon on the plastic back. Let these dry.

She gathered up two chunks of the green malachite, the small piece of amethyst and the rose quartz and taped the malachite over the mannequin's eyes for protection, the amethyst to its forehead for enlightenment, the quartz over its heart for love.

She took Cyrus's pocketknife from beside the bed.

He had not carried this knife with him when he stepped outside that morning.

She flicked open the knife and touched the blade.

Nicked her finger. Let some drops of blood fall onto the mannequin. Staunched the bleeding with her shirt. Then she took off her shirt and tore at the thin cotton until a strip ripped away. She used the material to tie the knife to the mannequin's wrist.

She needed one more thing.

She needed his ring.

But his ring was gone.

The police had it.

"Take my ring now," she said and removed the small silver band from her finger. Placed it in the mannequin's left hand. Without the ring, her hand felt foreign, too light, as if it might detach and float away.

Someone had killed him. Not only killed him but ragefully torn him asunder.

"Return to me," she said. "Cyrus Rivera, I speak your name. I speak your name so you may live again." And a chill ran through her body, as if her spine were a string of icy pearls pulled by an unseen hand.

Dog sat on his haunches, horn-ears perked. Motionless, as if he'd been carved from obsidian, except for his nose with its 300 million olfactory receptors. His eyes gazed at her with worry and with love. Her protector. She realized he'd been in this position the entire time she'd acted out this weird, compulsive ritual that she herself could not even begin to understand.

Izzy swallowed a Tramadol with as much water as she could stomach and lay down beside the mannequin. She had loved Cyrus so deeply and for so long that she had ceased to even think of it. The way she had forgotten that the ring on her finger was not a part of her hand, until the ring was gone. The same way her body had clung to life. A blind, driving obsession to stay alive, even in the years with Larry and Leanne before Izzy had found Cyrus, as if she knew she would find him. Now her body loved death like that. So she could be with him again.

Unless he could rise up, reassemble, return to her. Through some dark magic.

I Want Your Hands on Me

She lay beneath a man's warm, wide chest. For its muscular expanse, it was surprisingly full and soft, almost feminine. She held on to the strong slope of shoulders, the tensed biceps, she ran her fingers over the pectoral muscles, the abdominal muscles to the groin. The man's skin was so soft, like the satin of a woman's dress smoothed over the muscles and flesh. How was it that a young man's skin could be so soft? She tasted wine and salt. A sensation of great tenderness and of even greater desire filled her.

She opened her eyes in the dream and looked up at the man's face.

He was not Cyrus.

Here, in her dream, was Ever.

And yet this time she felt no regret, nor any guilt. Somehow, she knew.

Cyrus had sent him. Cyrus had sent him to her. He would know what to do.

❀❀❀

Cyrus had vanished on November first, Día de los Muertos. She had met Ever just weeks later. Maybe, she thought, some part of Cyrus's soul had slipped inside of Ever, as another part had slipped into Dog.

Dog Gone. Desperation, Izzy knew, could easily overcome doubt. But she was so far gone herself now that the thoughts only struck her as a little strange. Certainly not stranger than anything else that had occurred.

When Cyrus died, had he felt his soul leaving his body? In a violent death, did the soul leave differently? Did it find another body or bodies to inhabit?

Izzy picked up her phone and texted the man she had met.

❀❀❀

He arrived in less than an hour. She answered the door, with her shaved head and her wound. He wore a plaid flannel shirt over his T-shirt and jeans. The flannel added a breadth and width to his chest and shoulders that made her want to throw herself at him, like an animal seeking warmth. Dog must have wanted the same thing because he ran and leaped up on Ever, then turned a few circles.

Ever stepped inside and she smelled that whiff of comfort—coffee and firewood. Lavender laundry detergent and the freshly washed flannel. Dried lit sage leaves burned to silver-scented smoke. The scents brought her back to that first night when she'd sat on his couch with the cat in her lap, half-forgetting, in that moment, that Cyrus was gone.

"I'm so sorry," Ever said. He looked as if he might reach to touch the wound on her face, but then he dropped his hand heavily at his side. "What can I do? Aurora?"

She couldn't find words. "My name is Izzy," she managed. Outside of the shack, she could sense the wild reaches of the desert with its sinew, its blood and its bones. Cyrus's bones. She took the smiling photo of Cyrus from her wallet. "You look alike," she said. "Don't you look alike?"

She began to tremble.

Ever took a blanket—green with yellow birds—off of the bed, glancing quickly at the mannequin, glancing away.

She tried to explain, but he told her it was okay and lifted the mannequin off the bed, laid it carefully on the ground. He wrapped the blanket around her shoulders. Eventually her muscles softened into the weft and warp of woven cotton.

"You look alike," she said again. "Don't you?"

"A little."

"I met you right after he—"

"I'm not him, Izzy," Ever said. "I wish I could make everything better, but I'm not him."

Izzy wanted to sit on his lap—feel the hard denim beneath her—and let him take her in his arms—feel his strength beneath the soft flannel. Instead, in spite of the warmth from the blanket, she convulsed again with a shiver from deep inside of her, got up and let the blanket drop from her shoulders. She began to limp then, zombie-like, favoring one leg, toward the driveway. She didn't call for Dog, but he followed. She was going to go into the desert where no one could hear her, and she was going to scream and scream until she made a rift in the veil of the night.

But Ever was at her side with the green sky of yellow birds.

"Come back," he said. "Come on now."

She let him lead her back to the bed. Dog followed them and curled up on a rug while she and Ever sat on the mattress. She was still trembling violently though he had put the blanket around her shoulders again. Tears streaked the residue of sweat on her cheeks, and she could taste the salt of her eyes.

"Oh, I almost forgot," he said. He reached into his pocket and took out the stone woman—sheela na gig. He set it on the bedside table. "This is yours, yeah? You left her at my place."

Izzy looked at the little stone exhibitionist. For some reason, she didn't want to touch it, though when she'd stolen the thing, it had seemed to call for her to put it in her pocket. Now it grimaced at her with its various orifices.

"Can I stay here tonight?" he asked. "I don't want you to be alone."

Izzy nodded.

She let Ever undress her and cover her with the sheet, the blanket of birds. Ever took out his guitar, sat in a chair, and sang her a lullaby. Something about the moon.

"Liar," she whispered as she drifted off to sleep.

He stopped playing. "What?"

"You can sing," she thought she said. "Cyrus, when did you learn how to sing?"

❋❋❋

In her dream that night, Izzy held an infant in her arms, stroked its downy-brown head. Milk poured from her engorged breasts, letting down into its mouth. But the child didn't have a mouth.

Pain—as from something sharp. Blood on her breasts. A beak, this child had a beak. A baby falcon—an eyas—with a tooth-like beak for hunting insects, rodents, and reptiles. It would grow to a fledgling, and its wings would thin and taper for faster flight and hunting. The kestrel would hover above its prey before swooping down for the kill. She knew all this because of the tattoo on Cyrus's back.

Then the dream changed.

Izzy stood beneath a tall tree laden with brown pods and bright red flowers—silk tassels from which protruded sinewy stamens. A man crouched in the tree. He wore a crown of leaves, thorns grew from the tips of his fingers, and he held something in his hands—a wooden box inlaid with pieces of bone carved into different miniature body parts. Tiny heads, hearts, arms, hands, torsos, legs, and feet. The man opened the box and took something out. It was another child. Izzy saw the snout, the teeth, the slanted, predatory gold of the child's irises. The baby god of the dead.

When she opened her eyes in the dark, Ever was studying her. "What?" she said.

"You were crying in your sleep."

"And I look like her. Am I like her?"

"Like Emma? You're brave. And you look like her. Especially with your hair like that."

She didn't tell him that she'd seen the photo online. Besides, that wasn't why she'd shaved her head. Was it?

"Chemo," he added.

Izzy nodded. "I'm so sorry." She ran her hands over the bristles on her scalp. "I think I shaved mine as some kind of penance." And then, "It's strange that we found each other."

"I'm glad we did." He glanced worriedly at the mannequin lying on floor.

"I'm like her. And you're like him. And we are both lonely, right? We're both lonely?"

"Grieving and lonely." Ever turned back to her. She met the twin mirrors of his gaze. She did not look away.

※ ※ ※

Izzy woke later beside him. No bodily warmth could eradicate the pain that had cleaved her clean in half.

She picked up the stone woman she'd stolen from the retreat center and put her in a drawer. Then she sat on the couch and took out the box of photos. The box looked like a little coffin now, Izzy thought, searching through the pictures again, while Dog rested his chin on her knee.

Izzy came to the photo of her and Cyrus at the party at Seth's house where she, Seth, and Nephy had all met the new guy in town, the tall guy with the long black hair and greenish eyes. For the first time, she thought how young they both looked, as if they'd both aged a hundred years since he'd been gone. Even though now she would never see him age.

She looked over at Ever, asleep on the bed she and Cyrus had shared, and sniffed the skin of her arm, inhaling the quickly fading comfort of Ever's scent. Ever's jaw was not as angular as Cyrus's, his nose flatter, his lips a little less full. Even Ever's body was different, less muscular, a little softer through the chest and belly. His eyes were darker, and kinder, too, maybe. His left hand was dominant. Still, he had reminded her of Cyrus, just as she had reminded Ever of Emma. Ever and Izzy—each other's missing piece in a very literal sense. But as much as she wanted Ever to be Cyrus, no such magic had occurred. No, she had to face what had really taken place.

I Am Stretched on Your Grave

Joe called collect from CAL. Izzy had left her number on his list when she'd gone to visit him after Cyrus went missing. Now Joe had something to say: "I'm sorry I didn't help more when you came to see me. Sometimes I get pissed off in here. I didn't think—"

"I'm sorry, too," she said, sinking to the cold tile of the bathroom floor; she'd gone in there so as not to wake Ever.

She and Joe hung on in silence for a while. For a moment, she thought the call had dropped. Then she realized that Joe was trying to contain his emotion. "I'll kill whoever did this to him," Joe growled under his breath.

She hushed him. "Be careful what you say there."

"I want you to find out who did this," he said. "You're better than the SBPD. If it wasn't for you, some dog would be chewing on those bones."

"Stop," she said. "Okay."

"Where will you go?"

She told him whom she had talked to since she'd seen him at CAL. Selma and her Frankenstein henchman. The women at Miracle Manor. The House of Hearts Retreat Center. There hadn't been any legitimate leads. Nothing of substance. "Do you have any ideas?"

"What did Selma tell you again?"

"That she wanted to put barrettes in his hair when he was a kid. That I should go home and lock myself in a closet and face my ego."

"That's fucking bullshit."

"You think Selma's involved?"

Joe said, "You need to bring everyone together somehow. And watch them."

"What do you mean?"

"A memorial. Or a meeting. Something."

"I'm not ready yet."

"When will you be ready, Izzy? How much more dead does he need to be?"

Of course she would never be ready, but she would do what needed to be done.

❀❀❀

When she came out of the bathroom, Ever was up and dressed, staring out the window at the yellow-green shrubs waving at the sky like eldritch hands. She smelled coffee and heard the comforting castanet-click of eggs boiling in a pan on the stove.

"That was his brother from CAL," Izzy said.

"Can you talk about it now?" Ever moved to her side. She was struck, again, by the height and breadth of him, the warmth radiating through his clothes.

"He wants me to set up some kind of memorial. Watch everyone's faces or some such shit."

"The cops will figure this out."

She only had to look at him.

"I mean, isn't it different now?"

"It's not different. They still won't confirm it's him."

Ever put his arms around her, and she leaned her head against his pectoral muscles, felt his beating heart. "If this is what you want to do—" he said, and she felt the words vibrating into her.

"This is."

"I'll help you," Ever said. "Let's just try the cops first."

❊❊❊

But, as she'd expected, when they went to the police station, they were told the forensics still weren't back yet.

"What about the ring?" Izzy said. "That was his ring."

The cop—not Decker, another guy—told her that the ring could have been stolen. That the hand wearing the ring could have belonged to someone else.

Ever put his hand on her thigh to keep her from leaping up, from hitting the cop across the face.

"I promise we will tell you as soon as we hear something," the cop said.

Izzy turned to Ever.

"You were right," he said. He got up and took her hand with its twenty-seven bones, it's phalanges and metacarpal bones and carpal bones and many muscles, tendons, ligaments, sheaths, arteries, and nerve endings that provided the sense of touch. If you were alive. Cyrus was dead, but Izzy and Ever were still alive.

They walked out of the station together. He didn't let go of her hand.

"I have a recording session for a few hours. Are you okay?"

"I'm going to see Cyrus's parents," Izzy said.

❊❊❊

Del wasn't there. When Izzy bent down to hug Cyrus's mother, she almost gagged on the smell of chemical sunscreen with a faint undertone of spoiled milk. Jody stared, catatonic. She wore a housedress, sandals, and socks—her legs blue with swollen, erupting veins. Izzy knelt at her feet.

"I'm sorry." Izzy put her hand on the woman's rawboned arm. "I'm so, so sorry."

"I love my boys," Jody said.

"I know."

"I didn't do everything right all the time, but I love them."

Izzy stared straight ahead, blinking back tears.

"Joe said he'll kill whoever did this," Jody told her. "I'm afraid he'll get out and get sent right back in."

"No one knows what happened," Izzy said. "But I'm going to try to find out."

"Cops came by again. After they told me. Asking if I knew anything." Jody's eyes snagged on Izzy like silk on dry skin. "Why would anyone hurt a good boy like that? He was so good. Everyone loved him."

"I know." Izzy dug the nails of one hand into the meat of her other palm.

Cyrus's mother frowned, skin like sand dunes wrinkled with shadows. "What happened to you?"

"I fell," Izzy said.

Jody grabbed Izzy's hand, searched her face.

Izzy said, "What can I do for you? I want to help."

Silence.

"Can I give you a massage? Like I do at the inn. It might help some." She kept repeating that word: help, help, help—like an idiot.

No response.

"I could just rub your shoulders or something."

Jody nodded, and Izzy stood behind her. But Cyrus's mother flinched at the initial touch, so Izzy took it slow. What if Jody could feel the pain spilling through all those nerve endings in Izzy's fingertips? Still, she would try. Finally, she was able to knead her fingers into Jody's rigid muscles, and maybe Izzy had been right, maybe her pain, mixed with Jody's, was what tipped the scales. Because Jody was crying.

"He was my precious angel," Jody said. "He was everyone's angel. Especially yours."

Jackie's Strength

Izzy numbly set up a gathering. She chose Bombay Beach because it was where Cyrus had planted the three sisters. Though the plants had withered, Izzy felt, somehow, that the location was right—the place Cyrus had tried to brighten. She picked a date, rented the Silverlight Cinema, opened the wooden coffin-box, and gathered photos of Cyrus for a slideshow. Then she invited everyone she could think of. It seemed meaningless in some ways but better than doing nothing. And now that she believed she knew what had happened to Cyrus, she wanted to see these people all together; she wanted to watch their faces when they spoke.

✢✢✢

Ted, wearing his little round glasses and a black vintage vest over a white T-shirt, spoke first. He stood in front of the white truck facing the dead cars and talked about Cyrus growing up in the desert, teaching himself construction and landscaping, building the shack with Izzy.

"We don't know anything for sure," Ted said, though his face twitched when he said it. They all knew for sure. But someone, Izzy thought, someone here might know more. "The cops are working on it, but they don't have anything conclusive yet," Ted went on. A few moans and jeers from the crowd—no one out here trusted the cops. "But this is a way to honor him, to let him know we love him wherever he is and to try to help figure out what happened."

Ted read a Cahuilla poem about creation. Izzy vaguely remembered having read somewhere that the Cahuilla recited this poem when a man died—for women, they read a poem about the moon. So even though Ted had said he didn't know for sure if Cyrus was dead, he believed it too, she knew.

Izzy sat in the back holding onto Jody who slumped against her. Jody was crying, but Izzy didn't cry. None of this felt real. And she wasn't there to mourn—not yet. She was trying to learn what had happened.

Then Ted said that anyone could volunteer to speak.

Seth walked up, a cigarette butt jammed between his pointer and middle finger. "Cyrus, man, I can't believe you're not here."

Izzy heard Nephy sobbing from inside one of the junk cars.

Seth cleared his throat, and when he spoke, his voice sounded flat. "I love you like a brother, Cyrus," he said, his eyes darting back and forth like scattering pebbles. "I remember the first time I saw you. You were bigger, stronger, and better looking than anyone we'd ever met, and you could do anything with your hands. You caught every eye in the room. Especially Izzy's. The two of you were like one person for so long. Like you could read each other's minds. Nephy and I watched you. We wanted to be like that. We learned from you. It's possible to overcome shit and find love, that's what you taught us. It's still possible to love. I miss you, man. Find a way back to us somehow."

Seth wandered off to the side near Ever, who stood alone, leaning back, arms and legs crossed, against one of the cars; he and Izzy had decided it might bring up too many questions if they sat together. Seth dropped his cigarette butt at Ever's feet and stomped at it with his boot. Ever glanced sideways at Seth, then dipped his chin and raised his eyebrows in Izzy's direction. *I've got your back. I'm here.*

It was Del's turn to speak. He carried a beer in his hand and took a swig, spilling some as he set down the can. It seemed he had shrunken in width and height since Cyrus's disappearance.

"My son is missing," Del read from a tattered sheet of paper. "I like to believe things happen for a reason. Like the way Cyrus came into our lives. But now I'm wondering, what reason was there? There's no meaning. There's just shit. I'd rather die than lose a kid. And if someone hurt my kid, we're coming for you. You will never sleep again. Because we're coming for you."

Larry stood and walked over to Del, putting his hand on the other man's shoulder and leading him back to his seat. Then Larry walked back up front. "Everyone knew Cyrus Rivera and I had our differences," he said. A palpable quiet fell over the group. "I wanted to protect my little girl, is that so wrong? I will always protect my little girl. But I know now that what I was trying to protect her from was wrong. I was trying to protect her from Cyrus and all the while there was something else lurking, someone else in the dark, waiting out there. Who knows, maybe Cyrus was trying to keep Izzy safe? Maybe he'll make it back to us. Either way, he's gone now. I wish him back if only for my girl. And if you're gone Rivera, rest peaceful."

Larry sat down. Ever looked at Izzy as if he were about to come over, take her hand, and squeeze it. She drew her hands into her lap and pressed together her slick-with-sweat palms.

"Does anyone else want to say a few words?" Ted asked.

Some rustling, and then Selma Jenkins walked up with her guitar. She wore a crown of gauze and wire butterflies and a silver ring through her septum that made her already large nostrils appear cavernous. Her henchman Frankenstein crouched in the dirt to watch from the sidelines. Selma played "All Apologies," which, like everything she did, made Izzy sick.

After Selma finished, she spoke. "I remember Cyrus Rivera as a little kid. Those big brown eyes. Like a calf's. Always watching. So pretty. I wanted him to be my little sister. He got pissed at me when I tried to put make up on him once. Cyrus was big and strong, but he was vain and gentle as a girl sometimes. Which is why we loved him. Who could have done this shit to Cyrus? Whoever did this shit should be punished in the same way. I'm sorry for Cyrus's loved ones. Cyrus Rivera, you will not be forgotten. We love you."

"It's okay," Izzy said softly to herself. "They are all out of their minds. Remember why you are here."

Someone had set up a projector and the images of Cyrus that Izzy had collected flashed on the side of the white truck. The elementary school portrait. Dimples. Missing teeth. Hair slicked back, a button-down shirt, even a tie.

The high school picture with his long hair in his eyes, a Nirvana T-shirt, and a fierce scowl. *Such a tough guy.*

Izzy and Cyrus at the waterfall oasis at 49 Palms.

Izzy and Cyrus at his West Shores High School graduation with their arms around each other's shoulders. *Professor.*

Cyrus with his new Silverado. Both of them shining.

Cyrus, bare-chested, revealing the still-raw tattoo of her name. *Best ink ever.*

Izzy and Cyrus in front of the shack they had built together. *Desert Gothic. Home.*

Izzy and Cyrus on vacation at Miracle Manor. *Someday we should get married here.*

The black-and-white photo booth carnival images.

The photo of Izzy and Cyrus on the chartreuse couch on the night they'd met.

And, finally, the photo Izzy had used on the missing persons flyer. Cyrus, not smiling. If you zoomed in, he was just a million pixilated dots.

Then the still photos changed to film. Images floated—desert landscapes, fields, night skies, a sun rising, lotus blossoms opening, birds and insects flying, a woman's naked body up close, resembling a mountain range drenched in dawn-light.

Next: bleached twins shook on a bed; two jointed wooden dolls lay cast aside beside them. The man's chipped-black-nail-polished fingers shook too much to hold a cigarette. He broke a guitar, and the woman rode on his back in her baby doll dress, singing in her cigarette-rasped voice. A male voice, spoke: "The king and queen of nineties music in the act of destroying themselves reflect the devastation of our planet."

A rapper in a yellow suit and his girlfriend in a red dress walked in slow motion followed by two burly bodyguards. "Note the way this king and queen step regally through the crowd. The presence of the bodyguards reflects the danger that trails them at every turn."

The voice went on, over a clip of the famous 1968 speech: "In Tennessee, a day before his assassination, he imagined how he would fly in his mind and watch the people crossing the Red Sea to the Promised Land and beyond. And then, prophetically, he said that he would like to live a long life, but that his true purpose was to do God's will. There is no doubt that he reached the Promised Land."

The film of the former president falling onto his wife; she reached to hold him, then crawled over the back of the black limousine. She wore the infamous watermelon pink bouclé Chanel suit with the dark blue trim. The suit stained with her husband's blood.

On the makeshift screen of the white truck, an animated re-creation of the event showed in detail how the president crossed his arms over his throat before he collapsed.

Jody yelped.

"What is this?" Izzy said, standing up. "Who brought this? Turn it off."

She heard giggling and four red-haired children—the ones she had seen when she went to look for Cyrus—darted out of one of the cars and across the road to the blue windmill house.

While Izzy had her back turned, the film continued. A woman's voice said, "Let your goal be to make beauty in the slaughterhouse of the world. Then you can walk the flower path in peace. Loss is inevitable, but don't be afraid of it. The soul remains. It is the hope that allows light and love to flood and enter the void. Live with hope, with imagination, and with purpose."

Izzy turned back around. Sky from the House of Hearts stood there, projected larger than life on the side of the truck. Silver jewelry inlaid with blue, red, purple, greenish yellow, pink, and white adorned Sky's body and, even in her shock, or perhaps because of it, Izzy thought she recognized lapis, carnelian, amethyst, chalcedony, calcite, feldspar.

Ted walked over to the projector and flipped the switch. The sun had set and the area fell into darkness.

"That woman, that was the woman who used to come by the house," Jody's voice said in the dark.

"What woman?"

"In the movie. When Cyrus was a kid."

"Sky?"

"Who?"

"Her name is Sky."

"I don't know her name," Jody said. She cupped her palms over her face. "I don't even know where he came from."

"What do you mean by that, Jody? That you don't know where he came from."

Jody's eyes flicked up at her. "Cyrus just appeared one day. Del brought him home."

"You mean you adopted him. Right?"

"No, no. Something else. I don't know what it was but something else was going on."

"Jody," Izzy said, "you have to tell me everything you know. It's really important. Cyrus is dead. Someone killed him."

Cyrus's mother took a shuddery breath. "That woman. From the movie. She used to watch him play."

Cold ran through Izzy's limbs, wind rifling the branches of a dead tree in Bombay Beach.

"You have to tell me more."

"That's all I know." Jody's eyes glittered like paillettes sewn on burlap—large, flat, wet spangles in her wide, dry face. "You have to find her."

Izzy looked all around. The crowd had started to disperse. She grabbed onto a man's arm as he rushed past her. "Who brought that film?" she said.

He shrugged her off.

She left Jody and began to walk among the parked vehicles, shining her flashlight inside. Most had emptied out by now. A couple was making out in one of the cars. She shone her light on them and they glared at her, the guy giving her the finger; no one she recognized.

Izzy felt a hand on her shoulder and turned to see Ever.

"What happened?" he asked. "Why was Sky in the film?"

"I have no idea. Jody says that she used to come see Cyrus when he was a kid."

"What? Makes no sense."

"I want to find out who brought the video."

They both stopped and looked around in the darkness, but almost everyone had left. Where would she and Ever even begin?

She crossed the dirt road to the blue windmill house, opened the gate, went through the yard to the door, and knocked, but no one answered.

"What are you doing?" Ever asked, coming up behind her.

"I don't know. Those kids were laughing. Maybe they—"

A woman opened the door—the woman with the stroller Izzy had seen in front of her shack after the discovery in the mine. The woman was tapping her forehead and mumbling to herself. The four reedy, red-haired boys and girls peered out from behind her.

"Did you bring the video?" Izzy asked.

They didn't move. The woman kept tapping her forehead.

"Was that your video?" Izzy asked.

Then a man—over six feet tall, huge shoulders, red hair, and beard—appeared in the doorway. "Get back inside, kids."

"It was all for nothing," the woman said.

"What's going on here?" said the man.

"Did you play that video?" Izzy said. "Do you know Sky?"

The red-haired man stepped closer, glaring. He wasn't messing around. "Get the hell out of here," he said, but Ever was already leading her away.

When they had crossed the road, Ted came over to see if she was all right.

"Whose film was that?" Izzy asked.

"I have no idea. I think those kids might have put it in. Some kind of prank. What do you think it was about?"

"We have to go home," Izzy said. She turned to Ever. "Can you take me home?"

"Of course." He held her hand. It felt as if he had held her hand like this for years. His hands were warm and dry, and hers were cold and clammy. She let him lead her to his truck.

She could feel Ted standing there, watching them go. He still wore his sunglasses as if he hadn't noticed that the sun had set.

❁❁❁

Dog greeted Ever with the usual explosive dog-joy, jumping up and spinning in circles, while Izzy went to the drawer where she and Cyrus kept their important papers. There wasn't much—their social security cards, the deed for the car, the property documents for the house, and a bank account booklet with a twenty-three-dollar balance. Also their birth certificates. Izzy examined Cyrus's. She showed it to Ever. *Name: Cyrus Larkin. Born: 1/28/1990, Imperial County. Eyes: Hazel. Hair: Black. Parents: Melissa Larkin, Social Worker. Father: Unknown.*

"You think this means something?" Ever asked.

"I don't know." She went to the computer and typed in *Melissa Larkin Social Worker Salton Sea Imperial County* and a number of links came up but nothing to do with Sky. She typed in *Melissa Larkin House of Hearts Foundation Sky.* Nothing.

"What do you think is going on?" Ever asked.

"Something. With Sky and Cyrus. I need to go back there, to the retreat center."

Ever had a recording session starting late that same night but said that he would go with her the next day. "Do you want to come home with me now?" he asked.

She did, of course she did, but part of her wanted to be alone, to think about everything that had happened. And she knew she couldn't wait until tomorrow to go back to Joshua Tree.

"Lock the door and don't answer it," he told her. He knelt and looked into Dog's eyes. "Take good care of your mama, okay, buddy?"

Izzy could have sworn she saw Dog nod his whiskery head, but as she watched Ever leave, a part of her wanted to run after him, beg him to stay.

※ ※ ※

Izzy woke to her ringtone and reached for her phone, still half asleep.

"Izzy," Nephy said.

Izzy realized she hadn't seen Nephy after the meeting in Bombay Beach ended. She'd hardly seen Nephy there at all, just heard her crying from inside one of the cars. "What's wrong?" Izzy asked. "It's late. Are you okay?"

"I have to tell you something," Nephy said.

Izzy sat up and turned on the light. Dog, alerted, uncurled himself from his spot by her feet and sat on his haunches facing her, dutiful. She buried her fingers in the scruff of his neck for comfort. "What is it?" Izzy asked.

"Where did that video come from?"

"I don't know. I think those kids brought it. I tried to ask them but their father threatened me. Why?"

There was a long pause and then, finally, Nephy spoke. "That woman in the video," she said.

"What about her?" Izzy clutched onto Dog.

"She looked familiar. I—" Nephy stopped.

Izzy drew the blankets over her shoulders. "You what?"

"I think there's some connection between Cyrus and her," Nephy said.

"What do you know?" Izzy's voice came out louder than she'd intended and Dog flinched.

"Cyrus told me that he was looking for his bio-mom," Nephy said.

"Wait, what? He told you? Why the hell would he tell you?"

"He didn't want to freak you out, I think. I don't know. He told me about this woman. Well, he went to see her, I think."

"What woman, Nephy?"

"The woman in the video."

"And how do you know what she looked like?"

Nephy started to cry. Izzy gripped her phone. She wanted to throw it to the ground, smash the screen to smithereens, cut her hand on the glass shards.

"I went with him," Nephy said. "I'm sorry, Izzy. We went to this meeting this woman ran. Cyrus wanted to meet her, and he asked me to go with him. He didn't want to freak you out. It was some weird thing. I didn't understand it, really. I forgot about it until I saw the video."

"You forgot about it? You just forgot about going to a meeting with Cyrus to find his bio-mom without telling me? Neither of you told me? Because it would freak me the fuck out? Where was this meeting, Nephy? Was it in Desert Hot Springs? At Miracle Manor?"

"It was nothing," Nephy said. "I'm sorry, Izzy. I just thought since Cyrus—since what happened—we should look into everything. And this woman in the video was the same woman."

"What do you know?" Izzy shouted. "Tell me. What did you do? What do you know?"

She heard Seth's voice in the background, but she couldn't hear what he said.

Silence.

Then Nephy was gone.

Izzy sat staring at her phone for so long that the screen went black. She pressed her thumb on the button and the phone lit up.

Izzy went to Nephy's social media page. Most of the photos were selfies of Nephy sitting in the driver's seat of Seth's truck, looking up with big eyes at the camera, pursing her lips, showing off her acrylic-tipped, ring-garnished fingers. The only difference between the images was really just the T-shirts: "Lady of the House," "Queen." "Goddess-in-Training." That was a new one. "Heteroclite." It sounded so royal, almost, but it actually referred to abnormality, Izzy knew. She clicked through some more. Nephy as a girl with her tall, handsome Black father Otis and her little white mother Sarah. Nephy and Seth at their wedding at the West Shores Baptist Church. Nephy with a few of her day-care kids. Pictures of her favorite pop stars and rappers. More selfies. The pictures the photographer had taken of Seth and Nephy as kids, perched in the helm of the blue boat outside Seth's house. Seth, eyes lifted to the horizon, one arm raised, was pretending to sail the ship across the sand. Shirtless as usual. Ripped abs even then. Nephy, hands on hips, wore a white party dress and her hair waterfalled beneath the crown of a little tiara of twisted metal. Where had Izzy seen one like that before? She couldn't remember. She noticed the photo was tagged: Clay Wade Photography. She clicked on his name and was led to a webpage with a picture of a too-tan man in sunglasses, a camera around his neck. Izzy scrolled through some black and white images of desert people and city hipsters. There, among them, she recognized Amanda Flowers from the retreat center, and Izzy realized that the photographer who had come to take the picture of Nephy and Seth was the same man Izzy had seen at the House of Hearts.

Not sure how to process this, she clicked back on Nephy's page.

Another picture: Izzy, Cyrus, Nephy, and Seth as teenagers at the Salton Sea. Seth sat off to the side on a rock. Nephy sassed for the camera. Cyrus had his hands in his pockets and his head turned away, scanning the horizon for something. Izzy looked toward him; she was always looking toward him.

And then: a Polaroid from the night that all four of them met at the party at Seth's. They sat on the chartreuse couch, all in a row. Seth had his arm around Nephy, who smiled prettily. Cyrus looked somber; his gaze hooded. Again, even then, after they had just met, Izzy was looking at Cyrus.

Izzy stared at the phone screen. Then she noticed a date scrawled in pencil at the bottom of the Polaroid. 091305.

The date Cyrus met Izzy.

And got to know Seth.

And Nephy.

Izzy reached for Cyrus's cell phone. She typed in 091305.

Cyrus's phone unlocked.

He kept very little on there—Contacts and Maps and Music and a few photos. Cyrus said he didn't like to keep photos on his phone, he'd rather have printed ones, old school, although Izzy argued with him sometimes, wanting him to save more pictures of them together. "I don't need it," he'd said. "I see you every day, which is better." There was a photo of Cyrus and Izzy that Ted had taken at the Oasis of Mara. She had her arms around Cyrus, was gazing up into his face, while he—sunglasses on—stared into the camera. There was a photo of Cyrus's truck, and one of their house. A photo of Izzy, Seth, and Nephy from the day last spring in Bombay Beach. And a photo of Cyrus's birth certificate.

Engulfed by a shadow that came from within her, Izzy opened Cyrus's Notes. He never used his phone for this as far as she knew, but here he had typed the words: *What is this darkness? It's always inside of me. Like what Iz talks about. For her, it's almost a psychic thing. Like she knows when she's in danger. Maybe it's the same for me. Or maybe I'm just fucked up. But this Melissa Larkin. Something's not right. I can feel it.*

Most of Cyrus's texts had been erased. There were a few, though, under *Nephy*.

Did you take the test? Cyrus had typed months earlier.

And Nephy had typed *Yes*, with a series of happy face emojis; a row of little idiots, Izzy thought, feeling like one herself.

You sure it's mine?

Yes.

"It's not like this never happened before," Seth had said after Cyrus went missing. So many people she'd gone to hadn't seemed that concerned, like they expected him to leave her? Maybe she just hadn't wanted to believe it, not wanted to see. But there had been times, now and then, when he hadn't called, he hadn't come home. Denial is a stage of grief before pain, but pain can lead back to delusion, she knew, especially for those who are wounded early enough, and deep.

Something gnawed at Izzy, sharp and precise as Dog's teeth. It wasn't hard to see the pattern. How hadn't she known? She had not wanted to know.

Nephy with her smug smile, her talons, her secret bruise. Even in this benumbed state, Izzy could feel the fault lines in her body expanding like the ones under the desert floor, everything shaking. Blood whirled and pooled behind her eyes like the Salton Sea. She could almost taste iron on her palate.

Cyrus had gone to Miracle Manor with Nephy to look for his birth mother. He had gone with Nephy, not Izzy, to find his mother. Because it would *freak you out*, Nephy had said. The woman at the desk at Miracle Manor kept insisting he was with Izzy, and she'd thought the woman was referring to when Cyrus brought Izzy there in the past, but maybe the woman at Miracle Manor had confused Izzy with Nephy? Because Cyrus had fucked Nephy and gotten her pregnant. Maybe he'd been fucking her for a while. Years, maybe. It was all so extreme that in some ways Izzy couldn't feel any of it. Except. The other truth remained. Someone had killed Cyrus, cut him into pieces. And now there was a greater reason to believe that Cyrus was linked to Sky and the House of Hearts. Izzy knew she'd have to focus on this, only on this, if she were ever to learn what had happened to him.

She wanted to call Ever, but she could not call Ever—trying to call him felt impossible, like asking someone to return from the dead. And she was too damaged anyway. Walking damage and she had always been; she knew that now. She had been drawn to Cyrus because of that damage, and she had refused to see who he really was for the same reason. She could not rely on anyone else. Izzy had to go alone.

Petals

Izzy had lain awake all night, thinking about telling the police that Sky visited Cyrus as a kid, that Cyrus went looking for her, that she had shown up in the video, but Izzy decided against it. If the cops hadn't responded urgently to a severed hand bearing Cyrus's ring, why would they care about this tenuous lead? Izzy had lain awake telling herself to get up and go to see Sky right then, but she couldn't bring Dog, and it was too late to text Ted and ask if he could watch the animals. More, Izzy couldn't bear to leave the comfort of Dog's warmth in the bed and face the night. But morning wasn't much better.

❉ ❉ ❉

Still wrapped in a towel from the shower, water slithering coldly down her neck, she filled a backpack with her phone and charger, her canteen, a flashlight. She would, at least, be clean, organized, and prepared.

Izzy dressed—black underpants, black jeans, black tank top, Converse, a black knit cap, and her sunglasses. At the last minute, she removed the knife from the mannequin's hand, pocketed it, and snugged Larry's gun into the pack. And checked that the lipstick she'd stolen from Ever was still there, like a talisman. In the past, all her talismans—her ring, her crystals, even the herbs she grew and the candles she made—had been associated with Cyrus. She wanted none of them.

Izzy fed Yard and stroked his shell with her finger, blinking softly at him, promising she'd be back soon. She let Dog out and fed him, knelt to stare into his eyes. He lay there, long legs tucked under him, head erect, waiting for his next instructions. "My friend is going to come pick you up later today," she told him. "Yard, too. I love you, babies. I don't know if it will be safe for you where I'm going."

❀❀❀

White clouds galloped like horses through the blueness. She drove past mountains, ridged purple in the distance. A few wore light caps of snow, as if the clouds had come to rest there, but it wasn't much snow for this time of year. Izzy thought about Sky's lecture on global warming. Another way she lured all those people in.

Sky. Who was this woman, really? And what did she have to do with Cyrus? He had believed, somehow, that she was his mother. She had lurked around when he was a kid, and he had seen a flyer for her retreat and, without telling Izzy, he had gone with Nephy to visit Sky. It was easier to think about Sky than to think about what Cyrus and Nephy had done and what had happened to him afterward.

The cassette was still in the car stereo. Izzy pulled out the tape and looked at it. "For You," the label said. Cyrus had written that. For her. Or had he? The cassette tape had slid out from under the seat; what if the tape was for Nephy, and Cyrus had lied to Izzy when she'd found it?

She opened the window and tossed the music out of the window into the desert.

❀❀❀

On the way, Izzy stopped at the farm Larry managed. Fields stretched along the highway, crops of lettuce now frilly little noggins. The threat of drought hung over everything like a cloud of dust. Southern California had been restricting water usage for a while now. It could easily get worse. Cape Town, South Africa, for instance was already preparing for the taps to be shut off, people to line up for their rations.

She saw Larry supervising some farm workers. He came over, hugged her. She stiffened even more than usual at the wiry feel of Larry's arms and the bitter smell of tobacco.

"What's wrong?" he asked.

"What do you think is wrong?" She couldn't tell him anything more. She had forgotten her sunglasses in the truck, and even shielding her eyes didn't help. Sunspots danced. She half-imagined creatures with lettuce-heads rising up from under the earth and shaking down the rows.

"Find out anything else?"

"Do you know who brought that film to Bombay Beach, Larry?"

"What film?"

"The film. With the woman. You know what I'm talking about."

"Can't say I do."

"Jody says that woman was hanging around when Cyrus was a kid. That true?"

"How would I know?"

"Have you seen a woman with long black hair?"

Behind his sunglasses she felt his eyes waiting, serpents curled beneath rocks. "Only you. Or before you shaved it all off. And Nephy."

Izzy, nauseous, shook her head and refused the bottle of water he handed her. "Why'd you give me the fucking gun, Larry?"

His eyes darted sideways, suspicious, to see if anyone had heard. "Don't talk loud out here like that."

"Why'd you do it?"

"You were digging around in those mine sites. Not safe."

"Any other reason?"

"What are you getting at?" He cocked his scarecrow head at her.

"Tell me the truth," Izzy said. "You heard Cyrus went missing. You gave me a goddamn gun. I found his—I found his hand. Don't bullshit me, Larry."

"My little girl talking trash."

"What aren't you telling me?"

He flinched a little; she could see it.

Larry said, "You sound crazy like your mother. Leave it alone."

And though she thought she'd have faced death straight on to find out what had happened to Cyrus, something in Larry's expression made her recoil from asking more. She remembered the kitten dangling from the clothesline like a mourner's handkerchief when she was a kid, and the way Larry had lurched out of the trailer, pinched the clothespins, and let the body collapse flimsily into the dirt. He'd said the kitten must have gotten out, someone must have caught it and put it there.

What had really happened? This was the question, over and over again. What had happened when she was a child and, more importantly, what had happened to Cyrus?

She'd leave, but she couldn't leave this alone.

❋❋❋

Izzy arrived by nightfall at the retreat center in Joshua Tree. The stars glistened fish-like, as if the sky were made of water, and the air, too, gleamed with an aqueous cold.

The palm trees, silhouetted blackly against the sky, had been necklaced with phosphorescent Christmas lights.

Izzy entered the tiled courtyard and went through the door into the spacious front room lined with columns. The potted palms around the fountain twinkled with more white lights that turned the air diaphanous. *What date is it today*, Izzy wondered for a moment. When was Christmas? How had time passed when her heart had frozen so solid and still?

A small group of people—fewer than the last time she was there—mingled around the fountain, drinking beer and wine. Two life-sized wooden statues, a man and woman with inlaid black eyes, one wearing a cobra headdress and the other a wig of black curls, guarded the door, hands crossed over their chests. Izzy couldn't remember having seen them there before.

The bald, silent young man appeared with his tray of drinks and stood, staring at Izzy in a way that didn't just seem mildly creepy anymore; it chilled her.

"Is Sky here?" Izzy asked.

He shook his head, no.

Then Jeb materialized at her side—she hadn't seen him come over. "Hello, Aurora."

This time she was prepared for the name. "I'm looking for Sky," Izzy said, and then realized that she had no idea exactly what she would say to the woman when she did find her.

"What's wrong? You look gaunt," Jeb said. "Home life okay? You know, I like to ask this of every gaunt foundling who comes to our doors."

"I need to see Sky."

"She'll be here later tonight. This is actually a private meeting, but you are welcome to join." Jeb smiled pleasantly with a slight flap of his gauze-clad arms. "Beer? Wine?"

She couldn't afford to drink alcohol now. She had to stay on her game. "No, thank you."

"Get Aurora some lotus tea please, Ausar," Jeb said, and the bald man scurried off. "Make yourself at home," Jeb told her, and he left her there.

She sipped the tea the bald man had brought. It had a pungent scent, a subtle flowery taste, and a sharp anise-like aftertaste. Izzy finished the entire cup and set it down.

Then she went upstairs. Candles flickered in iron sconces. A balcony window overlooked the pool, vaporous with mist and stippled with moonlight, and Izzy heard the susurrating whisper of the waterfall; she imagined ghostly shapes in those vapors, transparent, swooning figures.

"Aurora," a woman squealed, and Izzy turned to find Amanda wearing a gold satin slip dress that revealed her cleavage and tattooed arms. Two wet spots showed at her nipples. "It's so good to see you," Amanda said, hugging her. Izzy's chest felt sunken, concave, especially in contrast to the other woman's milky voluptuousness. "How are you?" Amanda asked.

Izzy tried to answer. *My boyfriend was fucking our best friend. She's pregnant with his child. He was murdered.* She felt light-headed.

"I slept like a horse, and I'm hungry as a baby," Amanda said.

What? Was Amanda high?

"Sky hates clichés so she makes us mix them up," Amanda explained. "Original, visceral language—nothing derivative. She's all about the blazon."

"The what?"

"In literature. It lists the physical attributes of a subject. Eyes like this. Lips like that. Sky says it's kind of brutal. That's why it's so wonderful. Like you're making a recipe. Like you're going to eat them for dinner."

Izzy felt queasy, like she might be sick.

"Sky says poetry is the true language of the goddess. She exists everywhere," Amanda babbled on as if reciting the words. "Originally, she was in the myths, obviously, then, when Christianity threatened to banish her, she appeared in the folk tales. The sleeping princess in her glass coffin, in her briar-covered castle. She's shown up in the novel since the time of its conception, though. She may not have been called by name. And she's in the songs of many female singer-songwriters. She's even on reality television."

Definitely high. Or just crazy: Izzy felt like she was talking to Leanne. Her head hurt. "Please stop," she said.

"Were you looking for something?" Amanda asked. Had she narrowed her eyes when she said it?

"Just the restroom."

"Down the hall," Amanda said, pointing. "Are you staying for the ritual?"

What ritual? But Amanda didn't wait for an answer.

"Sky's the real deal. A mystagogue. That means someone who teaches the mysteries. A hierophant. That's another word for it. Really." Her smile vanished, and she lowered her eyes. "I had a big loss too," she said. "My first baby died. Sky nursed me through it."

Izzy felt the blood drain from her face and put a hand to her abdomen to touch the phantom pain, remembering her own loss. What would have happened if her baby hadn't died in the womb? Would everything be different between her and Cyrus? Would he still be alive now? "Oh, I'm so sorry," Izzy said.

"I'm better now. I have Kurt! I didn't want to make you sad. I just wanted to let you know it's good you're here and I understand."

Izzy nodded. "I'm sorry," she said again. And walked away.

###

After she'd used the restroom, Izzy stepped back out into the hallway. She remembered walking around this house the first time. She wasn't sure what she was looking for then, but her feet just moved her forward. Ever since Cyrus's vanishing, she had been restless for answers. But it seemed there were no answers. Except perhaps a clue in the video someone—maybe those red-haired children—had played in Bombay Beach and in what Jody had said.

Izzy's footsteps sounded on the tile, and she walked as lightly as possible, carefully trying a number of doors. They were locked.

Then, at the end of the hall, she tried a door painted with a large golden eye; this door opened.

Izzy entered a study with a large black lacquer desk inlaid in ebony and ivory, and a plate glass window overlooking the grotto outside. The desk, like the other furniture, had the golden feet of a lion. Against one wall of the room stood a large vitrine lined in carnelian velvet and full of small calcite statues, arranged on glass shelves. Books on history, anthropology, archaeology, and earth sciences covered the rest of the walls. What would it be like to have a room like this, a place to read and write, overlooking the palm

trees and the pool, the mountains and a sky that turned from pale
pink to pale blue with scudding clouds, to white-heat, to deep coral,
to darkest bluish black? She sat down at the desk and looked out at
the landscape, cold and spinning with stars. Then she began opening
the desk drawers with the small gilt knobs. One drawer was locked
and the others mostly empty except for a smattering of office supplies.

Izzy thought of the tools she had to help her search for Cyrus.
Not just technology, and Cyrus's truck, and the education Larry had
given her about mines. Not just the gun he'd given her, though she
still wasn't sure why. Not just Dog, though he had helped her most of
all, and part of her wished she'd brought him along.

Something else had helped her, could help her still: her hands.
She looked down at the shredded cuticles, the dry skin on her
knuckles. The massage client who didn't believe in global warming
had told Izzy, "Whatever you say." All she'd had to do was rub his
back. Cyrus wasn't the only one with strong, capable, loving hands.
Muscles melted wax-like under Izzy's fingers.

Another thing Larry had taught her, besides guns and trucks,
plants, mines, and minerals: how to use those hands and a paper
clip to open a lock. Izzy took two from the top drawer of the desk,
pulled one clip apart and slipped the end into the lock, jiggling;
then she pushed the end of the other paper clip into the bottom of
the lock and turned. It took a few cranks but opened. Inside, Izzy
found a folder of papers and searched through it. She chose the
photograph first.

Sky stood in the center of a group of four red-haired children,
her arms reaching out to embrace them, her smile spreading across
them all like the rising sun. Sky in her jewelry and gauze with her
flawless, fake-looking skin. Izzy recognized the children in the
picture: the kids from Bombay Beach. The ones who had run off
giggling on the night of the gathering. The ones who had probably
brought that video of Sky.

From the vitrine, the small statues watched.

Somewhere down the hall a door opened, then closed. Footsteps. Without thinking, Izzy dropped the picture, jumped up and left the room. The hall was empty, and she made it back downstairs unobserved.

"Where's Sky?" she asked Jeb. She felt strange and wondered if the tea had something in it. But, weirdly, she was starting not to care.

"You're in luck," he said. "She's just arrived. And she's eager to see you. Ausar will take you upstairs to her."

❀❀❀

Sky sat cross-legged on a large, low bed, its four posts carved into lotus blossoms from which hung white chiffon panels. She was admiring herself in a round hand mirror with the handle in the shape of an ankh. White roses in glass bowls had been placed around the room, white candles burned in sconces, and music—drums and flutes—whispered from hidden speakers. Sky's unnaturally smooth and brown skin had been recently oiled like lemon-polished wood. "I'm so glad you came, darling."

There was nowhere else to sit except the bed with Sky, so Izzy remained standing.

"Have something to drink." Sky got up, poured another cup of tea for Izzy, handed it to her, sat down again, and adjusted the white silk robe over her thighs. Izzy doubted that the woman wore anything underneath. The inner swell of one breast was visible through the opening of her robe. "I'm so sorry for your loss," she said.

Izzy said nothing.

"I see you've hurt yourself. And shaved your head."

Izzy reflexively touched her scalp as if protecting her head from a blow.

"The journeywoman often shaves off her hair as a sign of mourning as she searches for the beloved," Sky said. "She often becomes injured while on her quest. You intuited this. But I want to help you, so that you aren't so alone."

What the hell was she talking about? Was she high? Amanda had seemed high. Were they all high? Was Izzy high? "What do you know about Cyrus?"

"Do you believe in resurrection?" Sky asked then. "Because I do. I believe that in some ways the beloved is always with us."

Izzy rubbed her temples and shook her head from side to side to clear it, but the faint buzzing remained.

"I think everything is possible," Sky went on. "When the conditions are right. When the world is ready. Take King Tut's pectoral breastplate for example. Howard Carter, who discovered his tomb, thought the greenish gold gem, used to make the large scarab carrying the sun and moon, was chalcedony, ordinary quartz. But then minerals like lechatelierite and baddeleyite and also iron, nickel, chromium, cobalt, and iridium were discovered in the material. The greenish yellow material was made by a meteorite hitting earth, burning the sand, then cooling in the air and showering down on the desert.

"We are all sharing the earth's pain," said Sky.

The words the child had spoken, the child from Bombay Beach. They snapped Izzy back. "Why did you visit Cyrus when he was a kid? His mom said a woman with long black hair used to come around their house. Why did those kids play that video?" And: "What did you do to Cyrus?"

"Do you believe in resurrection?" Sky repeated. "Do you believe in rebirth and renewal? Perhaps your love lives on in some other way."

"He was killed," Izzy said "Cyrus. Chopped up into pieces." She had said it aloud at last. Was she screaming?

"I'm so sorry," Sky said. "We will try to help any way we can. I know how horrible this must be for you."

"You don't know me," Izzy said.

Sky's eyes shone in the candlelight. They looked, Izzy thought, familiar somehow. The white roses in the vase nearest her were rimmed in a thin line of red, as if they had been carefully dipped in blood. "I do, though," Sky said.

"No." Izzy's mouth had gone dry again, her head hurt, she couldn't think.

"I know you and I know him," Sky said. "You loved each other and—" Then she paused, and her eyes glazed over, looked somehow blind. "You are both my children. All four of you are my children."

"What do you mean?"

"I wanted children; that was all I wanted," Sky said. "But not just any children. Children who could change the planet, make everything right again. I knew I could make this happen if I birthed four children, two boys and two girls. And I did! Twice."

Izzy restrained herself, twisting her hands. They felt as if they belonged to someone else.

"You remind me of myself at your age," Sky said. "So fierce. So angry but also so full of love. I was poor, too, like you; I didn't have anything but my body. But I thought, this body is connected to some higher power, something sacred, and it can bring needed souls into the world. Children who can change the world! I will birth them and scatter some of them around the desert and then they will find each other and play out the myth as it is meant to be."

"What the fuck are you talking about?"

"The last four children, Osiris, Seth, Isis, and Nephthys, have the same father. With the four of you, each father was different, I promise, your real fathers—Del and Larry and Richard and Otis. They didn't know about each other. Cyrus's mother never knew about me, either, and Richard's wife left, but your mothers—yours and Nephy's—went along with it. Maybe they believed in me, or maybe they just didn't believe in themselves, didn't want to lose their men after the miscarriages. A woman in today's world has to find ways to feed herself."

"What the fuck?" Izzy said again. How did Sky know the names of all four of their fathers—not just Cyrus's but Izzy's and Seth's and Nephy's?

"Cyrus found me. And yes, she was with him. But you were the one he loved. He was just trying to understand himself, and he got lost along the way. I didn't know what would happen. I just let it all play itself out. And when I heard about your meeting at Bombay Beach, I asked the little ones to play the video to bring you to me.

The room spun and blurred, and Izzy steadied herself against the wall. "What? What's in this?" She threw the cup of tea onto the tiled floor, and it shattered.

"Lotus tea. To relax us. Sometimes thought of as a slight aphrodisiac. A little bit of opium to help with the pain," Sky said. "You might hallucinate slightly."

In Izzy's mind: the framed photo of herself at thirteen with Larry and Izzy who so little resembled her mother. As a child, when they were all in the car on the highway, Izzy would imagine Leanne screaming at Larry to pull over to the side of the road and telling Izzy to get out. "You're not mine," she'd hear Leanne say. It was both fear and fantasy. Now it was only fear she felt. Because if she was not Leanne's, then whose was she? *That woman. From the movie. She used to watch him play*, Jody had said. *You are all my children*, Sky had said. But how? And why? And what did this have to do with the fact that Cyrus had been murdered and dismembered? It was too much to fathom at once, but it meant—it meant something. Something unspeakable.

"I'm going to help you," said Sky, her voice a metronome, casting its spell. "At midnight in the courtyard. I will help you understand the key to becoming yourself."

What was the scent of darkness? Izzy wondered, as she drifted into the smoke of sleep.

❈❈❈

When Izzy came back to consciousness, her mouth even drier now as if she'd been sucking on linen, she was lying outside on a divan, looking up at the ultraviolet of an early evening sky. Black shapes swooped above her—a formation of birds. Hieroglyphs, she found herself thinking. She heard the glass-bead-tinkling of a fountain. Smelled fire in the air. Burning minerals.

Bare-armed and bare-legged, the cool of satin light on her thighs, someone had taken off her clothes, put her in underwear—lace underwear?—and a dress. A satin dress. White. The fabric caught lightly on her rough hands. She was aware of all of this but unable to fully respond or react.

"He was born in the desert," a man's voice said. Jeb's voice. "His mother laid herself out upon his father, the earth, her belly a great blue egg speckled with stars. His father impregnated her with his trees and his mountains, his fields of wheat stalks and corn. He and his sisters and his brother burst forth in the light of their grandfather Sun, the maker of all, the bright dung beetle in the sky, the golden scarab, the all-seeing eye.

"He and his sister-wife Isis bathed in the lotus pool, anointed each other's pulses with fragrant oil of myrrh and frankincense, adorned each other's brows with garlands, adorned each other's eyes with lapis, tourmaline, and emerald, adorned each other's lips and hearts with carnelian, adorned each other's skin with gold. Hummingbirds thrummed at their necks and wrists. Butterflies flew from their lips when they opened their mouths. Their scapulae sprouted wings. They let the wild flowers grow unfettered. Bees hummed in their hive and it sang like a lyre.

"He and his wife went forth hand-in-hand to irrigate dry land, to plant wheat and corn, to weave fine linen and make barley beer and date wine. They were not wasteful. They burned the wick all night and wasted no light. Draped in white linen and gauze, she knelt before him and offered her breasts and her thighs like cakes of saffron and honey. He offered her his cow's horn, his stalk of wheat, his golden staff."

The words had bound and drowned Izzy, seeped into her pores, as if they had been spoken directly to her. But she could not let them rule her. She tried to rouse herself, but she could not. The man's voice continued:

"When you create, you sacrifice a little of yourself, a little of your seed, a small blue egg. When two bodies struggle against each other in the war of love, a child may be conceived. Children are small deities, slick with blood as they arrive in this world. When you paint a story on the temple wall, you lose a little blood. But when you are done, you will walk the flower path dripping with hyacinth, fragrant with calamus, unfurling the blue lotus in the silver pool; you will go forth into the flower fields of peace.

"You were born to make beauty in the slaughterhouse of the world. You were born to toil. You were born to love. Offer yourself up to the light of the golden eye of the sun, to the silver mouth of the moon, to the gods and goddesses of love. The god and goddess reside within, but do not forget them in others. Gather your passions like precious gems, polish and refine them and give them to the world. Loss is inevitable, but do not fear it. It is the corpse without its stomach, intestines, lungs, and liver. But these organs wait in canopic jars to be reclaimed in the afterlife. Only the heart remains. It is the hope that allows light and love to flood and enter the void. Live with hope, with imagination and purpose.

"Osiris said, 'I have been imperfect. I have overlooked the goddess in my home. I have been lustful and full of fear. I have been ignorant. I have neglected the earth, I have neglected my beloved, and I have neglected myself. I have forgotten to kiss the dough and honey from my loved one's fingers, kiss her lips and hair in the blue dawn. I have listened to death singing in the courtyard and longed to go to her—lusted for her like a lover.'

"'See me,'" Jeb continued. "'I am Osiris, imperfect, but bringing light to the darkness, bringing water back to the desert. I am Osiris seduced by a sibyl-sister, night lady with her eyes like a panther's, her lips smeared in ox blood, her cloven hooves. I am Osiris rendered by a brother with his terrible snout, his self-mutilations blamed on the gods. I am Osiris, gathered up by a sorceress wife, with her eyes like grapes, her mouth like a pomegranate, her hair like a falcon's wings, her sex like a fig, her skin redolent of hyacinth, of olives and honey. I am Osiris resurrected by a son with the head of a hawk. He will be raped, his eyes plucked out by his murderous demon uncle. Everything that is lost returns. I have shed my skin and bones like a cloak of rags, but my heart remains intact like a lotus beating in a jar. I will return. I will return.'"

Izzy tried to speak but found she could not.

"Don't be afraid," Sky said, coming into Izzy's line of vision, leaning forward. "Every act of creation requires sacrifice. Art, sex, they all require giving up something of the body, of the self. Again and again the god is sacrificed so that he may arise again." She wore a long white dress, cut low to reveal her collarbones and a necklace of carnelian, lapis, and gold. Gold and glass bracelets chimed at her wrists. "I want to help you," Sky said.

"Help," Izzy managed.

"All that matters is that you are here now."

Izzy kept trying and trying to speak.

"I'm going to help you," Sky said again.

Then Izzy smelled the narcotic mix of resin, honey, and white roses. Falling into the deepening violet light, she wondered what it would be like for all her thoughts to stop.

※ ※ ※

Izzy opened her eyes. More time had passed. The sky hung, dark-amethyst now, over the garden.

"Why do we worship Isis?" a woman's voice asked. Sky's voice again.

Izzy realized that she had not moved for some time, that she could hardly move.

Jeb, dressed in black, stood beside Sky. The group had gathered by the waterfall. The night was colder now and clear. Izzy still lay, clothed in white satin, on the divan.

Over her hovered a man with the face of a bird—a falcon?—and another jackal-faced man. A cow woman with horns, a wet, black nose, a round, pink tongue hanging lasciviously from the cleft of her mouth. Her heavy head bobbed like a puppet's, and her arms were painted with flowers. A tall man, who resembled some animal with long furry ears and a snout, stood in the shadows.

"Why would the ancients follow her?" Sky asked. "A woman? A beautiful woman who could make love magic, vegetal magic, make plants grow, who could weave baskets and linen, make the waters rise and the evening star shine, who devoted her life to her husband, the king; a woman who gathered her beloved's bones and gave him immortality. Who wouldn't want that? And then she was abolished, sent away, underground. There she lived on and now we look to her again, in times of such great need.

"The girls and women raped and murdered. The guns shooting down our Black men in cold blood on the streets. Shooting our children in classrooms! The refusal to regulate these weapons. Nature rebelling. Ice melting, animals dying. It's like the apocalypse, truly. But did the goddess ever really leave? How many people go to psychics and hear, 'You were an Egyptian king or queen reincarnated?' Why not a plumber? Why not a beggar?" Laughter frothed like the waterfall hitting the pool. "No, an Egyptian king or queen. That's the message, over and over again. Because, within, we all are these Egyptian kings and queens, descendants of the gods and goddesses.

"And what are we doing here tonight?" Sky asked. "Trying to get you to assimilate the deities, to appreciate the feminine, to honor and restore her, so that the masculine, the powerful, good, kind-hearted king, can be restored to the throne as well." Sky raised her hand, beckoning, and the cow-woman stepped forward.

"Hathor, will you recite the invocation?" Sky asked.

The woman began to speak.

Re-membering Deities

Isis and Osiris, they were twins.
They loved each other even in the womb.
His brother Set chopped off Osiris's limbs.
She turned to falcon, raised him from the tomb.

From Isis's womb the child named Horus came.
Then, to avenge his father, he did go.
But Set was strong and raped and blinded him.
From Horus's eyes the lotuses will grow.

In pity, Isis freed Set from his bonds.
In anger, Horus severed off her head.
Replaced it with a cow's beneath the fronds.
Then Horus raised his father from the dead.

Like Isis I'm beheaded, Horus-blind.
Osiris I re-member, Set re-minds.

The words fell around Izzy like a shower of chilly petals. She could not quite catch them all.

The woman retreated.

Amanda?

Izzy tried to walk back through the lines of the poem.

Sky turned and looked at her. "Aurora, will you sit up, please."

It took Izzy a moment to recognize her name; then, as if hypnotized, she did as Sky asked.

Sky fastened a white papier-mâché mask over Izzy's face and tied it in the back with a ribbon. The mask fit too well, as if it had been made for her. Izzy tried to breathe normally through the tiny nostril openings; she stared out of the ragged eyeholes into the crowd of masked people.

"You will portray Isis this evening," Sky said. "And you—" She beckoned.

A dark-haired man with an eerily smooth white face came forward. Izzy gasped out loud. It was Ever. He was here. What was he doing? What were they doing to him? Why was his face like that?

"You will portray Osiris," Sky said. She lit a stick of incense on the candle flame and held it aloft. "Bless us as we enact the mystery of Isis and Osiris," she said.

Jeb stepped forward holding a sistrum that he shook lightly. "Lament with us. Osiris is dead! Dismembered by his brother, Set." He blew out the candles in the courtyard, one by one, until the only light came from the almost-full December Moon—the moon called Cold.

"Dismembered..." Izzy whispered. What were they talking about? What had happened? Dismembered...like Cyrus... By his brother, Set, like... She struggled to sit up, but she was too weak.

"Osiris saw the beautiful chest painted with wondrous images and lay down in it. But the chest had been made by his brother Set, made to Osiris's dimensions, and so he lay in it and died."

Sky said, "Now Osiris lives only in Isis's dreams." Izzy was shaking like the sistrum, now. She smelled more roses—always roses—and frankincense. "Repeat after me," Sky whispered.

"What's wrong with me?" Izzy asked.

"Repeat after me," said Sky, but Izzy couldn't speak.

"I, Isis, take the form of the kite, flying over the land to seek him as he dreams. In my womb, I carry his child, Horus," Sky said.

She went on, "I, Isis, search everywhere, and as I do, the people mourn with me." Her voice changed, became commanding once again: "Show Isis that you are with her in her search."

"Isis!" the company cried. "Isis!"

Jeb said, "All those who have lost a loved one, say the name of Isis's beloved."

"Osiris!" they chanted.

Faint, Izzy stumbled. Instead of helping her up, Sky, suddenly at her side, brought her down to her knees on the tiles and knelt beside her. Izzy closed her eyes and breathed Sky in.

"Now we will all meditate in silence and envision our lost loved ones here with us," Sky said.

In the quiet that followed, the only sound was the waterfall and someone sobbing. Izzy wasn't sure if it was she, herself, sobbing.

"Those who have lost a loved one have given their strength to Isis, and Osiris hears her and remembers," said Sky.

Ever tried to pull away but then seemed to collapse against Jeb. "Repeat the words," Jeb said to him. "I, Osiris, feel the love of Isis in my heart, but still I am disassembled, still I am imprisoned in the land of dreams."

Ever remained silent.

So Jeb kept talking: "Osiris feels the love of Isis in his heart, but still he is disassembled, still he is imprisoned in the land of dreams."

"Now we must all dance to help Isis in her work," Sky said.

Jeb shook the sistrum and music played from somewhere—flute, harp, drum.

The company began to dance with their hands in the air. "Feel the fire from the earth's core rising up through your feet, up your spine to your heart," Sky said. She lifted Izzy up from the ground and swayed with her in her arms. "Our Lady of Petals. The Great Mother," the voices said. Izzy collapsed into the other woman's flesh and scent.

Sky said, "As she dances, Isis remembers she is not a broken woman. She is a goddess! She is the daughter of the great goddess, Nut."

Izzy tilted her head and looked into the woman's eyes. Sky whispered, "Yes, yes, it's all right. Repeat after me—"

Izzy couldn't speak.

"My beloved, come back to your house, come back to me. I am Isis, your twin soul, your sister-wife, Isis. We are the children of the sky goddess, Nut," Sky said.

Something was happening to Izzy. She was changing. Transmuting. Becoming another. Becoming herself. No.

Jeb said, "And as Isis weeps, Osiris awakens from the slaughter-house of night, from his dream of death, the slaughterer, and returns to light and life." He gripped Ever's arm and whispered into his ear again. When Ever didn't respond, Jeb said, "Osiris hears the voice of Isis calling him back."

"And all our lost loved ones return to us," Sky said. "And we also, lost in the netherworlds of our grieving and self-doubt, return to life with them when we remember our true identities as incarnations of the deity. We are Nut, the firmament, stretched above in her dress of stars; we are Geb, the earth god, lying below the blue arc of her belly, absorbing her light; we are their children—wild Set, beautiful Nephthys, Isis who is love, and Osiris who is king and their son, Horus, the divine child who will be raped and blinded by his uncle. Awaken with Osiris to your true selves! Dance and awaken!"

They all began to undulate. Sky moved Izzy liked a puppet, turning her body this way and that. "She dances to the four directions, calling the parts of Osiris back to her. Priest, king, artist, wise man, lover, father, husband, brother. And as she gathers the parts of Osiris, so we gather the parts of ourselves together and find the goddess and god within ourselves!"

Jeb gestured for everyone to come closer. Then he took hold of Ever's shoulders and steered him toward Sky.

"Lie down," Sky said.

Ever looked at her. He knelt, then sat, then extended his legs and lay on his back. He was fucked up, as fucked up as Izzy. What had they been given? What hallucinogen? What aphrodisiac? The lotus tea? What—Sky gestured for Izzy to come and lie on top of him, and Izzy did as she was told.

"Ever," Izzy said. Beneath his clothing and his skin, she could feel his flesh, his muscles, the weight of his bones.

"What's happening?" he slurred behind the mask. She realized now, the whiteness of his face—it was a mask. "We need to leave."

"What?"

"—to leave," Ever said again.

"Did they give you something?" she managed.

"Just juice—"

"We can't drive," Izzy said, suddenly lucid.

"Have to leave," he said a third time.

"But we can't—"

"What did they do?"

"Drugged."

The company spoke: "Isis lays herself upon Osiris, brow to brow, heart to heart, limb to limb. He receives her breath into his mouth, into his lungs."

"Resurrect the God!" said Jeb.

"Resurrect the God!" said Sky.

"Osiris, awaken!" they said together. "Isis and Osiris are reunited!"

Izzy saw Jeb hand a silver ankh to Sky. She held it aloft. "Here is the sacred key that allows passage between the two worlds."

Jeb began to walk around the room, tearing pieces of bread from a large round loaf wrapped in blue cloth. "Partake of the wheat of Osiris."

Sky sprinkled water from a glass bowl on the foreheads of the now-kneeling company. "Partake of the water of Isis. Isis has brought Osiris back from the dead once again. The cycle continues."

The sobbing Izzy heard? It had emerged from her own chest and the depths of her throat.

The next thing she knew, Ever had somehow managed to get to his feet, lift her in his arms, and carry her away from the courtyard. No one stopped them.

But someone watched them as they left—Izzy saw: the man with the snout and fur ears.

❀ ❀ ❀

Izzy woke still half-drugged in a room in Sky's house. Her head a-throb with blood, Izzy blinked into the darkness. White rose petals floated on the dark water of the quilt—someone had strewn them there. The air scented with honeyed smoke—someone had lit candles, now burned to puddles of wax. Like a bridal chamber, Izzy thought. She couldn't remember anything that had happened after she and Ever had left the ceremony.

"Ever?" Izzy said now, but he wasn't there. She went back over what she could remember: the photo of the red-haired children with Sky, the spiked tea, the ritual, Ever. And before that: this thing that Sky had said about Izzy, Cyrus, Seth, and Nephy. That she was their mother? All of theirs? That she had slept with their fathers? What did Izzy have as evidence? The words of a bereaved Jody. The words of Sky, a crazy woman. One adopted child, three children who looked nothing like their mothers. A man and two women with black hair, thick enough, when you braided it, to use as rope. (Once this man and one of the women—maybe the other one, too, in private?—had joked about how much they looked alike.) And, somehow, whirling in her mind with no clear explanation, the image—taken by the photographer from the House of Hearts meeting—of the little tiara worn by Nephy in the photo of her with Seth on the dead boat, and the same headpiece worn by the little red-haired girl at Bombay Beach. The tiara was nothing, really, in the scheme of things, but it seemed to solidify it all, that little junkyard princess crown.

Izzy knew then.

Her lover had been more than her soul-twin.

He had been her blood.

They were all four—Izzy, Cyrus, Seth, and Nephy—they were all four blood.

If Izzy had a baby with Cyrus—

Nephy and Cyrus's baby—

"No," Izzy said aloud. She tasted bile and ran to the adjoining bathroom to vomit into the toilet. It could not be. It could not be. Everything had gotten to her, finally and completely. She had lost all semblance of sanity in the wake of Cyrus's death. But there was no way around the truth.

She went back into the bedroom and looked for her things. There was her backpack, her clothing, and shoes, the sweat-soaked remnants of the white satin dress. But where was Ever?

The darkness descended then, the worst one she had ever felt, the direst warning she had ever received. It almost blinded her. But she did not push it away; this time she let it guide her.

Izzy threw on her clothes, shouldered her backpack, and ran out into the hallway.

She ran down the corridor, calling Ever's name. In the large front room, the acolytes slept in piles, flowers and empty cups and bottles scattered all around them. Masks, too. The bird and the jackal and the cow and the strange unnameable creature had been masked people, of course. No sign of Jeb or Sky.

Izzy ran out the front door, through the courtyard.

Plata was parked where she had left it. Beside Plata, she saw Ever's truck.

Izzy ran back through the house, outside to the garden. The yard was empty. Ripples petalled out beneath the waterfall.

Izzy then heard a sound, and she turned. A woman stood there in the green-lit darkness, eyes glazed. Her stomach protruded and her nipples showed through her T-shirt, as if rouged. Pregnancy did that, Izzy knew. She wanted to grab Nephy by the perfect, round skulls of her shoulders and shake her to death.

Izzy asked, "Where's Seth?"

"What?" Nephy asked.

"Where the fuck is Seth?"

"I don't know."

"Where is he?"

Nephy bit her lip, screwed up her face, and shook her head like a toddler about to have a tantrum.

Izzy grabbed Nephy's firm little bicep, squeezed. "What happened? Tell me right now."

"Get off of me." But Nephy's voice sounded weak.

"Now!" Izzy screamed.

"Stop, Izzy."

"If you don't tell me, I will hurt you," she said.

Nephy pulled away, rubbing her arm. "I don't know, Izzy! I just found out Seth knew about me and Cyrus. I didn't think he knew. He made me tell him what you said to me on the phone last night, and I said I thought you were looking for that woman. So he brought me here. They gave us something to drink. He saw you with that man. He kept calling him Cyrus."

A dead calm wormed through Izzy's body.

"Izzy?" Nephy said.

"Izzy," Ever said weakly.

She turned and there he stood—the tall man in the mask she'd seen watching the ceremony. Seth. Holding Ever by the neck. Holding a knife to Ever's throat.

Izzy stared at him, stunned, a bird smashed into a window, electrified on a fence.

"Put the knife down, Seth," Izzy said. "Let him go."

Seth's eyes looked like scarabs, enameled in the death-mask of his face. "It has to be done."

"Seth—"

"Motherfucker had everything. Pretty boy Cyrus. Told me he didn't trust me. Accused me of all kinds of shit. That cat. But he's the one. And then he even got Nephy. I couldn't let him take anything more. He had to pay. I had to make him pay. And now he's back." Seth pulled Ever closer, and Ever's body jolted and he closed his eyes. "I have to kill him," Seth said.

"That isn't Cyrus," Izzy said, trying to keep her voice steady. Tears streamed down her face. "His name's Ever. You don't even know him."

"Please, man," Ever said.

"Let him go, Seth," Nephy said.

Seth looked over at Ever, blinked, with ophidian eyes.

And Izzy reached for the gun in her backpack.

Seth dropped his arm from Ever's neck and tore away. Nephy followed.

Izzy ran after them, around to the front of the house. She held up the shaking gun and started firing in the general direction of where Seth had gone. It was like the gun had a mind of its own, awakened after sleeping so long at her side. But the best-aimed bullet only hit and punctured the side of Seth's truck.

Izzy couldn't have fired directly at him anyway: now he had Nephy by the arm, a human shield, a shield pregnant with Cyrus's child. Seth dragged Nephy into his truck and drove off.

Izzy looked down at the gun in her hands. Dawn streaked the sky like blood diffused in water. The sun had begun to rise, reddening the dust.

Essence

Two weeks after the events at the House of Hearts, things were finally clear: Cyrus, trying to understand himself, had gone looking for Sky, and he had brought Nephy with him. Having realized what was happening between Cyrus and Nephy, Seth followed them to the House of Hearts and overheard the story of Osiris. Enraged by their indiscretion and incensed by the myth, Seth lured Cyrus outside that night, grabbed him from behind, hauled him into his truck, took him to the mine, and slit his throat, then dismembered the body and buried the parts in different mines. Months later, Seth had tried to kill Ever, believing he was Cyrus resurrected. By now, the police had fully recovered Cyrus's body and Seth was in prison for his crimes.

A woman's voice, thirsting for her lover's essence, wailed rawly through the speakers in Ever's house. Tonight was the first time Izzy and Ever had seen each other since everything went down. Both of them needed time apart, they'd decided, to try and understand what had happened. Izzy hadn't seen or talked to anyone—not her parents, not Del and Jody, not Nephy. She'd gone home and stayed there, with Dog and Yard.

Ever sat hunched over on his leather couch with his hands clasped in front of him. He did not look at Izzy.

That first night they'd met, Ever's eyes had taken her in. He'd nodded his head at her, so slightly. A smile sun-beamed out from his face, melting her icy body into rain. On Ever's roof, when the stars shot across the sky, she had not wished for Cyrus. He was gone, but Ever was there. Ever, who had held her in her sadness. She had moaned with sadness into his ear, but also with fierce, carnal relief.

Ever hit the remote to quiet the music. "Talk to me," he said. But he still wouldn't look at her. He fingered some stuffing that had broken through a tear in the brown leather, and she thought of the couch in Seth and Nephy's living room, the couch Izzy had sat on with Cyrus the night they met and many, many other nights since then.

"We all had different fathers," Izzy said. Because at least—that. She wondered if she disgusted Ever, sleeping with her half-brother. "Cult members. They didn't know about each other. My mom and Nephy's must have just gone along with it when our dads brought us home. Didn't tell anyone."

"Why?" Ever asked.

"Maybe they didn't want to lose their men. That's what Sky said. Maybe they hadn't been able to have children of their own."

Sky mentioned miscarriages, and Leanne had implied the same thing when Izzy lost her baby. *But out here by the Sea they all die.*

Seth's mother had left when she found out what her husband Rick had done. Only Cyrus's mother didn't know, had thought Cyrus was an orphan, not her husband's child.

"What about those other kids?"

"Sky had four more children by the red-haired guy from Bombay Beach. At least they know they're—that they're siblings." Izzy felt nauseous and leaned forward, pressing her hands against her belly.

Somehow—perhaps with the help of Nephy's father, Otis, or the photographer Clay Wade—Sky had given the tiara to Nephy when she was a girl and then taken it back to give to Nephthys, the little red-haired girl in Bombay Beach.

Cyrus and Nephy had betrayed Izzy and Seth, but it all started with Sky. She had damaged all four children from the beginning, hidden their identities, traumatized them in ways they had never quite been able to understand. She had birthed them because she believed that, somehow, they would play out the myth.

The police questioned Sky in connection with Cyrus's murder, but they had released her due to lack of evidence. All she had done was give birth to four siblings, had them adopted, the cops said. All she had done was to perform rituals in her home.

And illegally drugged people she'd seduced with her talk of saving them, saving the planet, and forced them to participate in her rituals. But without evidence, there was no way the charges would stick.

Ultimately, Izzy believed, Sky had started the chain of events that led to Cyrus's death. And she would have been responsible for Ever's death, too. Ever, who had nothing to do with any of this, but who had suffered anyway. Because of me, Izzy thought. And because of Sky.

Izzy, suddenly unable to breathe, went out onto the porch, and Ever followed her. A white Wolf Moon and its attendant wolf cub stars roamed the pearlized sky above the Joshua trees.

He took a pack of cigarettes from his shirt pocket, turned it upside down, and shook one out.

"You smoke?"

"Yeah. I do now. Again." He lit and took a puff, deep, blew the smoke away from her. "My mouth still tastes like death anyway."

He meant after what had happened. "No. Please," she said.

Ever leaned up against the wall, shoulders hunched, one hand in his pocket, the other holding the cigarette butt. Izzy thought of that dream she'd had once, the taste of salt and wine, the slide of warm, wet skin-against-skin, the thrust of Cyrus into her mouth and Ever behind her.

Cyrus was gone and here was Ever with his kindness, his music, his beautiful pain.

"I'm working on a song," Ever said. "It's about two people who look like each other's dead lovers. But then it almost destroys them."

Izzy stood there staring at him. He still would not meet her eyes.

"But like you said, you're not him. And I'm not her."

"No, you're you. I've never met anyone like you, Izzy."

"I'm sorry," she said.

He shook his head. It seemed so heavy on his neck, almost too big for his body now, and Izzy thought of the papier-mâché masks at House of Hearts.

"I'm going to leave," she told him.

"I don't understand."

"I have to leave."

Ever smiled—not a real smile. His dimples showed but they looked like someone had poked holes in his face. She could see his incisors. Sharp.

"I can't stay. I almost got you killed," she said. "And we hardly know each other."

Finally, now, he looked at her. His eyes were red and limned with tears. He and Izzy faced off, bodies tense as if for combat. She felt heat flash in her cheeks like grease in a pan. Her lips and nipples tingled, and this made her angrier.

"Izzy," he said.

She turned away.

"I'm sorry," she said again.

He didn't tell her goodbye when she left. He would go on with his life, she knew. As if he had never met her, as if he had never even spoken her name.

Part III

Under the Bridge

Aurora had wanted to forget who she was, so she'd changed her name. She had wanted to forget the people who reminded her of her childhood, so she'd left without seeing Leanne and Larry or Del. She had wanted to forget the people who reminded her of Cyrus, so she'd written goodbye letters to Jody and Joe, for they'd suffered, too, and went to see Ted for only an hour. "Don't be a stranger," he'd said. But she was already a stranger.

She wanted to forget her home, so she'd put the shack up for sale, packed her books and clothes and candle-and-candy-making supplies, brought Dog and Yard, and left the desert for Los Angeles.

She had not even been able to bring herself to stay for Cyrus's funeral.

The first week in LA, Aurora found a couch to crash on in a dilapidated, communal Craftsman house by the freeway, enrolled at UCLA, and landed a massage therapy job at a spa. On her days off, she drove to West Hollywood and Hollywood and Echo Park and Silver Lake and Westwood and Santa Monica. She drove through the canyons—Laurel, Topanga, Rustic, Beachwood, Beverly Glen. She drove to the San Fernando Valley—Studio City, North Hollywood, Shadow Hills. She repeated the words, the names of the streets and plants and trees aloud like a mantra: Melrose, Sunset, Jasmine, Rose; jacaranda, eucalyptus, magnolia, belladonna, bougainvillea, agapanthus, hydrangea, plumeria, oleander. One day she drove up into the hills below the Hollywood sign, hiked around the reservoir and found the bridge carved with the mournful heads of grizzly bears. She went to Venice and walked among the skaters and beach babes and tourists, listened to the drummers, and tried on straw hats and cheap sunglasses in the stalls. A pale-eyed, bearded man in a turban zipped by, playing discordant sounds on his electric guitar and the sound buzzed in her teeth.

She took off her shoes and walked down to the water, feeling her toes sink into the wet like sand crabs. She and Cyrus had gone there, too, late at night, after the concert. *You'll do massage and I'll work construction while we go to school, and we'll save up and eventually get a little house. Hike and read on our days off. Go to libraries and estate sales and clubs. Learn to surf.*

She walked into the waves and stood, now, feeling the cold water eddying around her ankles. *Desert child to the bone*, she thought. *And I will always be.*

Aurora imagined for a moment walking out into the sea. But she had a home now, she had school and a job, she had a purpose.

All these things helped Aurora forget her half-brother and lover; their half-sister who had carried his child; and their other brother who had been arrested for murder. Helped her forget Larry and Leanne. Aurora tried to forget Sky, too.

She did her best to forget her mother Sky except at night before bed when Aurora prayed to whatever there was left to believe in that Cyrus's death was a result of Sky's choices, based on her beliefs in a myth, and how those choices played themselves out through Seth. Cold comfort. But Aurora did not want to live so powerlessly under the weight of what felt like an ancient curse—the myth of Isis and Osiris, Nepthys and Set—unable to rewrite her own story.

All Aurora could do was study hard, become an attorney one day, try to right the wrongs of the past; or help someone at least. She could make a new home for herself and Dog and Yard, a home with honey-scented candles and chocolates shaped like roses, an herb garden in a window box, books and music, tea and yoga, and runs by the sea. She could try to forget Ever, too, the man she had rescued and then lost, but the more she tried to forget, the more she could feel pain running through her bloodstream to help form the baby growing inside of her.

The night she'd slept with Ever, they conceived a child.

Aurora had been so caught up in the moment that she hadn't asked him to wear a condom; later, she had been so distraught over Cyrus's death, she didn't realize she'd skipped her cycle.

But, yes, she was pregnant. And she had not told Ever.

###

When Aurora gave birth to Keaton nine months after she met Ever, the midwife had looked into Aurora's eyes, while she writhed on the cushions, and told her to breathe.

Aurora kept closing her eyes, and the midwife kept telling her, "Look at me! Look at me!"

She forced herself to stay present, stay there in the room.

"This isn't pain," the woman said. "This might hurt but it's not pain."

The baby was ripping Aurora apart. Literally. She felt her pelvis ready to shatter. The pain (it was pain) soared in crests. It made her feel as if she were levitating.

Ever. She wanted Ever. But he was gone. After what she had put him through, she felt she had no right to reach out to him again. She hardly knew him. And, if she were to be honest with herself, she feared more loss.

"Keep pushing," the woman said. "And look at me."

Aurora looked at her. All she saw was a sea of blood.

What if they had to cut her open?

He was bigger than they'd thought. Nine pounds, eight ounces. Huge. He was going to kill her.

But she loved him. She already loved him. She'd die for him, easily. She'd die, but then who would care for him? She couldn't die.

∰

Later, the baby, named "place of hawks," rested on Aurora's chest like a heart. His skin felt sticky and hot against her. His breath came evenly, making his ribcage—the wings of a bivalve seashell—rise and then fall. His crown smelled like petals. She whispered into the top of his head, "I have never loved anyone so much and I never will again."

He sighed in his sleep as if he'd heard her, and when she held out one finger, he curled all five of his around it. Though it took them awhile, when he finally latched securely to her raw nipple, it was as if they had never been apart.

She woke in the night and saw the baby watching her from the crib where the midwife had laid him on his back so Aurora could rest. That being, that perfect creature with his watchful brown eyes and black cap of hair and sweet-lipped mouth had come from her body? The thrill and shock of it made her wince with a kind of pain almost worse (better?) than what she'd gone through to deliver him. She had to tell someone! But whom could she tell? The only person she wanted to see, to tell, was Ever.

In her fantasies, she had stood in Ever's kitchen cooking and he came up behind her and ran his fingers up under her T-shirt, caressed her breasts, slid his hands down the slope of her belly, the jut of hipbones. She was so wet for him, and he slid his fingers into her just as his tongue slid between her lips. She wriggled away, fell to her knees, and unbuckled his belt. Slithered leather through belt loops. Metal clanked on the tiled floor. He pushed out through his boxers, and she took him into her mouth. He came almost right away, and she swallowed all of it. Her lips still tasted of him later when he came again inside of her.

But this was only her fantasy, and she knew she might never see him again, could not even tell him about the baby. They had only slept together once. *And I almost got him killed,* Aurora reminded herself, *and now I'm dead, too.* But you couldn't raise a child if you were dead. She could no longer give up everything for a man—which she feared she'd do again—no matter how much she loved him. She could not let herself love another man, especially not so soon after Cyrus's betrayal and death, so soon after she had begun to face the truth and find herself.

❅ ❅ ❅

Today, Keaton lay on his back, on a patchwork blanket Aurora had made from scraps of thrifted cloth, blinking up at glimmers of sky through the branches, blossoms, and feathered leaves of a *mimosifolia*, the blue jacaranda. An orange butterfly flew past, near enough for Aurora to have plucked it like a flower. Then a lustral hummingbird, shades of tourmaline, lapis lazuli, gold. *The colors of my love for you, my son, my truest love.*

Aurora lay beside her boy, watching the darting motions of his hands and his eyes that were the color of the jacaranda pods that would appear after the flowers died. The rest of him was still, entranced in a haze of blue petals.

Aurora saw something struggling in the branches. The hummingbird. Caught in a spider's web.

She tried to free the bird, but it fell to the ground. The cobwebs still wreathed its feet. It tried to fly, batting its wings, but the web held it down.

She scooped it up and cupped it in her hand. Keaton blinked at her. "Bird," she said. "Hummingbird."

She could have sworn he made the shape of the word with his mouth. *Bird.*

The creature stayed so still in her hand. Aurora opened her fingers just a bit, and it stuck its proboscis out. She slid her fingers along the fairy spear, removing the cobweb. Opened her hand some more. The hummingbird's chest glinted with green iridescence, hundreds of golden flecks. She let its feet dangle out from the bottom of her hand and slid the cobwebs off of the tiny talons. Then she set the hummingbird down on the grass. It didn't move.

Keaton looked at it, moving his mouth, waving his hands.

Aurora crooned to the hummingbird. Still, it didn't stir. She sprinkled some water from her cup lightly over the bird.

Then. It shook its feathers as if she'd resurrected it. Like Cyrus, she thought. Like Ever.

Like Ever.

The hummingbird beat its wings and lifted into the air. It brushed against her arm before it flew away. As if it were thanking her.

Aurora put Keaton in his stroller, and they walked back from the park to the little office that belonged to her new boss, an attorney named Toni Weller.

"Officially, you only work here," she'd said, handing Aurora the keys. Toni had glanced over at a cot in the back room. "But if you happen to fall asleep while working over-time, that's okay; the sheets are fresh. And animals are okay. Even exotics, should you know any. Just don't tell the boss." She had flashed a smile. "The shower works, too."

"Thank you," Aurora had said.

Toni, almost out the door, had not glanced back. "For what?"

Aurora had stood looking around the place. The front room, only three-large-men deep and one-tall-man high. The back room, even smaller, with the cot, and shelves lining the walls, ideal for books and candles. The tiny aqua-tiled kitchen with a window box, the pink-and-white-tiled bathroom with a shell-shaped sink. All the walls painted pale blue. From where she had stood, she saw a few palm trees and a ninety-four-foot steel sculpture of a rainbow on a movie studio lot. In the window next door hung a pink neon sign that read "Psychic," though Aurora hadn't noticed anyone come or go through the door beneath the sign. She'd seen flocks of escaped parrots in the eucalyptus trees and a lone peacock crying like a baby in the park among the ravens. A stringy-haired vampire girl, in a mask of white sunscreen and wearing a backpack thicker than she was, had walked with flat feet, lifting her knees, as if she had strings attached to them.

Just now, a man with an orange pylon on his head rode by, a little white dog perched upright in the bicycle basket. Like a beauty queen, he waved at Aurora, then chimed the bell.

Even here lurked things both beautiful and strange.

Lost Woman Song

Aurora woke predawn, the baby curled against her, his damp skin adhering lightly to her own. They'd fallen asleep that way, nursing, before she'd put him back into his bassinet. What if she'd rolled over on him in the night? What if he fell down between the bed and the wall? There was never a moment, even as she slept, where she didn't worry. And she knew this would last her entire lifetime, even when he became a tall, strong man. She watched him sleep now. He shuddered with a tiny sigh and waved his hands in the air. She held out one finger, and he curled all five of his fingers around, then stilled.

Just then she heard the sound outside of the bungalow.

It made her think of the way Cyrus had disappeared a year ago, vanished in the night. Why hadn't she heard any sounds; why hadn't she awakened? This fact still haunted her. They say you never sleep well again after the birth of a child, but Aurora had not slept well since Cyrus was taken. And every sound in the darkness or half-darkness now jarred her alert. Dog, too, as if he somehow knew. He was already awake, looking toward the front door. Yard lumbered behind them.

Aurora got up and slid her hands under the baby's star-fished body, lifted him as if he were made of wet sand, and set him in the bassinette. He didn't open his eyes. She kissed his damp forehead and walked to the door with Dog padding beside her.

She looked through the blinds, out at the parking lot and the little storefront with the pink neon "Psychic" sign. A woman stooped over, putting something on Aurora's doorstep.

She opened the door.

The woman stepped back, startled. Dog went to sniff her leg, then stuck his nose into the basket she'd placed by the front step.

"Nephy?" Aurora said.

Nephy, her half-sister, the woman who'd betrayed her, stood and looked at Aurora.

"What are you doing?" Aurora said. "How did you find me?"

Nephy had cut her hair short and she wore all black. Her long acrylic nails were gone, her skin bare of makeup. *She looks like me now*, Aurora thought, though her own hair had mostly grown back during the pregnancy.

"I kept asking Ted. He finally told me. I think he was worried about Jack."

"Who? Why are you here, Nephy?"

"I can't keep him," Nephy said. "Please, you have to keep him for me, Izzy."

"That's not my name." Aurora peered into the basket. The child lay there looking up at her with eyes like slivered obsidian. A shock of black hair stood straight up on his head.

"His name is Jack," said Nephy.

Cyrus and Nephy's child.

Cyrus, her lover. Maybe, though Aurora didn't want to believe it, they'd all been under some spell, under the enchantment of the myth. But if she were ever to feel that she had free will, she must accept that Cyrus did, too. And that he'd betrayed her.

"How the fuck did you even find me?"

"Please," Nephy said. "We drove all the way from the desert. Can we come in at least?"

The baby had started to whimper. Aurora stood back and let Nephy bring his basket inside.

Dog settled by Keaton's bassinette, boxy jowls hanging, eyes grievous and ever-watchful.

Nephy put the basket down, but she wouldn't sit.

"You can't just abandon your child," Aurora said. "What the fuck, Nephy?"

"You could take care of him," Nephy said. "Until I get myself together at least. I haven't been well since—"

Since Cyrus had died and it turned out that Cyrus, Aurora, Nephy, and Seth were half-siblings. Since Seth ran off with Nephy as his shield and was then arrested for killing Cyrus and trying to kill Ever. Since Nephy had given birth to her half-brother's child. Who could blame her for not being "well"?

Aurora wasn't sure she was either, though.

"You were going to just leave him there? On my doorstep? Like some crazy changeling shit?" she said, thinking of Leanne's stories.

"I'm sorry." Nephy put her hands over her face and began to cry. "I'm sorry for everything. Cyrus and me—it was just for a short time, I swear. It was my fault. I didn't know what I was doing. I just needed Cyrus."

Needed Cyrus? But Aurora had needed him that way, too, once.

She looked at the baby, Jack. He, too, was crying now, waking Keaton.

Aurora went to her child's bassinette and stroked the tiny round head. He reached for her, and she lifted him into her arms, sat on the edge of the sofa, and pulled out her breast. Her nipples tingled and the milk let down immediately. Sometimes she wondered who was fed more by the act of nursing.

Keaton—the only one she needed to worry about now. Him and Dog and Yard. And Aurora had to care for herself. She had to care for herself so she could care for them. Keaton patted the sides of her moon-breast with star-hands. He gazed up at the moon of her face with his star-eyes. His expression was one of agitation and fear (*Who are these people?*), but he also seemed to be trying to comfort her, batting his long eyelashes, gurgling down the milk.

"Pick up your baby," Aurora told Nephy.

Nephy's sobs turned to gasps as she gulped for air. She wiped her tears on her T-shirt and took a bottle of milk from her backpack. Then she picked up the baby and carried him over to the bed, holding him out to Aurora. "Take him," she said. "Please, Izzy."

Jack's eyes were not as dark as Aurora had thought—they had undertones of seaweed-green. Like her own eyes and like Cyrus's. Like Sky's.

Yard, who had retreated into his shell, now poked out his neck and head to look at Aurora. Instinctively, she reached out for Nephy's child.

Aurora scooped the baby into her other arm. He was older than Keaton, she knew, but scrawny with a slightly oblong head. The babies weighed about the same. She pulled up her T-shirt and took out her other breast. It was heavy, hot, sticking to the skin above her ribs. Keaton suckled harder, rolled his eyes up at her, patted his hands, and kicked his feet in agitation. What was she doing? The milk started flowing into Jack's mouth before Aurora could think of any other reason not to feed him.

While she was looking down at the two babies—her child with Ever and Nephy's child by Cyrus—she did not hear Nephy stand up and slip out the door into the night.

Losing My Religion

The next day, Aurora took Keaton and Jack to the blue jacaranda trees at the park. They all lay on a blanket looking up at the sky.

"How will I keep you? How will I raise you?" Aurora asked Jack. "Your mother, my sister, is gone."

He watched her with butterfly eyes.

"How will I trust you? How will I help you? How is there room in my heart?"

He stared with his butterfly eyes.

"I have no choice; I have no choice," said Aurora. And both children smiled with their butterfly eyes.

✢✢✢

Before the Beaux Arts dome of the Natural History Museum, rose bushes—planted in clumps of pink, orange, yellow, red, and white—flanked the entrance path to the Science Center, where a large shallow fountain sent an obelisk of copper-green water toward the overcast sky. At the sight of the water, the baby on her chest kicked his legs in the carrier, and Aurora wrapped her fingers around his thighs and lightly squeezed, bent her face to inhale the scent of his downy-black crown—as sweet as when he was born, when the bones hadn't yet closed so that his soul could filter all the way into him.

She'd heard the expression that being a parent is like having your heart walk around outside your body. But her baby had *given* her a heart where once, she realized now, there might have been only a chasm in her chest. And with that new heart, her child had also given her fears she could not have imagined.

Common parental fears. But, also: fear that he would grow up and be brutalized and blinded, just as the myth predicted, the myth that had ruled Aurora's life, the myth she was trying to forget.

The myth stirred something in her—her fear, but also her truth. And she must face it all. Especially now that she had Jack, too. Jack, the child on her back. Cyrus's child.

There had been a dis-membering. To counteract what had occurred she knew she must force herself to re-member.

Which was why she'd come with the children to the King Tut exhibit.

❀ ❀ ❀

Aurora and the babies stood in line and were then ushered into the Science Center. The visitors took the escalator upstairs to the exhibit. Waiting in the dark to enter, Aurora wanted to turn and leave. But Keaton made his little-bird sounds and continued to kick his legs and dimple-ankleted feet with delight. Jack remained quiet and still.

King Tutankhamun's tomb had been discovered, fully intact, in 1922 by an Egyptian water boy during an archaeological dig led by Howard Carter. Carter peered inside and reportedly announced he saw, "Many wonderful things." There, within, surrounded by more than five thousand ceremonial objects, rested the lithe, young vampiric king with the large incisors. His two stillborn daughters lay buried with him. Aurora thought of the baby she'd lost—she could understand King Tut's choice.

A sign on the wall told of the ancient Egyptian belief that the deceased had to pass through the twelve gates of the Netherworld, each representing one hour of the night, each guarded by another monster or demon, some in the shape of snakes, hippopotamuses, crocodiles, and lions. Aurora knew such demons—she had met them herself, in human form. At first, after learning their secret language, after learning their secret names and barely escaping their curse, she had been trapped in such a Netherworld.

And then Keaton had been born.

An alabaster lotus-shaped wishing cup, glowing as if it held a spirit within, bid them enter. What had King Tut wished for, Aurora wondered? A long, and happy life with his half-sister and wife, Ankhesenamun? Happy, healthy children? When he fell ill, did he wish for eternal life after death?

So many things had been prepared for his journey. A wooden traveling chest. A miniature ivory game board depicting the journey through the underworld. A gilded wooden bed with lion's feet. Tawret, the god with a hippopotamus face, and Bes, ithyphallic lion-headed guardian of newborns, had been carved into the footboard.

Aurora had not met these gods, but she would welcome them, she thought, in spite of their animalistic, phallic ferocity. For, in this world, her baby—her babies— needed all the protection they could get.

Life is a long, arduous journey. One must have guardians. Shabti.

Aurora had lost all her former guardians or left them behind in the land of forgetting. Now she was virtually alone, except for Keaton. And Jack.

A pair of large shabti, carved from wood then gilded, with eyes of volcanic obsidian, stood guard in their case, their arms crossed over their chests to hold now-missing crooks and flails. One shabti wore a headdress with a cobra uraeus and one a wig of tight curls, like small black grapes, also ornamented with a snake. They reminded Aurora of the two statues in Sky's house.

These two guardians will be together always, Aurora thought, even though it is in the beam of prying eyes. And then she thought not of Cyrus but, again, of Ever.

She had thought that they had parted because she did not love him enough or loved him less than Cyrus. No, it was not that, she knew now. She had banished herself, so that she could emerge from the underworld a different person, a whole person with a life of her own, a woman who could care for herself and raise two children.

After The Opening of the Mouth Ceremony, in which a blue faience vase shaped like a hieroglyph was used to pour liquid into King Tut's orifice so that the god Ptah would help him breathe, eat, drink, and speak in the underworld, a miniature wooden boat would ferry the king to his destination—the eastern sky. The oars of the boat were the fingers of the god Horus, and the sail was Horus's grandmother, the sky goddess, Nut.

Aurora turned her eyes from this. Nut. Sky. Aurora did not want to read her name.

The boat would take the deceased to the temple of Horus's father, the great god Osiris's temple.

Aurora did not want to read the forty-third spell from the *Book of the Dead* written on the museum wall for it commanded that the head of Osiris should not be taken from him and that the head of the deceased should similarly not be taken. The head was important to the Egyptians, second only to the heart, and must remain intact. Decapitation was considered the worst punishment. King Tut's head had rested on a stand of blue faience like a piece of sculpture. In this way, his soul, his Ka, a bird with the king's head, could fly to the land of the living each day and, at night, return to the mummy underground. Isis had restored Osiris's head, put him back together again so he could return to her.

Keaton, continued to chortle-coo through all of this. He did not seem disturbed by the darkness or the objects looming out of it. If anything, he seemed comforted. And Jack still remained quiet.

But then Aurora saw the king.

He is made of wood, then gilded. His face is broad with eyes in the shape of fish. His features feminine, as is the shape of his body with the swelling chest, the narrow limbs, the forward-striding feet.

He wears a high hat, pointed toward the heavens, a pleated, form-fitting kalasiris and sandals. He carries a crook. Here he is again, riding a black panther into the Netherworld. Here he is, colossal quartzite faintly traced with memories of turquoise-and-carnelian-colored paint, missing limbs but with a face of still-leonine beauty. Is he King Tut? Or is he something more? Is he the god, Osiris? Was this Tut's tomb or Osiris's sacred tomb?

"Osiris, Osiris," a recorded voice whispered.

Only then, did both babies cry out.

Aurora had to leave this place. She could not breathe here. It might as well have been an actual tomb. But a tomb that promised no resurrection. Or, perhaps, endless resurrection at great cost.

With the whispers of the recorded voice echoing the name— Osiris—in her mind, Aurora turned, her hands reflexively covering her baby's crown, her eyes volcanic rock. She wanted to run, to reject the myth, the origin of who she was, but she knew nothing was that simple. Still, she could not let herself be ruled by the past. She would choose her life. And this running and hiding was not what she chose. Instead, she walked out of the museum with the two babies, walked quietly back into the light.

❀ ❀ ❀

After the babies slept that night, Aurora regarded her reflection in the bathroom mirror. Aurora's hair—long again. The wound on her face had fully healed, leaving only a faded white scar. And the baby had changed her, filled her with milk and life and light. The journey into darkness to find Cyrus had changed her, too; she saw that now. Enough to find the strength to care for two children on her own and face the myth that haunted her.

This was what made it possible for her to text him, finally:

Dear Ever, I want to see you. I'm sorry for everything. Please meet me tomorrow at sunset on Mecca Beach near the sign.

But there was something else she had to do along the way.

All is Full of Love

The next day, Aurora put both babies into their car seats, strapping them carefully to avoid pinching the soft chub of their thighs. Keaton just gazed up at her wanly batting his lashes, his pointed chin pressed into the soft folds of his neck. Jack already looked like he was about to cry. If she got the car started fast, got driving, he'd calm down.

Dog jumped up into the front seat.

Aurora cranked the air conditioning, played some Navajo flute music. The reedy sounds had gotten her through Keaton's birth, though it had been hard to hear them over the sound of her own screams.

The San Jacinto and San Bernardino mountains swallowed the truck. Aurora drove through the Tehachapi Wind Farm where manic turbines spun. Cyrus once said he thought the four thousand windmills marred the landscape: "Planetary molestation." The clearing of the desert floor released carbon dioxide. The huge glass panels built to harness the sun at the plant outside Vegas fried birds to death, he told her. Like the electric fences at Calipatria State Prison.

"Someday we'll be like the dinosaurs," Cyrus said when he stood with her in front of the T-Rex and Apatosaurus statues in Cabazon. "Aliens will build steel and concrete statues of us along the side of the road."

Was it true? Was the planet coming to its demise? What world would her children know when she was gone?

But the spring wildflowers—gold, pink, purple, even the faint green buds—imitated a desert sky at sunset. Linear-leaved golden-bush, Acton's bristle brush, fourwing saltbush, blackbrush, California buckwheat, Nevada jointer, Anderson's boxthorn, California juniper, Indian ricegrass, big galleta grass, brownplume wirelettuce, Parry's nolina, desert needlegrass, Mojave aster. Aurora said their names in her head like a prayer for the earth, an incantation to help calm her mind.

✳✳✳

Although Aurora had changed, nothing about the place she'd grown up seemed any different. The aluminum siding of the Airstream trailer baked like a cookie tray in the sun. Leanne sat under the juniper tree sipping tea from a broken cup. The mannequin was still there, though she now wore a pink tutu—for spring, Leanne would say if anyone would listen. Aurora wondered if someone had claimed the male mannequin Leanne gave her after Cyrus went missing. The one with the painted tattoos, the stones taped to its eyes. The plastic figure she'd anointed with blood. Left in the shack when Aurora put the place up for sale. Probably in a dump by now.

Leanne stood and shielded her eyes from the light. "Is that you? Izzy? Is that you? What do you have there with you?"

Aurora, babies strapped to her body, walked toward Leanne—slowly. She didn't want Leanne to come too close.

Something had changed: Leanne looked older now.

"This is your grandson, Keaton," Aurora said. "This is Nephy's son, Jack."

Leanne froze and put her hands over her mouth.

"I brought you something." Aurora took some cash that she'd saved out of her jeans' pocket and held it out to Leanne, who snatched at it and tucked it in her bra.

"You okay, Leanne?"

Leanne stared at Keaton and Jack.

"Where's Larry?" Aurora asked.

Leanne said, "Around back. Chopping some wood."

"If you need me, you let me know," Aurora told her. "Once I get settled some more maybe I can come get you and bring you to LA with me."

She hadn't planned on saying this, and had Leanne even heard her? But Aurora was glad she'd said it anyway. It struck her for the first time how much Leanne had been a victim, too. How she'd tried to raise Aurora as her own, even if the whole thing clearly broke her. "And don't let Larry boss you around too much in the meantime," Aurora added.

"Speak of the devil," Leanne mumbled as Larry came around from the back of the trailer.

Land of devils. You were wrong, Larry.

"Izzy?" Larry said. "That you? Who's that there with you?"

"This is Keaton and Jack," Aurora said.

"You've been busy. Twins?" He laughed. "Your hair looks good, though. Grown out."

Aurora took a step back when he approached. "I'm here to tell you something."

Larry smirked at her. "Oh, yeah, what's that?"

"Remember the ghost stories you used to scare me with?"

In order to appease the ghost, the man had to fast in a dark room, leaving only to make daily offerings to the ghost. Food, clothing, objects, and finally body parts—a hand, an eye, a kidney. But nothing appeased the ghost and the man soon died.

"I recall you liked stories," Larry said.

"I couldn't sleep. I'd wake screaming in the night. Remember the pocket knife?"

Larry scratched his whiskered chin. "Made you brave in the end."

"Remember how you joined a cult and had sex with the leader and—oh, yeah—brought a baby home and told Leanne she had to raise her?"

He coughed into his fist—she thought she could hear the dust and smoke in his lungs.

"Remember the kitten?" she said.

"That cat incident had nothing to do with me—"

"Right. That's what you've told me for almost twenty years. Who else could it have been, Larry?"

"Seth," he said.

"What?"

"I caught him throwing rocks at roadrunners, things like that. I had some concerns at the time. But I figured it was mostly harmless."

"You knew that? Hurt *animals*? Like nascent serial killer shit?"

"I didn't know for sure. Still don't, but with everything that happened...I do know it wasn't me."

"You never fucking told me that you thought he killed my cat."

"Stop," Leanne said. "Izzy, stop."

Aurora took a breath. Anger would no longer serve her now. "These are your grandchildren, Larry. You get to see them this once. And I never want you coming near them the rest of your life."

She turned and walked back to the car, took the children out of the carrier, and buckled them into their car seats.

Then she drove away from that trailer for the last time.

❋❋❋

Aurora stopped at Nephy's, then. But the pink house had been boarded up. Her sister was gone.

"You're mine forever now," she told Jack. "And I am yours."

❋❋❋

Clouds floated lotus-like in the lake of the sky. Aurora looked out at the Salton Sea reflecting the sun like the polished copper or bronze of an ancient mirror, with a handle carved of bone, she thought, in the shape of a goddess.

But there was no goddess, no resurrected god. Nothing had changed. Like Sky had said: the ice was melting, the forests burning, the animals dying. The denial, the fear, the brutality. The Johns, the Janes, the Baby Does. Cyrus's death had meant nothing. The world would still come to an end from man's doing. And if she were still alive by then, she might have to face the end alone.

Ever might not come today.

But—the babies. She had them now.

She turned to the sound of her dog crying. Dog Gone, a silhouette, otherworldly against the mother-of-pearled sky. He began to gallop toward a distant black speck of a figure walking down the beach.

Dog Gone. The dog that had come to her after Cyrus vanished. Just as Ever had come to her.

And then Aurora knew. Sky perverted the myth by trying to control it, by trying to claim it as hers alone, but in some ways the truth of it remained.

Isis was born in the desert. Her mother-betrayer laid herself out upon her lover, the earth, her belly a great blue egg speckled with stars. Geb impregnated Nut with his trees and his mountains, his fields of wheat stalks and corn. Isis and her brothers and sister burst forth in the light of their grandfather Sun, the maker of all, the bright dung beetle in the sky, the golden scarab, the all-seeing eye.

She and her brother-husband bathed in the lotus pool, anointed each other's pulses with fragrant oil of myrrh and frankincense, adorned each other's brows with garlands, adorned each other's eyes with lapis, tourmaline, and emerald, adorned each other's lips and hearts with carnelian, adorned each other's skin with gold. Hummingbirds thrummed at their necks and wrists. Butterflies flew from their lips when they opened their mouths. Their scapulae sprouted wings. They let the wild flowers grow unfettered. Bees hummed and their hives sang like lyres.

They went forth hand-in-hand to irrigate dry land, to plant wheat and corn, to weave fine linen and make barley beer and date wine. They were not wasteful. They burned the wick all night and wasted no light. Draped in white linen and gauze she knelt before him and offered him her breasts; she straddled him and offered his staff to the cleft between her thighs.

When you create, you sacrifice a little of yourself, a little of your seed, a small blue egg. When two bodies struggle against each other in the war of love, a child may be conceived. Children are gods and goddesses, slick with blood as they arrive in this world. When you paint a story on the temple wall you lose a little blood. But when you are done, you will walk the flower path dripping with hyacinth, fragrant with calamus, unfurling the blue lotus in the silver pool; you will walk forth into the flower fields of peace.

You were born to make beauty in the slaughterhouse of the world. You were born to toil. You were born to love. Offer yourself up to the light of the golden eye of the sun, to the silver mouth of the moon, to the gods and goddesses of love. The god and goddess reside within, but do not forget them in others. Gather your passions like precious gems, polish and refine them and give them to the world. Loss is inevitable, but do not fear it. It is the corpse without its stomach, intestines, lungs, and liver. But these organs wait in canopic jars to be reclaimed in the afterlife. Only the heart remains. It is the hope that allows light and love to flood and enter the void. Live with hope, with imagination and purpose.

When someone dies, it is said the dead are still with you. It is never enough. But it is true, too. And Aurora knew then that Cyrus, imperfect as he had been, was still all around her. They had come from the same womb, and later they had shared the womb-home they had made together. A part of him was in the dog that had run to her. In the music. In the betrayal of Nephy's child. In Aurora and Ever's child. In the sky now, full of clouds, with one smear of rainbow light—yellow, green, blue, purple, violet—a fire rainbow, just above her head.

She had not been able to attend Cyrus's funeral, but she would honor him here and now.

I have been imperfect, Aurora thought. I have been lustful and full of fear. I have been ignorant. I have neglected the earth, I have neglected my beloved, and I have neglected myself. I have forgotten to kiss the dough and honey from my loved one's fingers, kiss his lips and hair in the blue dawn. I have listened to death singing in the courtyard and longed to go to him, lusted for him like a lover.

I played the role of Isis, betrayed by my brothers. Betrayed by my sister. Gathering up the parts of my beloved and calling him back to me. But I am not Isis. I am far less sacred than the missing-and-the-dead found along the roadsides and in the mine shafts. The raped, the murdered, the mutilated and dismembered. The unclaimed Johns, the Janes, the Baby Does. I am less sacred, but like them, like everyone, I embody the sacred in me, too.

See me, I am imperfect, but trying, as we all must try, to bring light to the darkness, bring back water to the desert, carry the lotus of love in our hands.

I am Aurora now.

And everything lost someday returns.

The distant speck on the beach had become a man. His shoulders swaying, arms loose at his sides, legs long, head down. He wore a hoodie and aviator sunglasses that hid his eyes. The dog ran toward him, rose up light as air, and put his paws on the broad shoulders of the man in black—a kind of dance. Had she seen it right?—Dog walked like a horned god on his hind legs beside the man.

Nephy and Cyrus's child murmured. Aurora cooed his name and put her hands around the other child strapped to her chest, holding him against her like a small blue egg from which a deity is born. Then she took a breath and looked back into nacreous light at the man on the beach.

He lifted his head to greet her.

Author's Note: *Awakening Osiris: The Egyptian Book of the Dead* by Normandi Ellis, *Isis and Osiris: Exploring the Goddess Myth* by Jonathan Cott, and *Egyptian Magic* by E. A. Wallis Budge, as well as the photography of Theresa Havens, provided inspiration for this book.

Acknowledgments

My deepest thanks to my wonderful friend and agent Christopher Schelling for sticking by me through everything, and to Tyson Cornell for publishing this book. Also, thanks to my professors Stephen Graham Jones, Joshua Malkin, Jill Alexander Essbaum, and Tod Goldberg, and to my cohort, especially Greg Tower, Billy Minshall, Stephanie Kotin, Felicity Landa, and Anjali Becker. Thanks for input and support: Laurel Ollstein, Reina Escobar, Mary Pauline Lowry, Denise Hamilton, Lauren Strasnick, Tracey Porter, Molly Bendall, Hillary Carlip, Sukha Gildart, Sera Gamble, Laura Lee Bahr, Jennifer Becherer, Lisa Locasio Nighthawk, Hope Rieser Farley, Vince Gerardis, Marjo Maisterra, Lexi Rosen, Liz Dubelman, Richard Nash, Lydia Wills, Howard Paar, Leza Cantoral and Lorinda Toledo. I am grateful to Hailie Johnson, Alexandra Watts, Kellie Kreiss, everyone at Rare Bird, my publicist Bruce Mason, and to Scout LaRue Willis for the vinyl recording. My love, as always, to Jasmine, Sam, Chris, and Gregg.